THE RUSSIAN KEY

A NOVEL

JERI LABER

Arcade Publishing • New York

Arcade Publishing books may be purchased in bulk at special discounts for sales promotion, corporate gifts, fund-raising, or educational purposes. Special editions can also be created to specifications. For details, contact the Special Sales Department, Arcade Publishing, 307 West 36th Street, 11th Floor, New York, NY 10018 or arcade@skyhorsepublishing.com.

Arcade Publishing® is a registered trademark of Skyhorse Publishing, Inc.®, a Delaware corporation.

Visit our website at www.arcadepub.com.

10 9 8 7 6 5 4 3 2 1

Library of Congress Cataloging-in-Publication Data is available on file.

Jacket design by Brian Peterson
Jacket illustrations credit: Getty Images

Print ISBN: 978-1-951627-72-0
Ebook ISBN: 978-1-951627-73-7

Printed in the United States of America

For my daughters

Abby, Pam, and Emily

Praise for *The Russian Key*:

"*The Russian Key* is a captivating Cold War thriller. Its clean, clear prose and artful plotting kept me turning pages into the wee hours. Laber has had an illustrious career doing clandestine human rights work behind the Iron Curtain, and she draws on her deep knowledge to create a story as authentic as it is entertaining." —Joe Weisberg, creator of *The Americans*

"I picked up *The Russian Key* and couldn't put it down. As a founder of Human Rights Watch, author Jeri Laber builds her novel on knowledge acquired in dozens of missions into the underground in the Soviet Union and Eastern Europe. In our era, in which heroes wear capes and fly, it is a joy to be able to hang on to an ever-provocative story which describes an attractive and unusual love affair."—Hannah Pakula, author of *New York Times* notable book *The Last Empress*, *The Last Romantic*, and *An Uncommon Woman*

"In this fast-paced and often witty book, Jeri Laber combines her deep knowledge of totalitarianism with the ups and downs of a thriller. She writes from the inside, conjuring multiple societies and the players within them, and the story she tells is ultimately both alarming and delightful."—Andrew Solomon, PhD, author of *Far and Away*, *Far From the Tree*, and *The Noonday Demon*

"I was surprised and delighted by Jeri Laber's *The Russian Key*. Its protagonists—lovers and spies, friends and enemies and CIA officials—kept me intrigued from the first page to the last. A terrific read."—Rose Styron, poet, journalist, and human rights activist

"*The Russian Key* is one of the most refreshing spy novels to come along in some time, a remarkably realistic exploration of the human costs of the espionage game. Set in the Cold War era of the 1950s and 1960s, it tells the tale of a relationship between two spies, and two countries. Along the way, Katherine Landau emerges as an unlikely hero, one of the more compelling and authentic characters in American spy fiction. The author's first-hand knowledge of the Soviet Union and Eastern Europe shows throughout this taut, thought-provoking novel. A great read."—James Lilliefors, author of *The Children's Game* (as Max Karpov)

[Russia] is a riddle, wrapped in a mystery, inside an enigma.
But perhaps there is a key.
—Winston Churchill, October 1, 1939

One

Washington, DC, November 1964

"Maksim Andreevich Rzhevsky. Does that name mean anything to you?" The two intelligence officers—one CIA, the other FBI—looked at me intently, awaiting my response.

I'd been summoned abruptly to a large office on the CIA's seventh floor. I wasn't dressed for an interview; I'd barely had time to brush my hair. Relatively new to the CIA staff, I worked in a cubicle doing translations and seldom met with any of my coworkers, and certainly not with the top brass. But I'd straightened my blouse and skirt and pulled myself together with youthful confidence, hoping this summons was about the position I'd been angling for.

Instead, they were asking me about the past, taking me back ten years, to my ill-fated trip to Moscow, to Max and our brief, romantic fling. The adventure that had ended badly, with me, an American college girl, in a Soviet jail.

Max. Maksim Rzhevsky. I'd never forgotten him. I'd never expected to hear his name again.

Now, years later, Max was about to reenter my life—not as a friend, but as an enemy.

And I would begin an exciting new assignment—and a life full of danger and duplicity.

I would become a spy.

Two

Smith College, Northampton, Massachusetts, 1953–54

Let me start back at Smith when I was sixteen, the youngest girl in the freshman class. Being the youngest was nothing new for me: I'd been skipped ahead, not once but twice, before I started high school. Looking back now, I find it hard to recognize the girl I was back then—a pampered only child, inept at making friends, intimidated by the sophisticated-looking girls who were my classmates, some as much as two years older than me.

I arrived at Smith a day later than planned and without my parents. My mother had come down with pneumonia and my father was at an important lawyers' conference. They hired a driver to bring me to Northampton, where I was deposited with all my luggage at the front door of Sessions House, the historic brick building where I would be living. I struggled inside, carrying two suitcases and pushing another along with my foot. Luckily, my room was only one flight up, and I made it up the stairs in two short trips.

Jeanie was sitting on a bed near the window, reading a book. Blond hair, blue eyes, a suntanned, freckled face. She jumped up with a big smile and helped me with my bags. "So you're here, at last!" she exclaimed. "I've been waiting and waiting to meet my roommate. The house-mother told me all about you: 'Katherine Landau, a precocious Jewish girl from New York City.' That's how she described you. I expected a little girl with big glasses. Not someone tall and beautiful like you, Kathy."

"Kate, please," I replied, blushing a little at the compliment. "Call me Kate, not Kathy, okay?"

"Sure thing, Kate. Call me Jeanie, full name Jean Johnson. Can you think of a more boring name?

"Here, let me help you unpack." Jeanie was already opening my bags. "Let's see your New York City duds. I'll bet they're a lot more chic than mine. My folks are die-hard Bostonians, really square. Right down to the clothes my mom makes me wear."

Jeanie was hanging up my skirts and dresses and neatly folding my cashmere sweater sets, murmuring appreciatively as she did so. She came across my saddle shoes, not the conventional brown and white ones, but black and tan instead. "How smart!" she kept saying. She couldn't get over them.

"So, tell me all about you," she demanded.

"Well, I'm from New York City, as you know. Manhattan. My dad's a lawyer and my mom's a housewife; she does a lot of volunteer work."

I didn't say we lived on Park Avenue. I assumed Jeanie was from a rich family, but she didn't seem at all boastful and I followed her lead. I knew, even back then, that her kind of rich—Boston Brahmin rich—was different from the first-generation wealth of my parents.

But I wanted to show her I was a regular girl, not a "precocious" bookworm, as the house-mother had implied. "I'm into sports," I told her, "the riskier the better. I like to ski, surf, and rock climb. I hunt and fish with my dad, at our place up in the Adirondacks. I've even taken up skydiving."

"Skydiving? You mean jumping out of a plane with a parachute? You call that a sport?"

"Yup. It's thrilling. You free-fall through the air before you open the parachute. There's nothing like it."

Jeanie was quiet for a minute, wide-eyed. *Good*, I thought, *I've impressed her.*

Then she asked: "Do you sail? Sailing's my thing. I have my own boat, got it for my sweet sixteen. It's in Newport where we go for weekends and summers. I spend all my time there sailing."

"I've done some sailing, but I don't really know how to sail."

"I'll teach you," Jeanie declared, "during spring break. Now hurry and wash up. I'll show you around campus. I've already scoped it out. I spent four years in an all-girls school; these schools are pretty much the same. I'm eighteen, by the way. My birthday's in May."

"So is mine!" I answered, then paused in confusion. I didn't want to mention my age.

Jeanie got it right away. "Don't be embarrassed," she said. "I know you're really young. You don't *seem* so young. What's age anyway? Just a bunch of numbers."

I really liked her. I'd lucked out.

We made a striking couple, Jeanie and me. Both of us tall, about five-foot-eight, both with long, shoulder-length hair. Mine was black and wavy; Jeanie's was thick and straight, so blond it looked almost white in the sun. With our small breasts and narrow waists and hips, we could easily fit into each other's clothes. And we were both planning to major in art history. We seemed meant for each other, perfect roommates.

Jeanie took my arm and led me around the campus. I was a bit in awe, taking in the wide expanses of lawn, the ancient trees, the imposing brick buildings; this would be my home for the next four years. Jeanie kept stopping to talk with girls we passed. Some of them she'd already met, while with others she quickly introduced herself, and me as well. She had a way about her; she seemed to like everyone and everyone liked her. She asked personal questions, questions I wouldn't dare ask a stranger, but she did so easily and with such interest, it made them feel special. And, I came to see, she remembered everything she was told, which made people feel like she really cared.

Thanks to Jeanie, I soon found myself included in a circle of friends that ate together each evening in the Sessions House dining room. There were about twenty-five girls living in Sessions, ranging from freshmen to seniors. We took our meals there, sitting at round tables that were set with fresh linens and handsome china and cutlery. Our little group was not a clique; Jeanie was always asking other girls to sit at our table or to join us for after-dinner coffee in the living room. She had a way of bringing me into the conversations. She'd say: "Katie was saying just the other day . . ." and I would find myself talking easily, no longer feeling young or shy. No one seemed to care about my age. Still, I never felt like I really belonged among these older, mainly Christian girls.

Jeanie, however, was a real friend, the first close friend I'd ever had. We shared a lot: our clothes, our makeup, our taste in music and movies, our interest in art. I opened up to her about things I'd never discussed with anyone before. She made it easy, for she did the same.

"My dad's hopeless," she told me one day. "Completely involved in his work, not interested in anything I do or say. He hardly ever comes to Newport; he's too busy and stays in Boston most of the summer. He's just not around, for big chunks of time.

"And my mom, she doesn't care what I think either, as long as I do what she says. I didn't want to go to boarding school, but she gave me no choice. She went to Rosemary Hall and I would, too. The same with Smith. I had to follow in her footsteps and go to these all-girl schools. No wonder I've never had a boyfriend. If I didn't have a kid brother, I wouldn't even know what a penis looked like."

"With me, it's different," I confided, surprised to find myself chatting freely. "My parents won't leave me alone. They want to share everything with me—fancy restaurants and plays that don't interest me, dinner parties with people their age. They got so involved in my high school work, it was like they were taking the classes themselves. They keep telling everyone how smart I am. It's embarrassing."

"Doesn't sound so bad to me," Jeanie said. "At least they appreciate you."

"You don't know how hard it's been, how lonely. How I've wished for a sister or brother, or at least a close friend. I was always being skipped ahead in school, with new kids older than me. It was hard to make friends.

"I did have a boyfriend for a while during my senior year. I kept it secret from my folks and never brought him home. We hung out in his house instead where his parents, thank God, left us alone."

***

We were hanging out in our room one Friday evening, soon after the Thanksgiving holiday. Jeanie had her hair in curlers; she was getting ready for a blind date the next night with a boy from Dartmouth. One of the girls in our house had set it up.

"I love your straight hair," I told her. "I wish my hair was straight. Why do you want to curl it?"

"Because I like yours better than mine, of course. Don't we always want the opposite of what we have?" I stopped to think about that, wondering if she was right.

Jeanie meanwhile was trying on one of my good dresses; she and her date were going to a dancing party. We readily shared our clothes, though Jeanie was more likely than I to be the borrower, since my clothes were much nicer than hers. The dress she chose was black velvet, with a tight bodice and flared skirt. Its V-neck was trimmed with a white cotton piqué collar and the three-quarter sleeves had matching white cuffs, a striking contrast to the velvet.

"I'll bet your mom's really stylish," Jeanie remarked, twirling in front of the floor-length mirror. "Does she pick out these clothes for you?"

"Yeah, she's a style-setter all right. Her picture's sometimes in the paper, all dolled up for some charity event. She's always bringing home clothes for me; she knows I hate to shop."

"Tell me," Jeanie said, "is your family religious? I mean, do you practice your religion, go to a Jewish church?"

"No," I told her. "We don't go to temple and we don't celebrate Jewish holidays. I'm an atheist. I've never actually asked my parents, but I'll bet they'd say the same."

"Well, my family's not very religious either," Jeanie said. "We go to church on Sundays, First Presbyterian, but it's mainly a social thing. And, of course, we celebrate all the holidays—Christmas, Easter. They're national holidays, after all. My mom's family dates back to the Mayflower. She's a Daughter of the American Revolution and, boy, is she proud of that! I think that's her real religion."

I hadn't told Jeanie the whole truth: that we *had* celebrated Jewish holidays when my grandparents were alive; that my parents, though not religious, identified strongly as Jews; that they belonged to an elite Jewish country club and were acutely upset by those clubs and vacation spots where Jews were not allowed.

Nor did I tell Jeanie that I'd probably been accepted by Smith as part of an unacknowledged "Jewish quota." Most colleges and universities had them at that time, designed to limit the number of Jewish students they admitted. Jeanie probably knew nothing about that.

Three

"**D**o you have a secret passion?" Jeanie asked me a few days later. We were washing up, getting ready for bed. "I don't mean boys, or movie stars," she went on. "We all have our crushes and fantasies. I mean something you dream about, something that's precious to you and you don't easily share with others.

"Mine's sailing," she continued. "At night, before I fall asleep, I imagine I'm on my own big, beautiful boat somewhere in the Bahamas, sailing smoothly over turquoise water, palm trees in the distance, waving in the breeze. I'm going to have a boat like that someday, with a blue hull, thirty-five feet long, big enough to live on for longish periods of time. I haven't decided on a name yet. What about you? Do you have a secret passion?"

"Yes, I do. It's Russia."

"Russia?" Jeanie looked perplexed. "Why Russia?"

"Russia has always intrigued me: it's mysterious, the country of my ancestors. My grandparents fled from Russia and never wanted to talk about it. And my parents also avoid the topic, especially now, with the Cold War and all, when everything Russian is considered bad. But *my* secret dream is to visit Russia someday. I had a book of Russian folk tales when I was a kid. It had beautiful illustrations: fairy-tale palaces, onion-domed churches, and landscapes all covered in snow. And the stories, well, they were hardly for kids—some of them were really terrifying, like the one about Baba Yaga, a hideous witch who was planning to eat two lost children. She goofed and put her own daughters in the pot by mistake, ended up eating them for dinner."

I went on to tell Jeanie about the great Russian writers I'd read in high school—Tolstoy, Dostoevsky, Turgenev, Chekhov—their deep, provocative thinking, their devotion to their homeland. "But Russia today," I pointed out sadly, "is more remote than ever before, off-limits to foreigners under the Communists. I haven't told you this, Jeanie, but I've started studying the Russian language. They don't offer it here at Smith, so I found myself a private tutor in Northampton. That's where I go on Tuesday afternoons when I say I'm at the dentist."

"Hey Katie, you've been keeping all this from me? I'm glad you're finally owning up!"

"Please . . . don't say a word about this, Jeanie. My folks would die if they knew I was studying Russian. I'm not sure the college would like it, either. People get suspicious when you praise anything Russian these days."

"Don't you worry," Jeanie assured me. "My lips are sealed. You know, I read *Anna Karenina* in high school. I loved it so much, it's so romantic. They should make a movie of it."

"They did, an old one. With Greta Garbo. I've seen it. I wish we could watch it together."

***

One Tuesday, a week or so later, I came rushing back to campus, a little late for dinner. Jeanie was holding court at our usual table, talking to a group of girls. As I slipped into my seat, I tuned in to what Jeanie was saying: " . . . So yes, sailing is my passion. That's my fantasy every night as I fall asleep—the boat I'll have someday and the trips I'll take in the Caribbean."

I was taken aback: Jeanie revealing the "secret passion" I thought she'd shared only with me. And then it got worse. "Hi Kate," she said, waving to me. Then, addressing the others: "Katie has a secret passion, too. Hers is Russia."

I froze. How dare she! I had sworn her to secrecy.

All eyes were on me. "Russia?" Lucy Humphrey asked, giggling. "Are you a Communist, Kate?" Lucy was rather flighty and often spoke without thinking. This was the McCarthy era, when being a Communist was no laughing matter.

"Not Soviet Russia, not Communism," I hurried to explain. "I'm interested in Russia before the Communists. Nineteenth-century Russia, where there was the greatest flowering of culture at any time since the Renaissance. Great writers, great philosophers, great composers." I was talking fast, not sure how I was coming across.

"But wasn't there always repression there, even before the Communists?" another girl asked. "Isn't that what led to 1917, to the revolution?"

"Yes, you're right, there was. But somehow culture flourished under the Tsars, some say in response to all that repression. Russia has such a rich history. And the country's so vast and beautiful."

"It sounds really cool," Lucy said, while several others nodded in agreement. I relaxed. They were getting it.

Then Stephanie Evans butted in, ruining it all. Stephanie was a year ahead of us; she'd been appointed a "sophomore sister" to me and Jeanie, if we needed help in adjusting to school. She was a stocky, athletic, red-headed girl whose single room was diagonally across from ours. Jeanie liked her and often got into long chats with her. I found her arrogant and unfriendly.

"Russia's not cool, it's cold," Stephanie declared. "It's a cold, cruel, backward place with tyrannical leaders who want to take over the world." Stephanie gave me a disparaging look. She'd clearly pegged me as a naive, romantic young kid.

Someone quickly changed the subject. I sat there, feeling heat rising to my face, a mixture of anger and embarrassment. I couldn't look at Jeanie. She'd betrayed me and set me up for ridicule.

★★★

"I'm so sorry," Jeanie blurted out the minute we were back in our room. "I don't know what came over me. I started talking and I just couldn't stop. I know I upset you. I'm really sorry."

"How could you do that? If you want to expose *your* secret yearnings to the world, that's your business," I sneered, though I was actually deeply hurt to see Jeanie sharing her private thoughts with all those others. "But you have no right to be revealing *my* confidences. You said your lips were sealed."

"I know. I'm sorry. But it wasn't all that bad. They were interested in what you had to say. It's not a shameful secret to be fascinated by another country and its culture."

"Yeah, well, they might've been interested at first, but not after your pal Stephanie dumped on me. She made me seem like a fool."

"C'mon, let's drop it," Jeanie implored.

I turned off my bed light, got under the covers and turned my back to her. "What? You're going to go to sleep? Just like that?" Jeanie was dismayed. I didn't answer. It was a long time before I actually fell asleep.

We barely spoke over the next few days. Jeanie made herself scarce, studying at night with Stephanie across the hall. I couldn't get over my sense of betrayal.

After a few days, I calmed down. I needed Jeanie, I realized, much more than she needed me. She was my only real friend at Smith, while she had many friends and found it easy to confide in them all.

"I'm ready to drop it," I announced one morning. We hugged, laughed a little, and things soon returned to normal. Months later, however, I would think back on this early betrayal: it should have tipped me off, shown me how fragile Jeanie's loyalty to me really was.

★★★

I spent part of spring break with Jeanie in Newport. We were there with her thirteen-year-old brother and her stern-looking mother, who referred to me as "Jeanie's roommate," not by my name. Their house was old and rambling, austerely furnished with no cozy spots to settle into. It was too cold and windy to sail, so we hung out in the cabin of Jeanie's docked sailboat, which had just come out of winter storage. We wrapped ourselves in blankets, feeling snug and increasingly confidential as we sipped sherry from a bottle Jeanie had filched when her mother wasn't looking.

Our conversation turned to sex. We were both virgins, we confided, but Jeanie, unlike me, had virtually no experience with boys.

"What did you two do?" Jeanie wanted to know. "You say you're still a virgin."

"Just about everything we could think of, short of intercourse. I was afraid I'd get pregnant if we went all the way. Doctors won't prescribe diaphragms for young, unmarried girls, you know. And I've heard horror stories about illegal abortions."

I didn't tell Jeanie I was really into sex. I was wary of telling her things so deeply personal. And she was pretty clueless when it came to sex. She would have been shocked to hear about my fantasies and yearnings, about how eager I was to have a passionate love affair.

"Anyway," I told her, "I wanted to save my virginity for someone really special. I saw no point in wasting the big moment on some high school kid I happened to be dating."

"And who would that special someone be?" Jeanie asked.

"I have no idea. But sooner or later I'll meet the man of my dreams."

Four

Time flew by; soon we were studying for finals. One Sunday afternoon, taking a break, Jeanie and I sprawled out on her bed, thumbing through illustrations of ancient Russian icons in an art book I'd found in the library. "Most of these are in the Tretyakov Gallery in Moscow," Jeanie observed. "Wouldn't it be great to see them in person?"

"You know, it just might be possible," I conjectured. "It's been more than a year now since Stalin died; things may be loosening up there. An American lawyer recently traveled in Russia on a tourist visa, something that would have been unthinkable under Stalin. And my Russian tutor told me about a group of German students who got to go there on an art tour."

"Why don't we apply for visas?" Jeanie was excited. "I have a cousin who works in DC. I'll ask him how to go about it."

A week later, Jeanie received an envelope from her cousin containing three visa applications to fill out and mail to the Soviet Embassy in Washington. "Maybe we should ask Steffie to apply with us," Jeanie suggested. She'd begun calling Stephanie "Steffie," at Stephanie's request, and she'd suggested I do the same. "Steffie's an experienced traveler. Her dad's a political science professor at Yale and they travel abroad almost every summer. And she's very focused, a good organizer."

I frowned; a familiar demon of jealousy was rising in me, despite my efforts to repress it.

Jeanie continued: "If there are three of us, we'll seem more like a delegation, like an art tour." She had a point there. I went along. The chances were so remote that the trip would ever happen. Why make an issue over Stephanie?

But try as I did, I could not suppress a nagging suspicion that Jeanie's cousin had not made a mistake when he sent her three applications. Had Jeanie asked him for three, with Stephanie in mind?

Stephanie quickly took over in her bossy way. She inspected our visa applications to be sure they were consistent. She announced that we had doctor appointments for a series of inoculations that we would need for our trip. I objected to spending time and money for shots when we hadn't received a single word in response to our visa requests. But Stephanie insisted: "If the visas *do* come through, there may not be time to get all this done. We have to be prepared."

Summer came; no word from the Soviets. We each went home, Jeanie to spend the summer sailing, Stephanie to a job her dad had gotten her at the Yale library. I joined the hordes of New York City kids, home from college for the summer and looking for work.

Then, in mid-July, a letter for me arrived at our city apartment. It was from "The Embassy of the Union of Soviet Socialist Republics, Washington, DC." In it was a visa, giving me permission to travel as a tourist in the Soviet Union during the month of August. Jeanie and Stephanie received their visas, too. Going to the Soviet Union as tourists? We might just as well have been touring Mars.

The Cold War was at its height. American passports expressly forbade US citizens from traveling to the USSR. The State Department had to give us special permission to go on the trip, which came only after a week of negotiating, during which our professors, families, and friends had to vouch for our loyalty.

My parents, who always encouraged my adventurous spirit, were uneasy because the trip was to Russia. They said I was too young to travel so far away on my own. "I'll be traveling with older friends," I pointed out. "You agreed to have me skipped in school, so don't complain now when I'm doing things older kids do." My father grudgingly agreed to give me the two thousand dollars I needed for the trip.

Stephanie, Jeanie, and I met up in Washington at the State Department, where we had been summoned to receive our amended passports and to be briefed by Paul Larkin, a State Department official.

"You are lucky gals," he told us. "You're about to see a place most Americans will never see. There are scholars and journalists who would trade places with you in a heartbeat. They'll want to know everything when you get back, so take good notes and lots of photos. This is a serious undertaking. The Russians may try to use you for propaganda purposes. So be careful. Don't go to any Communist rallies. Don't talk to anyone from the Soviet press. Be polite, but not effusive. Don't give them a chance to say you love the USSR and wish you could stay there forever."

"That'll be the day," Stephanie muttered. Larkin nodded approvingly.

"You'll be surprised at how backward the country is," he said rather smugly. "I know. I was there for two years with the Embassy. All their money goes into heavy industry and the arms buildup. They don't give a damn about their people."

"Why do you think they're letting us go there?" I asked. "Why *us*?"

"As far as we can determine, you girls are a test case, a first step perhaps in establishing some kind of student exchanges. They've fallen so far behind the West in technology and research. They may need to open up a bit to close that gap. You know, of course, you'll be watched and followed. Everyone is. It's a police state, a very effective one. They have recording machines everywhere. Watch what you say in your hotel room and in cars. Don't take any letters or packages from strangers. Be on your guard at all times. Here's a name you should have, Frank Stoudemeier, and here's his phone number at the Embassy." He handed each of us a card. "He'll be your contact there, if you need him. He's not going to compromise you by seeking you out—Embassy personnel are considered spies by the Soviets—but you should call him if you have any problems. He knows all about your visit."

★★★

"Whew!" said Jeanie. "He doesn't make it sound very inviting." We were out on the street, looking for a place to have some coffee.

"It sounds exciting to me," I said. "Like being in the middle of a spy novel, or something."

Stephanie looked at me with disdain. I knew she saw me as a frivolous kid, more interested in adventure than in culture. There was more than a little truth to that; I knew it myself, even back then. I just didn't find it shameful.

"I wish we were going to Paris," Stephanie muttered. "There are plenty of good paintings in the Louvre."

So why don't you go there? I wanted to say, but I held my tongue. Our trip was just beginning. It was important that we get along.

As news of our plans began to circulate, we found ourselves loaded down with requests, some from people we didn't even know, asking us to gather specific information for them. Editors at *Life* magazine gave us cameras and thirty rolls of color film; they were eager to run a photo story based on our trip. "Rare Views from Behind the Iron Curtain," or something like that. We were eager to oblige: the money from the article would help pay for the trip.

We left in early August on a flight to Helsinki, where we would transfer to Aeroflot for the last leg to Moscow. My parents drove me to the airport. Jeanie and her mother were already there, and Stephanie and her father arrived soon after. Stephanie's dad took charge: He lined us up for photos and made a little send-off speech: "Have a great trip. Stay focused and alert. This will be the adventure of a lifetime." We nodded, knowing he was right.

But for me it would be much more than a one-time adventure. It would be a life-changing experience. It would send me on a quest, a search for a meaningful life.

Five

Moscow, August 1954

I opened the French doors in my hotel room, stepped onto a small balcony and gazed in awe at the scene before me. I knew it well from countless photos but never expected to see it in person: the crenellated walls of the Kremlin with its medieval towers topped by brightly lit Communist stars, the vast expanse of Moscow's Red Square, the sleek, granite Lenin-Stalin tomb and, in the background, the brightly colored onion domes of St. Basil's Cathedral. I gazed starry-eyed at the scene. Others might have found it ominous, the seat of Soviet power. For me, it conjured up scenes from Russian history—the ancient fort, its thick walls enclosing churches and palaces, the historic residence of the Tsars, the site of wars, scandals, and intrigues.

It was early morning, but people were already lining up to view Stalin's preserved body, recently added to Lenin's inside the tomb. Two elderly women in smocks, using primitive-looking brooms, were listlessly sweeping the immaculate sidewalk in front of the hotel. An army van slowly crossed the square, a child's toy in that enormous space. Traffic was permitted in Red Square in those days, but there were almost no cars on the Moscow streets except for official vehicles. Private cars were pretty much unheard of.

We'd been given three of the best rooms in the National Hotel— three suites, side by side, each with a balcony facing Red Square. The hotel had been built in 1903, well before Communist rule. It had many vestiges of its former elegance but had seen better days. At breakfast that first day, we compared notes.

"Don't you just love the alcove for the bed, how you can close it off with those dark red velvet curtains?" Jeanie asked. "And those huge marble bathrooms?"

"Yes," I added, "and the big sitting room with its plushy furniture and fringed lampshades. I can't believe we're actually here."

Stephanie was dismissive. "Looks like the place was furnished fifty years ago and hasn't been touched since. Talk about dust and fading Victorian splendor."

Spoil-sport, I thought, turning toward Jeanie and rolling my eyes. But Jeanie was busy studying the menu. "There's caviar for breakfast!" she announced with glee.

After breakfast we reported, as directed, to the Intourist office in the hotel where we would plan our trip. Intourist was the only tourist agency in the Soviet Union, closely tied to the KGB—the Soviet secret police—and used to keep track of visiting foreigners. We knew, we had been forewarned, that Intourist and its guides would report back to the police. Their job was to watch us and steer us in the right directions.

"For nineteen dollars a day, you will have a first-class trip," the middle-aged official told us in fluent but heavily accented English. He affected a bored expression, the whiteness of his face accentuated by his crudely-dyed black hair. "First-class hotels, four meals a day in your hotels, chauffeur-driven cars, guides and interpreters when you wish. It has all been arranged. This is your itinerary."

We would visit major sites and museums in Moscow and travel to the republics of Uzbekistan and Georgia. Altogether we would cover more than three thousand miles within the USSR.

"Don't we have anything to say about this?" Stephanie asked him. "I'd like to go to Leningrad, to visit the Hermitage Museum."

"Your trip has been approved by the Soviet government," the official replied firmly, ignoring her question. "This is your itinerary."

Maya, our guide in Moscow, was only a few years older than us and hardly my idea of a police agent. I liked her immediately: her open face, her well-scrubbed, wholesome looks. She was amused by the way Jeanie's name had been converted into Cyrillic: *Dzhin Dzhonsonova.*

My name slid mellifluously into Russian as *Katerina Landova*. I loved the sound of it; it gave me a rare feeling of belonging.

Our presence on the Moscow streets invariably created a sensation. Bystanders would follow us. Our clothes, our shoes, our hairdos, and our makeup—everything about us was curious and foreign. They would accost us, demanding to know "*Otkuda vui?*" ("Where are you from?"). I always got special notice because of my long dark hair and my face, pretty enough to attract attention even on the busy streets of New York City. Jeanie, with her blond hair and blue eyes, did not stand out the way I did among the mainly fair-haired Russians. And Stephanie always remained on the fringes, looking bored and restless.

I encouraged people to gather. It was a chance to practice my Russian and a way to get to know ordinary Russian people. I would delay answering their main question—"Where are you from?"—by asking them to guess. Their guesses were often wild ones: "Bulgaria?" "China?" And when I finally told them we were Americans, some in the crowd would back off nervously, afraid to be seen with us. Many seemed frightened by our cameras; they did not want their pictures taken. Some even reported us to the police, which led to annoying delays, the checking of papers, the making of phone calls, and eventual apologies as we were sent on our way.

Moscow was a discordant blend of things Russian and things Soviet. Everything Russian spoke out to me—the palaces and churches, the famous monasteries, the Bolshoi Theatre where we would see *Swan Lake*. I loved the elegant, fading mansions in the center of town and the ancient wooden cottages on the outskirts, dilapidated but still charming with their ornately carved and painted window frames.

The Soviet side of Moscow seemed uniformly backward and sleazy. New apartment houses, with laundry flapping in the courtyards, were already shabby and showing signs of decay. Clerks in the stores used abacuses to tally up bills. Elevators didn't work. Water ran brown. The showpieces of Stalinist architecture were built in a layered, ornately decorated "wedding-cake" style that belonged in Disneyland, not in an ancient, world-powerful capital.

The people on the streets, with rare exceptions, seemed grim and suspicious. They were obedient and orderly, probably in response to the omnipresent uniformed militia men, two or three to a block. Shop windows were half-empty, boring, and bland. There were long lines for food. With the Soviet government controlling all production, there was no entrepreneurial competition. An occasional billboard announced in unattractive script: DRINK TEA.

***

From the start, there was a disconnect between me and my friends. They were focused on art, eager to visit as many museums as possible, taking diligent notes as they went along, writing in their notebooks each evening when they returned to the hotel. Tired from the day's excursions, they were ready for sleep. I, on the other hand, wanted to go out, to see what Moscow was like at night. I was interested in meeting ordinary Russians. I wanted to see how they lived, find out what they thought. I wanted to try out my language skills. But I was wary about going out alone at night. I would attract too much attention; it could be dangerous.

"Let's go out tonight," I suggested on our very first evening in Moscow. "Take a walk, get a taste of Moscow night life." We had spent a long day sightseeing and were now having dinner in our hotel. "No way," they said, almost in unison; they were too tired. When I made the same suggestion the following night, Stephanie looked annoyed. She gave Jeanie a pained look, and Jeanie just shrugged. And so I was forced to retire early, grumpy, and discontented.

I felt like I was hovering outside of Russian society, looking in through a glass wall. I had barely talked to a Russian, other than our official minders. I wasn't all that interested in Russian art, I realized. I wanted to meet real Russians. I wanted to see what it was like to live in Russia.

I was about to get my chance.

Six

A few days into our trip, we visited Moscow University, a large complex in Sparrow Hills, then on the outskirts of Moscow. Its recently finished main building was built in the wedding-cake style that the Stalinists loved. There, in a small lecture hall, a group of about a dozen English-speaking students, all male, had been recruited to act as our hosts. They were studying the English language and American civilization and had access to materials about the United States that were off-limits to other Soviet students. "Spy factory," Stephanie whispered to me as we were being introduced.

But I wasn't worrying about spies. My eyes were fixed on a young man standing near the window and I couldn't tear them away. He was tall, slender, and beautiful, with a sensitive thin face and curly dark hair. His blue-purple eyes seemed to be beckoning me from across the room, and an elusive half-smile flickered across his face. It was as if we shared a secret, the secret of mutual attraction. I made my way toward the window and stood beside him. His arm brushed lightly against mine as a young instructor explained their study program to us.

Soon it was time to tour their facilities—their classrooms, their library, a science lab. I fell into step alongside the young man who introduced himself: Maksim Rzhevsky.

"I'm Katerina, Katerina Landova," I replied in my best Russian. Then, continuing in English: "Everyone calls me Kate."

"Well, I shall call you Katya, if you agree."

I was delighted to hear his fluent, almost unaccented English. Speaking Russian was an effort for me back in those days.

"Of course," I replied. "And I shall call you Max."

He had the lithe gait of an athlete, an easy way of talking and a dazzling smile. I felt an electric charge between us, something I'd read about in novels but never experienced before. I wondered if he felt it, too. As we followed the group, moving from classrooms to the library, to the lab, we exchanged polite talk about where we grew up, our families, and what we were studying. Our conversation was innocuous and had nothing to do with the drama that was quietly unfolding between us. We were exploring each other with our eyes, while our mouths formed the words we were expected to be saying.

"Americans say their country is more free than Soviet Union," Max commented. "But look, you have permission from Soviet government to travel here with your two friends. I am student of American life, but American government will not give me visa to travel in your country."

"That seems to be changing," I said. "I hope so. When Americans talk about their freedom, they mean freedom of expression, the freedom to criticize our own government. People aren't punished for their beliefs." I felt on somewhat shaky ground as I said this, thinking about Senator Joseph McCarthy's ongoing pursuit of American Communists. I wondered if Max knew about that, whether it would come up.

But our visit was coming to an end. I wasn't ready for that. I moved closer to Max and said softly: "Can I see you again? Maybe you will show me around Moscow tomorrow?"

"*Nevozmozhno*" ("Impossible"), he whispered, shaking his head and backing away from me. I didn't try to hide my disappointment. A few minutes later, when we said our goodbyes, he pressed a small piece of paper into my hand. I slipped it into my pocket and did not read it until later, when I was alone in my hotel room.

I expected to be teased by my friends as we made our way back to the hotel. I had behaved shamelessly by completely monopolizing the best-looking guy in the room. But to my surprise, they hadn't even noticed.

"A bunch of spies-in-training," Stephanie declared. "It was so obvious: they'd been briefed about us and told what to say. About how great the Soviet system is and how superior it is to ours. Little robots!"

Jeanie was nodding and laughing in agreement. "I almost lost it when that guy asked me about *Mr. Sowltenzall*. It took me awhile before I realized he was talking about Senator Saltonstall. Katie, can you believe it? He'd researched where I lived and was trying to impress me by knowing the name of my senator!" I smiled, though I failed to see why it was so amusing. I was counting the minutes till I was in my room, able to read the paper Max had slipped me.

"*Tomorrow, 12 noon, Upper Garden, Alexandrovsky Sad. Tell no one.*" I was bursting with excitement, but I kept it to myself. I had a date, a secret date, with a sexy Russian student somewhat older than me, someone who was clearly attracted to me and willing to risk seeing me again.

★★★

The next morning I feigned an upset stomach and begged off from the scheduled visit to the Tretyakov Museum. There were paintings there that I'd been eager to see, like Andrei Rublev's famous *Trinity*, and Valentin Serov's *Girl with Peaches*. I wanted to see the icons, and all the Repins. But the passion that fueled me that morning had nothing to do with art. I retired to my room and studied the map, figuring out the best way to get to the Alexander Gardens. They turned out to be near my hotel, running along the western Kremlin wall. I could easily walk there. Dressed in the most inconspicuous clothes I had with me—a below-the-knee, black, A-line skirt and a tailored white blouse—I made my way as quietly as possible out the side door of the hotel.

I knew I was doing something risky, going off to meet a total stranger without telling anyone, not even my two companions. But I assumed they wouldn't approve, and I didn't want to hear their objections. This was *my* adventure. I didn't want anyone to spoil it. The secrecy and the hint of danger made it all the more exciting.

There was no way for me to go unnoticed in Moscow. The concierge stationed on our floor in the hotel took notes on our comings and goings, and the doorman at the side door bid me good-day. There were plainclothes police at every lobby entrance, observing everything, though their main job, it seemed, was to keep ordinary Russians from entering the hotel. I walked out briskly, my head held high, and no one seemed to take special notice.

I discouraged all approaches from people on the street, walking quickly with my eyes down, pretending not to hear the questions that were being fired at me. I was reasonably successful. As I ducked into the park, the people following me seemed to fade away.

Max had not said exactly where to meet him. I found a bench in the upper garden that seemed centrally located, sat down and buried my face in a book. I was too excited and confused to actually read. What did Max have in mind? We couldn't go strolling in the park; Max would not want to be seen with me. He had written: "Tell no one."

If I had met Max in the United States, or in any other free society, this would have been our first date. We would talk, get to know each other a bit, maybe kiss before parting, plan to see each other again. But this was the Soviet Union. He was taking a great chance, just by meeting me. And I was on a closely monitored trip, scheduled to take off for Uzbekistan the following day. So where could this possibly lead?

It was a while before I saw Max approach. He sat down at the other end of the bench and, like me, took out a book. After a time, he said softly, in English: "Go to trees behind you. I will come soon."

The park had many formal flower beds, juxtaposed with clusters of large, ancient trees. Max caught up with me and led me behind a huge tree that sheltered us from the views of passersby. I leaned back against the tree, facing Max. He didn't seem at all nervous. I relaxed.

"You are beautiful American girl," Max said and then, correcting himself: "*A* beautiful American girl." Though his English was close to perfect, Max sometimes forgot to use "a" and "the," which don't exist in Russian. "Please, tell me, how is it to be a beautiful American girl?" He was being flirtatious, his eyes lively, a smile on his face.

I countered lightly: "I'll bet you say that to every American girl."

He became more serious: "You are the first American girl I know."

"So, are you asking me what it's like to be an American or what it's like to be beautiful?" I was flirting, too.

"No," he said slowly, pondering my question. "Not American. If I ask that, we will talk politics and I do not want that. Tell me about beautiful instead. You must have many men, men that want you."

I smiled, but said nothing. There was an awkward pause. I broke the silence: "And you, with those amazing eyes. There must be many girls chasing you."

"Yes, there are many," he said matter-of-factly, then added very seriously: "I never hoped to meet someone like you."

He was enthralled by the fact that I was American. Just as I, my heart beating fast, was thrilled to be there with him, a handsome Russian.

Max reached out and touched a strand of my hair, twisting it lightly on his finger. Seconds later, we were kissing, soft, timid kisses at first, becoming more and more passionate as the minutes went by. He put his hands on my butt, pressing me close, his groin hard against me. When we finally pulled apart, I was breathless. I didn't want to stop.

"Meet me exactly here tonight." There was a thrilling urgency in his voice. "Come at nine, when it is dark, to this tree. Park closes at ten, I think, but do not worry. I know special exit." He took off in a slow run, not looking back.

I sat on a park bench for quite a while, thinking about Max and what had just transpired. We had hardly talked, we knew nothing about each other, yet the sexual tension between us was overwhelming. For me, this was something new, an attraction to a man that was so intense I was ready to abandon all caution. Was it the same for him? Or was he a Russian "Don Juan," used to seducing girls with his compliments and his ardor? Did it really matter? Our rendezvous that evening would be a one-time encounter, nothing more. We would do our best to communicate, through sex, all that would forever go unsaid and unknown between us. Like the movie *Brief Encounter*. Heartbreaking, and very romantic.

At dinner that evening, I listened as Jeanie and Stephanie described what they'd seen at the Tretyakov. They were excited, eager to return there, there was so much yet to see. I tried to show interest, but my mind was on Max, on what I was about to do later that night. I was fighting the temptation to tell Jeanie about it. Would she try to dissuade me? Did part of me, the sensible part, want to be dissuaded?

After dinner, we went upstairs to our rooms. I was still toying with the idea of confiding in Jeanie. Her room was next to mine, but when I turned, expecting to see her at her door, she was down the hall, entering Stephanie's room instead. A sharp pain tore through my chest, a sudden reminder of how I often felt as a kid, vacationing with my parents. My folks would be with me all day long, the three of us inseparable. But at night they would retire to their shared hotel bed, while I, feeling abandoned, would enter my adjoining room alone.

Fuck Jeanie. I'd always been on my own. I could handle this by myself, and I would.

Seven

There was still some dusky light at nine that night when I found Max waiting under the tree. He'd brought a blanket with him; it was spread out on the grass. We sat down on the blanket, cross-legged, facing each other. He took my hands in his. "You are from a dream," he said, "my deepest dream. My dream to see United States. I want to go there, to see, to understand. But you know, it is not allowed."

"*My* dream has always been to see Russia," I replied. "And look, I'm here now. My dream has come true. Maybe yours will come true, too."

"I will make it come true," he declared firmly. "I have been accepted by the highest Institute. I will study and become a diplomat. And, with good luck, they will send me to United States. . . . And then, I will see you again, my first and only American girl."

I was touched. He seemed to be holding out the unlikely prospect of a future meeting. Like me, he must have realized the enormous leap we were taking—about to have sex, knowing we would never see each other again.

Max stood up and quickly stepped out of his pants. He folded them into a neat square and set them on the blanket. Then, kneeling beside me, he guided me onto my back, using his folded pants as a cushion for my head. I had dressed for the occasion, wearing a wrap-around dress that opened easily with just one tie. No bra underneath, just a pair of nylon panties. Max found the tie and unwrapped my dress, spreading it out on each side of me. I raised my hips to help him remove my panties. He quickly removed his own clothes, inhaling softly and appreciatively as he gazed at me, lying there in the warm night air, naked and dazzled by my own abandon. And then I was in his arms, our bodies wrapped around each other, hearts pounding.

I'd been saving myself for something special. And what could be more special than this Moscow night, the air heavily scented with freshly mown grass and the mixed perfumes of summer flowers? The sky was illuminated by countless stars, against which the dark silhouette of the Kremlin wall loomed silently, mysteriously. And I was in the arms of a soulful Russian boy who kept whispering melodic Russian words in my ear. He called me Katya, Katrina, Katusha. I was transported.

He was slow and gentle, as if he knew it was my first time. He explored my body with his hands, as if trying to memorize its feel. Attentive to my reactions, he seemed quick to learn what felt good to me. I grew wet with desire and we came together with ease. It was over quickly, too soon for me.

Our second time lasted much longer and swept me away. I felt things deep inside that I'd never felt before, feelings both intense and exhilarating. I was straining for a climax, yet wanting it to go on forever. At last I lay there exhausted, his arms around me protectively, as my involuntary shudders slowly subsided.

Max fumbled with his pants, taking something from the pocket. It was a small, homemade cardboard box he had clearly fashioned himself. "This is for you," he said simply. I opened it and found inside a small, delicate gold key. "What is this?" I asked. *"Klyuch k moemu serdtsu,"* he answered. ("Key to my heart.")

"Meet me here again tomorrow, same time," he said insistently.

"I can't," I almost sobbed. "We are flying out of Moscow—to Uzbekistan and then to Georgia—first thing in the morning. I'll be gone for ten days."

I could feel his disappointment, mirroring my own. "But I'll be back in Moscow for a few days before I leave for home," I said hopefully. "I can see you then."

He was quiet for a while, then slowly began reciting a poem in Russian. It was beautiful to hear, though I only understood the first few words: *"Ya vas lyubil,"* which means "I loved you"—*loved*, in the past tense. "The poet Pushkin," he explained, and then he added: "It is better to say goodbye now. This is beautiful thing we have, we *had*. I will always remember you."

"But . . ." I began, as he put a finger firmly on my lips, silencing me. Somewhere near us, there was the sound of a branch cracking. The park was very still, deserted, a little spooky.

We dressed quickly. "Come," he said, folding up the blanket and taking my hand. "Don't be afraid, I know the way."

He led me to an iron fence at the perimeter of the park, to a spot where one of the iron rails was missing. We were able to slip through without difficulty. I felt a familiar pang of jealousy, wondering how often he had done this before and would do it again, with other girls, not with me.

We were standing on a Moscow sidewalk, not far from my hotel. Max looked uncomfortable. People were passing by, looking at us curiously.

"Goodbye," he said quickly, kissing me lightly on the forehead. "Remember me." And he was gone. I made my way back to the hotel, torn by mixed feelings of ecstasy and despair.

Eight

Our handlers had chosen Uzbekistan and Georgia, two of the fifteen Soviet republics, to show us the vastness and diversity of their country. During the next ten days we traveled thousands of miles by air and automobile and wore out our shoes in the dusty streets of ancient cities like Bukhara and Samarkand. There, camels and donkeys jostled us in the blazing heat, old men sitting on tables sipped tea in open tea houses, and veiled women haggled in the bazaars. We visited a famous mosque in Samarkand that had become a Soviet "museum." It was in total disrepair; we collected broken pieces of beautiful mosaics lying among the refuse at its base. There were loudspeakers along the busy streets, blaring out music and news. We cringed at the broadcasts denouncing US "imperialists," even as we talked, with the help of our interpreter, to friendly, incredulous crowds of people who gathered around us wondering who we were. Some even asked if we were from Moscow, revealing how remote they were from the center of Soviet power.

I took pictures of the pigs that roamed the streets of Tiflis—now called Tbilisi—the capital city of Georgia. I photographed a little girl in native dress who reached out to touch my arm, as if to see if I were real. We were taken on a breathtaking mountain drive to see Stalin's birthplace in the town of Gori, about sixty miles west of Tiflis, a little shack protected from the elements by a marble pavilion. We visited model collective farms and museums of the revolution. We saw Young Communist League and Pioneer camps where uniformed children sang spirited songs about the glorious Communist future. At night, as I nursed my blistered feet, I thought only of Max, the wonder of him eclipsing the fantastic world in which we were traveling.

★★★

On our first day back in Moscow we went to the Tretyakov Museum. I had missed the first visit and was happy to have another chance. Jeanie and Stephanie were leaving for home the following day. I had one additional day to spend in Moscow, having somehow bungled my return reservation when I made it back in New York.

Walking back to our hotel from the museum, we saw a crowd forming. It was a familiar pattern by now—first, a group of people, somewhat at a distance, would gather together to observe us: "Who are they? Where are they from? Let's go ask them. Come on." A throng would then besiege us, asking questions all at once.

"I'm tired of these crowds, let's get out of here," Stephanie muttered. "C'mon, walk quickly," and she led the way with her broad shoulders, head down, discouraging any contact with the people following us.

"Hey, Steffie, let's not be rude," I said.

"Me, rude? They're the ones who are rude." And she proceeded to mimic them: *How long did it take you to get here? Which is better, Soviet Union or United States? How much money does your father make? Does everyone in America have a car? Do you have a car? How much did it cost? Why does America want war? Why do you lynch Negroes?* Jeanie was laughing; Stephanie did good imitations. But I wasn't amused.

"Listen," I said, catching up to them. "It's not fair to make fun of them. They know nothing about the outside world, and they really want to know. I feel for them. You know, if my grandparents hadn't gone to America, I might be in that crowd."

Stephanie seemed bewildered by my outburst. Jeanie filled the breach. "Hey Steff, don't mind Kate. She can be super dramatic at times." I pulled Jeanie aside and hissed at her: "Are you explaining *me* to Stephanie? You should be apologizing to *me* for *her* behavior!

It was your stupid idea to include her in this trip." I didn't know if Stephanie could hear what I'd said. I didn't really care.

We had an early dinner in the hotel dining room. It was their last night in Moscow and it should have been a celebration of sorts, but we were all feeling moody and upset. Finally, during one of the interminable waits between courses, Jeanie suggested we sum up our impressions.

"I'm not sorry I came," Stephanie volunteered, "but I can't wait to leave. The people seem so grim. I feel like I'm being watched all the time. This place gives me the creeps."

Jeanie chimed in: "I found it all very interesting, especially the art. But I'm eager to get home. I can't wait to go sailing. We still have two weeks before we're back in school."

"I'm not ready to sum up yet," I said. "I have to give it some thought." I didn't mean to sound dismissive, but my thoughts were elsewhere. I was busy hatching a plan.

***

The next morning, at breakfast, things were cheerier; they were looking forward to their trip back home.

"First thing for me is some milk and Oreos," Jeanie declared.

"I'll settle for a cheeseburger," Stephanie said, "with lots of fries on the side. Oh, the good old US of A. I can't wait."

"What will you do today, Katie, all alone in Moscow?" Jeanie asked. She seemed a bit concerned. Maya, our guide, had said her goodbyes the day before. She didn't seem to know I was staying on.

"I'm going back to the Tretyakov," I said. "There are some paintings I want to revisit."

"Oh, will you try to find a postcard for me," Stephanie asked, "of that Repin painting, you know, the one with the religious procession?"

"I'll try," I promised.

We hugged and said our goodbyes. They went upstairs to finish their packing, and I took off. But I didn't go to the Tretyakov. I went to the university instead. I was going to find Max.

Nine

I had not stopped thinking of Max for a moment. Continually replaying our night in the park, I was consumed by desire. I had to see him again, to make love again, to feel that way just once more.

I had no trouble finding the university building and the right floor. But when I entered the room where we'd previously assembled, it was empty, except for a girl with long, stringy blond hair, sitting at a desk and gazing off into space. She had a classic Slavic face, round with high cheekbones and almond-shaped eyes. She turned to me, an inscrutable expression on her face.

"*Pozhaluysta, ya ishchu Maksima Rzhevskogo*," I said softly in Russian. ("Please, I'm looking for Maksim Rzhevsky.")

She looked me over slowly, got up from her chair, walked into the adjacent hallway and yelled at the top of her voice: "*Maksim!*"

He appeared almost immediately, looking startled and then very pale as he saw me standing there. He came up close: "What are you doing here?" He did not look pleased.

"I wanted to see you. I had to see you," I said.

Max took my arm and led me into an empty classroom, locking the door behind him. "You should not be here. You are not allowed to come here." He was angry.

"I'm sorry," I said, walking up to him and putting my arms around his neck. I pressed my body close, rubbing against him, thrilling to the feel of him. "I miss you so much. I want you so much. I'm still here, we can still have one more night together."

Someone tried the doorknob, calling out in Russian; Max answered, also in Russian. I didn't get what was said. Max looked at me helplessly, clearly in conflict. I could see and feel his desire. He pulled away from me and said curtly, "It is not possible."

I took out my camera and snapped a picture of him, standing there looking torn and confused. I wanted something to remember him by.

"No!" he said, truly alarmed. "You must not take picture. This is much trouble for me."

"It's okay," I assured him. "I will bring it back home undeveloped. I'll print out one picture, then destroy the negative. One picture. Just for me. To remember you by. I'll put it under my pillow every night."

"Do you promise?" he asked.

"Of course, I'll sleep with it every night," I said, but then he added: "You promise you will destroy it?"

"Yes. Don't worry. No one will see it. I will destroy the negative as soon as I get home."

"Then goodbye," he said. "I am sorry. But this is not good."

He slipped out the door, leaving me behind in the room. When I left a few minutes later, he was nowhere to be seen. As I reached the stairs, I saw the girl with stringy hair standing there, looking at me impassively. Burning with anger and humiliation, I made my way back to the hotel.

***

I was still upset the next day as I packed my suitcase for departure and went down to the dining room for a solitary breakfast. The room was pretty empty, as usual, except for an older man sitting at a table by the window. He was probably in his early sixties, but he looked ancient to my young eyes. I'd seen him there before.

He came over to my table, a half-empty cup of coffee in his hand. "You're alone today. May I join you?" He had a bit of a New York accent.

"Yes, please," I said, happy for the company.

He introduced himself as Sy Dulchin, an American fur trader. He asked me how I had enjoyed my trip.

I told him what we'd seen in the Caucasus and in Uzbekistan, how the Soviet authorities had bent over backwards to make the best impression on us. "It's all very heady," I said. "After all, we're just three college girls, interested in art."

I was surprised to learn that Mr. Dulchin traveled frequently to the Soviet Union and had been doing so for years. "I thought Americans weren't allowed here," I said.

"There are exceptions to every rule," he said with a sly smile, "especially when money is involved. The fur trade is very lucrative here, for me and for them."

It was time for me to leave for the airport. I said goodbye, got my suitcase and headed off in the hotel car. My heart was heavy with anger and disappointment; I was smarting from the way Max had treated me the day before. And I was angry with myself. Why hadn't I left him alone? We had parted for good. It was a loving farewell. He had given me that little key, the key to his heart. But I hadn't been satisfied. I wanted more. I still did.

***

At the customs table I opened my suitcase with easy confidence; I had nothing to declare. I assumed that the fifteen rolls of color film in my suitcase, each cassette in its little yellow box, would not be a problem. Paul Larkin at the State Department had assured us we could bring home undeveloped film. "Just be sure not to photograph any bridges or military bases," he told us. "Everything else is now okay."

To my dismay, I was told I had to leave the film behind. I began to argue with the two officials behind the table, telling them they were wrong, that the law had changed. "No, no," they said. "We are the law. You must leave all film here. We will process it and send it to you through US Embassy." My film was Kodachrome, a new kind of color film in the United States that could only be properly developed in a

Kodak lab. When I tried to explain that it was a secret process, things got even worse. "Our Soviet scientists can process all film," they said proudly. "We will process and send to you." The more I argued, the worse it got.

I could see a plane out on the runway. It was past the time for it to leave. It was waiting for *me*. I didn't know what to do.

In a separate place in my suitcase, tucked into the corner nearest to me, was the film I'd used to take Max's picture. I'd inked a little star on the box so it wouldn't get confused with the other film. *Whatever happens, I can't let them have that.* Feigning urgency, I headed for the ladies' room, just a few feet away. As I left, I put my hands in the suitcase, ostensibly straightening out my clothes. I cupped the starred box of film in one hand, hoping they wouldn't notice. I had to destroy it, but how?

Locked in a bathroom stall, I used my little pocket knife to pry open the slot in the cartridge, enough to reach an edge of the film. I pulled on it and was able to unroll the entire film, twenty frames in all, exposing them to the light, ruining them. Then I bunched up the film as best I could and buried it under the garbage in a trash can near the sink. I straightened up, turned around, and found myself facing a uniformed woman who was standing near the door, watching me. "What are you doing?" she asked in Russian.

Pretending I didn't understand her, I rushed out of the room. My suitcase was still open on the table, the other boxes of film neatly stacked alongside it. "I must not miss my plane," I cried out in mock hysteria, snapping my case closed and running out with it toward the plane, leaving the remaining film behind. One of the officials was running behind me, calling for me to stop. I just kept going. He dropped behind. I could see him talking on a phone connection out in the field.

The plane had clearly been waiting for me. There were only a few others aboard. As soon as I entered, the doors closed. I fell into the nearest seat; there were no assigned seats or seat belts on those Soviet planes. My heart was pounding loudly with excitement and then with wild relief as I heard the engines begin to rev up. The plane stood still as the engines gathered power. Then, suddenly, they died. The doors opened and the two customs officials entered the plane. "Come with us," they said grimly and escorted me from the plane.

Ten

I was driven to a police station and left by myself in an empty room. After a long wait, a police captain entered, dressed in a snappy uniform and accompanied by a slight, older man who turned out to be an interpreter. The captain carried a large envelope, which he emptied on the table. There before me was the crumpled, ruined roll of film, fished from the trash can in the airport lavatory.

"What is this?" he asked me. "Why did you try to destroy it, to hide it?"

I didn't answer. I didn't know what to say. He repeated the question.

"I'd like to call the US Embassy," I said. "I am an American citizen."

"In good time," he replied. "First, please tell me why you did this." After a long silence, in which I said nothing, he added: "Your trip here has been approved and welcomed by the Soviet government. You have been extended every courtesy. I hope there is some misunderstanding here, but we will not know unless you explain why you destroyed this."

I asked once more to call the Embassy.

He leaned forward, placing his clenched fists on the table in a threatening manner. The interpreter shot me a warning look. I stared back at the officer impassively, trying to imitate that tough blond girl at the university. There was no way I could tell him the truth.

Throwing up his hands in disgust, he escorted me to a telephone. I called the Embassy number I had been given by the State Department in case of trouble, hoping to reach Frank Stoudemeier. It was late, I realized, probably too late to reach anyone.

A woman answered the phone, speaking English with a heavy Russian accent. I asked for Frank Stoudemeier. "No one here," she said. "Call tomorrow."

"This is an emergency," I said. She hung up.

I called again. "Please, listen to me. My name is Katherine Landau, *Katerina Landova*. I'm being held by the police. *Militsiya*. I must speak to Mr. Stoudemeier. Do you have his telephone number? At home? *Doma?*"

"It is forbidden to give number," she answered. "Call tomorrow, call in morning."

"Please contact him now," I said firmly. "This is an emergency."

"I will try," she said and hung up.

I was taken to a locked cell, my room for the night. A woman warden brought in a thin blanket and a shabby pillow which she placed on a cot with a bare mattress, the only furniture in the cell. She escorted me to the bathroom, watching me all the while. Later, I was served a meal on a tray: lukewarm potato soup and a piece of stale bread. They were treating me like a criminal, I realized. I could end up in prison, accused of taking forbidden photos and trying to smuggle them out of the country.

But what could I tell them? Surely not the truth. By destroying the film with Max's picture on it, I had made things with Max seem much worse than they really were, much more sinister than a simple tryst in the park. Max could get in serious trouble if I mentioned his name. *No, telling the truth now would be a disaster*. I was wide awake, surprisingly calm, as I sat there thinking and planning what I would say. Around 4 a.m., I fell asleep.

Frank Stoudemeier woke me about four hours later. "I've been going from jail to jail, looking for you," he said. "I was out last night and didn't get your message till very late. Then I didn't know where to find you. Now, tell me, what happened? Something about some film?"

I told him about *Life* magazine, about the many rolls of film, about the assurances we received from the State Department that we could bring home undeveloped film.

"Yes, I know. There's been some misunderstanding. But I'm told you destroyed a roll of film. Why? What was on it?"

"Just some silly stuff I didn't want them to see. You know, photos we took in our hotel room, of my friends and me, half undressed, in sexy poses. I thought it might cause trouble if those photos ended up in *Pravda* or *Izvestia*. They could use them to discredit us, our whole trip." I smiled lamely.

Stoudemeier did not look amused, but I could see he believed me. "Let me go talk to them," he said.

He was gone for a long time. I could hear him talking in a neighboring room. I could hear other voices speaking in Russian. But I couldn't make out the words. After a while there was some laughter. I began to relax. They were buying my story.

Stoudemeier came back to the cell. "Okay, you're getting out. But I have to tell you, this has not been fun. I'm disappointed in you and your friends. I'll have to pay a price for this. Every 'favor' in this country has a price."

"What about the rest of the film?" I asked.

"That stays here. They're wrong about the rules, of course, but it's a matter of face-saving at this point. They'll develop it and send it to me. I'll get it to you when I can."

"It will be ruined," I said, "you know that."

He didn't respond. "C'mon, I'll drive you back to your hotel."

★★★

I found myself back at the National Hotel, scraping together the remnants of my money to pay for another night's stay. No view from a balcony this time around: small and undistinguished, my room was in the back, facing a courtyard. It seemed to reflect the downward turn of my luck in Moscow.

Sy Dulchin joined me at my breakfast table the next morning. "You're still here?" he inquired. "I thought you'd left." He seemed concerned. I thought of my parents, how concerned they must be.

Did they have any way of knowing what had happened? They had been planning to meet me at the plane.

"I had some trouble at customs," I explained. "Ended up spending a night in jail."

"Oh?" He was curious, of course.

"I'd rather not talk about it," I said. "There were some problems with the film I was taking out. . . ." I was relieved when he didn't press me. I sensed he had ways of finding out what he wanted to know.

"Stephanie and Jean must be home with their parents by now," he commented. "Do your parents know what happened here? They must be very worried about you." He must have been reading my mind. "If you want, I can get word to them."

"Oh, that would be wonderful," I said and scribbled down my home phone number. Then I stopped short. "You know Stephanie and Jean?" I asked, surprised.

"I met them here. They asked me for advice when they were leaving."

"What kind of advice?"

"You'd better ask them," he replied, then added: "I'm sorry I couldn't have done the same for you, about your film, that is. I wish you'd asked me. I could've arranged for you to send it out in the Embassy pouch. They're not allowed to search it."

"I didn't expect any trouble," I replied. "It never occurred to me to ask."

Then I asked him for another favor. "I spent my last cent for the hotel room last night. My ticket's paid for, but I'll need a little cash, just some pocket money to get me home. Could I borrow some from you? I'll send you a check as soon as I'm back home."

"How much do you want?" he asked, reaching for his wallet.

"Twenty-five dollars," I said. He peeled off five ten-dollar bills. "You'll need a bit more than that, I think."

I asked for his address. "Don't worry about it," he said, but I insisted. He scribbled down an address in Helsinki, to which I sent a check as soon as I got home. Weeks later the envelope came back unopened, marked "*addressee unknown*."

Eleven

Changing planes in Helsinki was like entering the Land of Oz. The sparkling shops and food stores in the airport, the bustling activity of well-dressed people, and the noise—especially the noise—were dazzling to me after the hushed drabness of Communism. I felt a sense of deep relief, as if a great burden had been lifted from me. I couldn't wait to get home.

When my plane landed at Idlewild—now John F. Kennedy—Airport, I hurried down the steps, surprised to find a young man ready to whisk me through customs and into a waiting car. He was from *Life* magazine and had come for the film. As I was explaining what had happened to the film, I found myself surrounded by reporters asking questions: "Is it true they took naked pictures of you?" "What was it like in a Soviet jail?" Flashbulbs were popping, all aimed at me.

"No. No, it was nothing like that." I tried to correct them. "It was just a few pictures we'd taken . . ."

My parents had made their way through the crowd, my mother smiling and waving, my father looking grim and lawyerly. He greeted me tersely, without a hello: "Don't say anything to the press. Let's get out of here." And we did, fighting off questions as we made our way to the car. Ruggles, our ancient Lab, was sitting patiently in the back seat, panting. I climbed in and curled up with him. "We are *so glad* you're home!" Mom exclaimed. Despite myself, I began to cry.

***

The press had a field day for the next few days, and I was the game. My picture was in several tabloids, with headlines like "Coed Jailed by Commies for Withholding Naked Photos," and "Soviets Demand Nude Pics, Lock US Girl in Jail." Fortunately, the interest was short-lived. I refused all requests for interviews, and the story died on its own. My parents did not ply me with questions. They accepted my version of what had happened, found it somewhat distasteful, and chose not to discuss it further.

Two days after I got home, I received a phone call from a John Bradbury of the FBI. "We'd like to debrief you, a routine debriefing, about your trip to the USSR." I invited him to our apartment, but he preferred to meet me in the lobby downstairs. He led me to his car, where another FBI man, I never got his name, was waiting. The interview took place in the car. Bradbury did all the questioning. "Did anything unusual happen?" "Did anyone ask you to deliver a package, or to bring out a letter?" "Were you pressured to attend any Communist party rallies?"

"No," I replied to all.

"Did you receive any gifts?"

"No," I lied. That little gold key was none of their business.

"Now," Bradbury said, "let's talk about that film. We know there weren't any naked pictures. We've already debriefed your girlfriends."

"Can I speak confidentially?" I asked. I didn't want to lie to the FBI. He assured me I could.

So I told them about Max, that we had seen each other a few times, that I had taken his picture and promised to keep it out of official Soviet hands.

"Why do you think that was so important to him?" Bradbury asked.

"He didn't say. But he was part of a select group at the university. I guess he didn't want any blemishes on his record. Friendship with an American would look bad."

"What's his name?"

"Do you really need to know? Yes, well, it was Maksim, Maksim Rzhevsky. He's just a student. No one important." Bradbury wrote it down.

"Well, Miss Landau, you're certainly one to keep your promises. The hard way, I'd say." He shook his head from side to side. "You girls are quite a crew," he said, with a note of admiration. It got me wondering what Jeanie and Stephanie had told him.

★★★

Jeanie was on the phone. I'd been expecting her to call. "What the hell is going on, Kate? Nude pictures? In our hotel room? Nothing like that happened and you *know* it. What in the world are you trying to do?"

"Oh, I know. I'm sorry," I said. "I can explain it all, but not right now. When I see you. It'll take time."

I'd been looking forward to unloading to Jeanie, my best friend, my confidante. I was waiting till we were together again so I could tell her everything: Max, the park, the photograph, jail. But Jeanie wasn't waiting.

"You'd better tell me now," she demanded. "My folks are furious. They can't believe that we three—student ambassadors to a hostile country, representing the United States of America—would behave like college kids partying during spring break. I'm not sure they really believe me when I tell them nothing like that happened. 'Cause no one can understand why you would say something like that. For the *publicity*? To get yourself in the papers? It doesn't make sense."

I was silent, searching for something to say.

"You were so weird in Moscow, Kate. I mean, I know we come from different backgrounds, but I thought you'd overcome yours. It was as if you went native. Did you really identify with those crude Russians, those brainwashed Commies?"

"Overcome my *background*, Jeanie? Is that what you just said?" My voice was rising. "What a snotty thing to say! I think it's *you* who hasn't overcome *yours!*" I didn't use the word "anti-Semite." She knew what I meant.

There was a long silence. I thought Jeanie might be crying. I felt bad, sorry I'd raised my voice, sorry I hadn't been open with her in Moscow. But I couldn't talk to Jeanie without including Stephanie, and I really hadn't wanted to involve *her*.

"Listen," I said. "We'll be back in school in a week. We'll have a real talk then. I have so much to tell you!"

Jeanie cleared her throat. "I'm going to be rooming with Steffie this year. My folks think a change will be good for me. Steff and I got really close during the Russia trip. She's very special."

"Special? You mean especially grumpy and unpleasant. You must be kidding, Jeanie."

"No, Kate, I mean it. You and I need a break from each other. We seem to be moving in different directions."

I was stunned, but I tried not to show it. "Okay, if that's what you want. Maybe you're right. Maybe we *do* need a break. I'm sure *my* folks will agree." I hung up the phone abruptly, without saying goodbye.

***

"Fuck you, Jean Johnson," I yelled out loud, to no one. "And fuck your snobby mother!" I had felt her mother's condescension when I visited Newport. Oh, she tried, she was polite. But I knew she looked down on me as a nouveau-riche Jew from New York.

I was in despair. How could this have happened? Jeanie, my best friend from the very first day of college. I thought we'd be friends forever. We wore each other's clothes, and even each other's shoes. We liked the same books, the same movies, the same food. What had come over me in Moscow? Why did I get so carried away? I was infatuated with Max, not just because he was handsome and sexy, but because he was Russian. I was thrilled by the secrecy. And the danger. I'd destroyed that goddamn photo, just to keep my promise to him. I could have been charged with espionage, ended up in a Soviet prison for the rest of my life. And all because of a total stranger I knew nothing about. And he certainly hadn't seduced me. I'd thrown myself at him!

No one else was home. I could let go, and I did, cursing out loud, pounding the pillows on my bed in anger and frustration. Ruggles whined beside me, rubbing his cold nose against my cheek as I finally dozed off, falling into a heavy sleep. I awoke around 3 a.m.; they'd let me sleep through dinner. They must have known how tired and upset I was.

I felt calm. I was going to be all right. I knew what I would do. I had some important changes to make, changes that would alter my life.

I would switch my major to political science, with a specialty in Russia. I would master the Russian language, do graduate work in Russian studies, and plan to use my skills in some sort of meaningful work.

I didn't need Jeanie. I would move to another house at Smith. I didn't need friends at all. Friends brought out the worst in me—feelings of jealousy and anger that I found hard to control. I would learn to be alone without feeling lonely. And my aloneness would make me strong.

***

I knew I should forget Max, push him out of my thoughts. But I didn't. I couldn't. When I arrived back at school that fall, I had a slim gold chain around my neck. Attached to it, a little gold key.

Twelve

Washington, DC, 1963–64

I hadn't planned to work for the government. But when two CIA recruiters approached me in early 1963, I decided to apply. I was excited by the prospect of doing undercover work. I was sure I'd be good at it. I was pleased with the way I'd handled myself in that Soviet jail back in 1954, proud of the story I'd invented to explain why I'd destroyed that roll of film. I had the makings of a good operative, or so I thought.

Nine years had passed since my Moscow trip. I was a doctoral student at Columbia University's Russian Institute in New York City, working on my dissertation, uncertain about my future career. I was writing about Isaak Babel, one of the greatest Russian writers of the early Communist years. Babel's life was fascinating. It was full of lies and secrets. He had affairs with more than one woman at a time, and had three children by three different women, only one of whom was his legal wife. Babel was drawn to intrigue and danger, something I understood.

A new president, John F. Kennedy, was in the White House. I thrilled to his words at the Inauguration: "Ask not what your country can do for you. Ask what you can do for your country." Working for the CIA, using my knowledge of Russia and the Russian language—that was something I could do for my country and also for Russian people victimized by Communism. I saw the United States as a beacon of freedom. I wanted Russia to change, to learn from our example.

I had learned a lot about the ravages of Soviet repression: that an estimated fifty to sixty million people had perished in one way or another under Stalin's reign. Soviet people lived in fear of arbitrary arrest, of being sent to slave labor camps where they would be tortured and starved. The "thaw" that had followed Stalin's death—when my two classmates and I were allowed to visit the USSR—had been short-lived. It was soon replaced by more arrests and repression under a harsh new leader, Leonid Brezhnev.

Months went by before I actually got the CIA job, months of traveling back and forth from New York to Washington for interviews and written exams, language tests and psychological assessments. I passed a lie detector test, an important step in the process. I found it ironic that a lie detector test was essential for a job in which lying would become routine. Indeed, my ability to lie, and to lie easily, would turn out to be one of my assets in the job.

In July 1963, I began work at Langley, the CIA campus in McLean, Virginia, in a new, imposing structure that seemed designed to make me feel like a very small cog in a big machine. I was imbued with a sense of mission, of "what I could do for my country." Four months later, President Kennedy was assassinated.

Like most Americans, I was devastated. The beautiful young family in the White House, the President who spoke of ideals I understood and shared—all gone with the speed of an assassin's bullet, an assassin who was probably a Communist and had spent time in the Soviet Union. Kennedy's death strengthened my determination to help protect my country from its Communist enemies, using whatever tactics were necessary.

My work for the CIA was a dark secret. If anyone asked, I was "translating documents for the State Department." My parents didn't push me to tell them more, though I assumed they knew. They had only one question: "Will you be traveling for this job?" "No traveling," I lied. I didn't want them worrying about me being arrested as a spy in some foreign country. They were clearly relieved.

As it turned out, there really was no traveling. I was assigned to translate Russian materials, sitting at a desk in a small cubicle on the second floor where everyone wore ID cards and opened locks to enter their assigned sections. The people in the cubicles around me appeared to be doing similar work, though we never discussed it. My specialty was Soviet defense spending. I translated all day long, learning the specialized vocabulary I needed as I went along. I was fast and accurate and my boss, Ross Coleman, kept congratulating me on my talent and hinting at a promotion that never seemed to materialize.

I shared a dreary apartment in DC with two women from the Agency. One knew Chinese, the other was an economist. It was a relief not to have to lie about where we worked, though we never discussed the substance of what we were actually doing. Suzy, the China expert, liked to cook. Sometimes, on weekends, we cooked together. She taught me some Chinese dishes that her mother, raised in China, had taught her. Mary, the economist, liked movies, and we often went to movies together. Occasionally, we would all attend a party given by other Agency people. Such office parties weren't very lively, but at least I didn't have anyone asking me: "What do you do?"

I avoided meeting new people because I couldn't be open about my work. I wouldn't have minded if I were doing exciting, covert work. But to lie about the boring translations I was doing—that began to seem absurd.

I had a boyfriend, Steven Erickson, but he was far away. We had met in New York City more than a year before, on a warm spring day, sitting on a bench in Riverside Park. I was engrossed in a book; he had been jogging. "What are you reading?" he asked me, a complete stranger, in a warm, friendly manner that reflected his Minnesota upbringing. It was as if we'd known each other forever. He told me he lived on a houseboat at the 79th Street marina and invited me down to see it. We soon became inseparable, and our friendship became love. But our career paths were leading us to cities very far from each other. Though not formally engaged, we reached an understanding that we would marry in two years, once Steven finished his studies at Stanford Law School.

Steven was my complete opposite—a serene, purposeful man following a straight path to his future. He was unaware of my deep need to step out of the ordinary, to do something meaningful, something that took courage and daring. If he suspected I was working for the CIA, he didn't let on. He frequently chided me for abandoning my research in New York to do translations in Washington, and often urged me to resume my studies out in California where we could be together. Discouraged with the way things were going for me in DC, I was beginning to like that idea.

*****

More than a year had passed, and I was still translating. I went to Ross Coleman to complain. Coleman was an undistinguished-looking man of average height and build, with bland coloring and a thin, pinched face. He wore horn-rimmed glasses and favored bow ties, which seemed to emphasize his protruding ears. He had an unnerving way of averting his eyes when I looked straight at him. It made it seem as if he was hiding something.

"Don't worry," he told me. "By the end of this year, you'll be doing analysis, and that's the interesting part. Searching for trends, unearthing secret programs, writing reports to be sent to State." I looked at him questioningly and he looked away.

"I'm not up to much more of this," I told him. "I joined the Agency because I wanted to be a case officer, to work in Russia, to recruit agents there, people who were fed up with the Soviet system and wanted to work for *us*. My conversational Russian is excellent, I understand the Soviet mentality. I would think you could put me to better use than sitting at a desk."

Coleman looked me over with a half smile on his face. "You haven't the looks or the personality for covert work," he muttered. "I can't see *you* fading into the woodwork." I didn't like the way he was looking at me; it was creepy. Then he stood up and walked behind my chair, putting his hands on my shoulders. "You have to learn patience," he said.

"I have a fiancé," I blurted out, shrugging off his hands. Coleman moved away. To smooth things over—he was my boss, after all—I quickly continued: "My fiancé's in law school for the next two years. This would be the perfect time for me to travel, before I settle down."

"The government moves slowly," Coleman said. "As for covert work, very few get to do that."

Maybe I should call it quits, I thought, as I left Coleman's office. *I'm stuck in Translation, with a lecherous, repugnant boss.* But before doing anything rash, I went to see someone in Human Resources and told him I was bored with translating and wanted to work abroad. His response was similar to Coleman's: "Very few get to do covert work. You will move ahead in research. Stick to it and you'll find yourself doing important analysis. And anyway, it's my understanding that Bud Riley never uses women for undercover work. Except in those cases where only a woman can do the job." He gave me a meaningful look.

"You mean by seducing men and setting them up for blackmail?" I asked. I'd heard there were such women in the Agency; they were known as "swallows."

"Exactly. And I assume that's not what you're looking for."

"Definitely not. But tell me, who's Bud Riley?"

"He's one of the big bosses, the one in charge of covert operations. I've never actually met him, but I hear he's a real pro."

At last, I had a name. Bud Riley, head of covert operations. I would write to him directly. I knew, of course, that I would be defying protocol: I would be going over the head of my boss, Ross Coleman, in an effort to advance my career. But Coleman would do nothing for me, I knew that by now. I had no choice.

November 3, 1964

Dear Mr. Riley:

Forgive me for writing to you directly with my concerns, but I have received no satisfaction through normal channels. I joined the Agency in July 1963 with the expectation, given my training and abilities, that I would be sent to do undercover work in Moscow. Instead, I have been translating documents for more than a year, with no end in sight. My Russian is fluent. My studies at the Russian Institute at Columbia University have given me a deep understanding of Soviet politics and culture. I believe I could serve my country best by working in Moscow to develop assets there.

I enclose a copy of my resume. I would very much appreciate an opportunity to meet with you in person to discuss my future career.

Thank you for your time and attention.

Yours,

Katherine Landau

Three weeks went by without an answer. The only change in my status had to do with Ross Coleman, who avoided me when we passed in the hall, refusing to greet me. He must have known about my letter to Riley. I wondered when he would confront me.

At last, Coleman summoned me to his office. He was irritated. "Bud Riley up on seven wants to see you," he said. "The man you've been trying to see. You must have pulled some pretty important strings."

I ignored his insinuation. "When does he want to see me?" I asked, trying to hide my excitement.

"He wants you up there right now."

Thirteen

Bud Riley had the assurance and good humor of a man who is comfortable in his job. He was nice-looking, in his early sixties, with graying temples and sharp blue eyes. "Please, sit down," he said, pointing to one of the two black leather chairs facing his desk.

"So," he began without preamble, "you want to be a spy. Trench coat and dark glasses, that sort of stuff?"

He was teasing me, but his manner was friendly and cheerful, and I decided not to take offense. "I have excellent conversational Russian," I began. "I can mingle easily, make friends, find people in Russia to work for us . . ."

Riley interrupted: "Russia is a police state, a very dangerous place. We don't send people there to wander around making contacts. The case officers we send there are highly trained, yet they're frequently arrested and expelled. Their Russian assets pay a much higher price: they're arrested and executed on the spot. Anyway, we've never sent a woman operative to a place as lethal as Moscow."

"Well, there's always a first time," I suggested and began to cite my skills again. "I speak good Russian, I . . ."

"I like your spirit," Riley cut in, "but forget it. It's not going to happen. However, I do have a proposition for you. It involves undercover work you can do here in the United States. It's not without its risks, of course. Do you think you'd be interested?"

"Yes!" I said too eagerly, then backtracked. "I mean, it depends on what you have in mind."

"You're about to find out," he said and picked up his phone. "Send Baxter in," he said crisply.

Baxter was a huge man, tall and broad-shouldered; his large, puffy face bore the telltale reddish glow of heavy drinking. "Jim Baxter, Federal Bureau of Investigation," he said, extending a sweaty hand to me.

"Katherine Landau," I replied, shaking his hand. He sat down in the leather chair facing mine. Bud Riley remained behind his desk. He nodded to Baxter to proceed.

★★★

"Maksim Andreevich Rzhevsky," Baxter announced, watching me closely. "Does that name mean anything to you?"

Max! I felt myself tumbling back into the past, but I kept my outward cool. So much had happened since that summer night, ten years before, in a Moscow park. I was no longer a romantic schoolgirl. I'd had several serious relationships, and then Steven, of course. And I'd learned a great deal about the Soviet government, about the evil measures it used to keep people under its control. I no longer wore the little gold key Max had given me; I put it away when I graduated from Smith, replacing it for a time with my Phi Beta Kappa key. Yet Max was always there, somewhere . . . in my dreams, in my fantasies. They say you never forget your first, and Max was a very special first.

"I met a Maksim Rzhevsky when I was in Moscow in 1954," I told Baxter. "I don't know about the Andreevich, I never knew his patronymic."

Baxter removed a black-and-white photograph from a folder he was carrying: it was a murky picture, dark and blurry. It looked like it had been enlarged from a passport or visa photo. "Is this the guy?"

The picture showed a man with short, well-trimmed dark hair, eyes of indeterminate color, a serious, almost grim set to his mouth.

I remembered Max with longish, curly hair, shockingly blue eyes, a thin poetic face and a beautiful smile. I sat there staring at the photo, looking for some resemblance.

"Well?" Baxter jogged me into alertness.

"I don't know," I said. "It was ten years ago. The Maksim Rzhevsky I met was a boy, a student. This is a man."

Baxter began to read from a dossier: "Maksim Andreevich Rzhevsky. Born 1932 in Moscow. Father, Andrei Rzhevsky, engineer. Mother, Sofia Alekseeva, bookkeeper. Older sister, Ekaterina Rzhevskaya, teacher.

"Yes," I interrupted, "he had a sister named Katya, same as me, I remember that. . . . And she was a teacher, I'm pretty sure that's what he told me."

Baxter continued: "Studied American economics at Moscow State University, did graduate work at the Moscow Institute of International Relations. Married 1958 to Viktoria Gruzinskaya, divorced 1961." Baxter looked up at me: "I think this is the man you met, the man whose picture you destroyed to keep him out of trouble. He owes you something for that."

It was like a long-forgotten dream. I remembered telling the FBI about Max when they debriefed me in 1954. Of course, they'd kept his name from that debriefing. And mine. I had no idea where this was leading.

"Maksim Rzhevsky is now living in New York City. He's with the Permanent USSR Mission to the United Nations, their 'cultural affairs officer.' We think he's KGB, one of their top intelligence guys. The Mission is teeming with spies, and he's one of the bosses." A long pause. "And that's where you come in."

"Me? How? I haven't seen Max in ten years. He's probably forgotten all about me. And I'm not sure I'd recognize him."

"This is what we have in mind," Baxter explained. "You will renew your friendship with Mr. Rzhevsky. Get close to him. Get him to trust you. Learn all about him and his activities. He'll be happy to see you, I think. Everyone has a weakness, and this guy's weakness appears to be pretty women."

"Let me get this straight," I said. "You want me to spy on Max and find out if he's KGB?"

"No, that's not it. We know he's KGB. That's about all we *do* know about him. He's left no paper trail. We don't know what he's done for the KGB or where he's been before this. We know nothing about his friends or family. He's clearly highly trusted by his superiors: they send only their most loyal people to the United States, people who won't defect. This guy, Rzhevsky, he knows a lot. We're wondering if he's someone we could turn, someone we could get to work for *us*. We need to learn more about him. Now get this straight: We're not asking you to try turning him. That's a highly skilled business, requiring years of training. What we want is an assessment: We want you to find out everything you can about him, his background, his work, his interests, his politics. You can help us prepare a profile. Help us decide whether he's worth pursuing. Rzhevsky's job here, we believe, is to recruit and maintain contact with American spies, receive secret, classified documents from them and pass them on to Moscow. The Soviets have a network of spies in our country. Some are Americans in high-level positions who've turned traitor, either for money or because they've bought into the Commie dream. Others are Russians who've taken on American identities and live among us pretending to be ordinary Americans; 'illegals,' we call them."

So Max, the soulful boy who'd recited poetry to me that night in the park, had ended up in the KGB, the Soviet Union's vast, ruthless intelligence service. How disappointing. I had thought he'd become a diplomat, an ambassador. It made sense to use my connection to him, slight as it was, to find out whether he seemed susceptible to changing sides and working for us.

"Count me in," I said, surprised to feel my heart thumping loudly. Was I scared? Excited? Or just thrilled to be getting out of Translation? "When do I start?"

"You can work that out with Clarence here," Baxter said. "He'll be your handler, your control. This is a joint FBI-CIA operation. Rzhevsky is in a position to expose American spies and sleeper cells in this country, which is FBI business. He also must know plenty about the KGB's activities abroad, which interests the CIA. So we both have a stake in getting him to cooperate. Clarence and I will be working together on this. But he'll be your point man, your boss—for training, reporting, and advice." He stood up, shook my hand, nodded to Riley, and left.

★★★

"Your name isn't Clarence," I said to Bud Riley as soon as Baxter was gone. "Why does he call you that?"

"It will be Clarence to *you* from now on. That's my code name for this operation, OPERATION PLAYBOY. And Max will be known as PLAYBOY."

"PLAYBOY?" I raised my eyebrows.

"Why not? He's a ladies' man, likes a good time. That seems to be his style. Now here's how we're going to work this," Riley went on. "You'll report to me, as Clarence, on a special secure phone line that goes directly to me and exists only for you. We'll set up a regular, weekly phone call for you to report in. You'll also be free to call me at any time, day or night, if you have any questions or problems. Is that clear so far?"

"Very clear." I tried to hide my excitement. This was the kind of clandestine work I'd been hoping for.

"We'll figure out a strategy for you to meet up with Max again. After that, it will be up to you . . . to get close to him, close enough to find out where he goes, who he sees, what he thinks, what he does with his time."

"When you say 'close' . . ." I began, but he cut me off. "That's up to you. How you win his confidence, his trust . . . That's your business, not ours."

I knew, of course, what he was implying. And he knew, of course, that I knew. To "get close" to Max meant to sleep with him. Did he see me as a "swallow," using sex to get close to Max? I was about to voice my objections, but I decided to hold my tongue. Maybe I would find another way.

"First, you have to learn some tradecraft," Riley went on. "We don't have that much time. We want to utilize your connection to Max while he's still in New York. He could be called back to Moscow at any time. So we'll have to give you a crash course—a few months, maybe a little more, at the Farm where we do our training. It's in a secret location about a hundred miles south of here. They'll decide what you need for this job: surveillance and counter-surveillance techniques, lock-picking, eavesdropping, covert photography, that sort of thing. They'll help develop a cover story for you. I'll get all the paperwork done tomorrow. Report to my office on Monday. You'll get a pay increase commensurate with your new work."

He continued, "Oh, and one more thing—we'd like you to send us written reports as you learn things about him. And Katherine, this is very important. Under no circumstances are *you* to try to turn him, to bring him over to our side. That's for us to decide, based in part on your findings. So don't get ambitious, just report what you see and hear."

"I will."

"Thanks." He smiled. "You're gonna be great at this."

I smiled back, but my heart wasn't fully in it. In his amiable way, Riley had sent me some very mixed messages. True, he was offering me challenging undercover work, secret work that I'd been seeking. But he'd begun our interview by teasing me for "wanting to be a spy," implying I was in it for the "trench coat and dark glasses." He had told me bluntly that he didn't trust women to do dangerous case work. And he had deftly set me up to be a kind of "swallow," by telling me to get close to Max while refusing to discuss exactly what that would entail.

Fourteen

New York City, 1965

In April 1965 I was back in New York, with a cover story and a plan. To Steven, to my parents and to the world at large, I had left the government and was back at Columbia, writing my dissertation. In reality, I was on contract with the CIA.

My salary was tripled overnight, a tacit acknowledgment that the demands of my new job might exceed the normal call of duty. I was uncomfortable with this raise in pay grade: I was being paid to sleep with a stranger. It was demeaning, even if it was for a higher cause. But then, I rationalized, no one had actually ordered, or even directly suggested, that I sleep with Max; they'd left that up to me. And sometimes the hint of possible sex can be more enticing than the act itself. I would see how it went. I could always resign, if I felt I had to.

I was given a cozily furnished, three-room apartment, the front half of the second floor of a New York City townhouse on East 76th Street, near Lexington. The rooms were small, befitting a single person, but the bedroom had a queen-sized bed.

I knew the East Side well. I had grown up and gone to prep school there. My parents still lived in the family apartment at 83rd and Park. But it didn't seem appropriate for a student to be living in such elegant surroundings. I had suggested that I live up near Columbia, but Clarence vetoed it. "We want you on the East Side. The UN is there. The Soviet Mission is there. Max lives in that part of town. It will make it much easier to see him."

"But how will I explain this fancy place to my parents and my friends? Students can't afford to live like that."

"You'll find a way," Clarence said. And I did. I rented a shabby room down a long corridor in an old lady's apartment on 115th Street near the Columbia campus and used it as a mail drop and message center, giving that address to my parents, Steven, and my Columbia contacts. Periodically, I would check my phone messages there and pick up any mail. Sometimes I even slept there on the lumpy mattress, bracing myself for the frantic scattering of roaches when I turned on the light in the communal bathroom.

As planned, I joined the *Russky Kruzhok*, the Russian Circle, an organization of Russophile students at Columbia devoted to Russian culture. They were planning a special evening of Russian folk music and dance. I suggested that we invite some "real" Russians from the Russian community in New York. They immediately liked the idea. I volunteered to make the contacts.

This was the start of the strategy Clarence and I had worked out. As a student at Columbia, I was busily publicizing a Russian cultural event. I kept it apolitical. I sent an announcement of the event to the *Novoe Russkoe Slovo*, an anti-Soviet Russian newspaper in New York. I posted an announcement on the bulletin board of the Four Continents Book Store, the only exclusively Russian bookstore in New York City, known to be sympathetic to the Soviets. And then my real work began: I went to the Soviet UN Mission and asked to speak to the cultural affairs officer. Feigning ignorance, I asked for and was given his name: Maksim Rzhevsky.

It wasn't easy gaining access to the building. I think my fluent Russian did the trick. My driver's license was held at reception, my bag was searched, several phone calls were made. Finally I was ushered into a waiting room where a young man named Gleb was sent to receive my materials. "I want to speak to Mr. Rzhevsky in person," I explained.

Gleb frowned. "He is very busy right now. He has no time. I will bring these to his attention."

"Please," I said, "bring him my card." I had printed up special cards for the purpose, with my name, the Russian Circle, and Columbia University on them.

The wait was short, but seemed interminable. Gleb reappeared. "Mr. Rzhevsky will see you now," he said.

***

Max was standing behind a desk in a large, airy office. He held out both his hands and clasped mine as I came within reach. "Katya!" he said, "I've been looking for you!"

"Max!" I replied. "I couldn't believe it when they told me your name. It really is *you*." I suddenly felt my knees go weak.

The man I was facing was impossibly handsome. His cheeks had filled out and his jaw was quite square; he was tall, broad-shouldered, and trim. His dark hair was cut short, not the tousled curls I remembered. But his eyes were the same deep purplish blue, and his smile, his even white teeth, made my heart beat fast. It was Max all right, a grown-up Max, a Soviet official, a spy. He looked like he could be the CEO of some major American corporation, except for his ill-fitting, slightly shiny Soviet suit.

"I've tried to find you in the phone book," he said. "In Northampton, Massachusetts; in New York City. Where have you been hiding?"

"I've been right here," I said, "studying at Columbia University. Russian, and things Russian." I said this in effortless Russian, pleased to see how surprised he was. "I've brought you this announcement," I said, dropping my hands, which had remained in his all the while, and searching in my shoulder bag. I brought out the invitation to the Russian Circle event at Columbia. He took it, but barely glanced at it. "Yes, of course, we'll send someone. But now I want to hear about *you*."

The strategy I'd worked out with Clarence had been to play it cool, to wait and see if Max remembered me, to be a bit standoffish and get him to pursue me. Instead we were like long-lost lovers, bypassing any preconception I had had of our initial meeting. I could hear Clarence speaking: *Nothing works out exactly as you plan; be prepared to improvise.* And so I did.

"I've never forgotten you," I said to Max. "It was so long ago, but it was also so very special."

"And I the same," he answered. Then, with an intensity I remembered well: "I must see you. When? When can we meet?"

"Why don't you come to my apartment for dinner," I said. "Is Wednesday all right?" I set the date a few days ahead, not wanting to appear too anxious. "Seven p.m."

I wrote down my address.

I was thrilled with my success. I couldn't wait to tell Clarence how well it had gone. It was also thrilling to see Max again. But I had no intention of telling *that* to Clarence.

Fifteen

I prepared a Russian-style dinner for Max. Ice-cold vodka with two small shot glasses and a tray of *zakussky*—an assortment of appetizers including pickled herring, boiled potatoes, sour cream, sliced sausage, pickles, cucumber salad, and slices of dark bread. I set it all out on the cafe table in the bay window of my living room; my apartment had no dining room, just a square living room, a tiny kitchen and that bedroom with its queen-sized bed.

Max tried to kiss me on the lips when he entered, but I averted my head and let the kiss brush my cheek. He was wearing a tweed sport jacket that looked American-made and stylish, a white shirt and a tie, which he soon loosened, opening the top button of his shirt. He smiled appreciatively when he saw the spread I'd set out. We sat down at the little table.

"To us," Max said, as we downed our first shot of vodka. "Now, tell me about your studies. You're a student of Russian, I did not know that."

I told him about Columbia, about my dissertation, about my affinity for the Russian language. He listened closely. "Is all this because you travelled to the Soviet Union?" he asked. "You were studying art when we met. When did you become interested in Russia?"

I was pleased that he remembered and impressed by his thorough command of English. His speech was somewhat formal but he spoke with hardly a trace of accent. "You're right, it all came after my trip to Russia. But you know, my family dates back to Russia. I think it's in my genes."

I asked about his impressions of New York, how long he'd been here, how long he intended to stay. "I came here about six months ago," he told me. "I like it here. I want to stay as long as possible." We downed a second shot of vodka, accompanied by a little food. Max took off his jacket and removed his tie.

I couldn't stop staring at him. I was searching for the Russian boy I'd fallen for a decade before. I found what I was looking for in his violet eyes and his seductive smile. I found it in the courtly way in which he addressed me and in a sexual intensity that was almost tangible.

Max was studying me as well. "Please, Katya," he said. "Will you loosen your hair the way it was when we first met?" I had put my hair up in a French knot that was very fashionable at the time. I pulled out the pins at his request and let my hair fall down to my shoulders. Max gave an appreciative sigh. We sat there in silence for a full minute, or maybe even two, just studying each other. The air between us was highly charged. We were both at a loss for words.

"I'll get some water," I said finally, and started for the kitchen. Max stood up quickly and barred my way. He was about to kiss me, when I said, with a mock pout: "I still can't forgive you for refusing me a last night in Moscow. You really hurt my feelings."

"Let me make up for it now," he said, and led me to the bedroom.

***

We weren't the kids we once were. I was 28; Max was 33. Yet we came together with the same eager passion that had fueled that magical night back in Moscow. The experience we had each acquired over the years made it even better. Some time in the early morning hours, we lay naked, side by side, and began to talk.

"Why *did* you refuse to meet me on my last night in Moscow?" I asked Max. "I was so eager to see you just once more and you seemed to want me just as much."

"Let me explain," Max replied. "I had just been accepted into the Institute of International Relations, a very prestigious school where I would train for a diplomatic career. It was an honor to be one of the students picked to meet with the first visiting Americans. It showed that my professors considered me smart and trustworthy. They gave us strict rules. 'Be polite, show your knowledge of the United States, say nothing negative about the Soviet Union. Do not establish any relationships with these American students. You are not to see them again, even if they request it.' I broke the rules by meeting you, not just once, but twice. And I probably would have done it again, if you had stayed on in Moscow instead of leaving for the republics. But then, when you came to see me a week or so later at the university, that was compromising. People saw you there. I had to explain that I had nothing to do with your visit, that you had come on your own. I certainly could not meet you again, not after that, not with everyone watching."

"Everyone?" I asked.

"First, my fellow students, they were the first to hold me to account. They accused me of fraternizing; they wanted to show their own loyalty to the state. Then my case moved on to the faculty. Fortunately, it did not go any further. My record remained clean."

"I don't know how you managed to live with such rules, such suspicion," I remarked. "It sounds like they controlled every little thing you did."

"And you? Did you not have questioning when you returned home from Russia?"

I remembered the FBI men who debriefed me in their car. It was not quite the same, but perhaps he had a point. The Cold War worked both ways.

"I have to tell you what happened to me on my way out," I said. "With the photo I took of you . . ." And I began describing my confrontation with Customs at the Moscow airport. "And then, they took me to a jail . . ." I was saying, when I suddenly stopped. I had picked up on something in Max's expression. "You already know all this, don't you?"

"I do, but I'm really interested in hearing it from your point of view. I assumed it had something to do with the photo you took of me, but I wasn't really sure until now. I owe you much thanks."

"How did you hear about it? It wasn't in the press, was it?"

"No. I have a friend in a high place. He told me."

"Well then, now you know the whole story. I had promised you I would protect your photo and I did, by making up a silly story that involved my friends, the girls I traveled with. That was the end of our friendship."

"That's just as well," Max said. "That red-head was up to no good. Did you know she smuggled out anti-Soviet literature?"

"Red-head? You mean Stephanie? No, I have no idea what you're talking about."

"She brought out writings by the anti-Soviet traitor Sochinsky. Got away with it, too. It was some time before we figured out who the writer really was and how his writings got to the US."

My head was spinning. I knew all about Sochinsky. I had written about him and several other dissident writers in my Masters thesis. Sochinsky had been a highly regarded member of the Soviet Writers Union, published widely in the USSR, until it was discovered that he was also writing under the pseudonym "Titov" and publishing critiques of the Soviet Union in the West. It took the Soviet authorities five years to unmask Sochinsky, charge him with anti-Soviet propaganda in a highly publicized trial, and send him to prison and hard labor for twelve years.

Yes, it figured. "Titov's" works were first published in a New Haven journal associated with Yale. That was where Stephanie's father taught. He must have put her up to it. And Jeanie must have helped her.

No wonder they were so angry with me for publicly trivializing our trip. Even if they had known my whole story, it would not have changed things. They had accomplished a dangerous political mission for which they could never take public credit, while I was telling the world stupid stories to protect my Communist Party lover. I cringed inwardly with embarrassment: what a naive romantic fool I'd been! Well, I would make up for it now. As enchanting as it might be, lying here with Max in my bed, I would not get carried away. He was the enemy; my job was to outfox him.

With all that was whirling around in my mind, my newly trained professional ear had not missed Max's statement: "It was some time before *we* figured out who the writer really was. . . ." He said "we," implicitly aligning himself with the KGB investigators. I wondered if he was aware of his slip.

★★★

"It's going very well," I told Clarence during our regular weekly phone call. "We had dinner Wednesday night, talked about our time in Moscow, all very amicable. And we're having lunch on Saturday and then going to the Met to see the new show, 'Three Centuries of American Painting.'"

"Good," Clarence replied. "It sounds like you're off and running. Remember, you have to gain his trust."

I didn't tell Clarence that Max and I had already slept together, that we had picked right up again as lovers. It was too personal, and too embarrassing to share with him. And Clarence had made it clear that he wasn't interested in those specifics. Of course, Clarence expected me to sleep with Max, that was what he was implying when he kept telling me: *Get close to him. Gain his trust.* It gave me a queasy feeling: What must Clarence think of me? That I would prostitute myself to gain an enemy's trust?

It was different with Max. I found him irresistible. I would have gone to bed with him even if it were not part of my job. But suppose they had assigned me to someone else, some ugly, vulgar Party commissar, and told me to "get close to him." I could not imagine going that far, job or no job.

I did feel guilty, however, guilty about Steven. We were committed to each other; I was violating *his* trust. But sex with Max was so exciting, it made me question my love for Steven. Thank goodness Steven was so far away. I didn't want him to know about Max. I didn't want to hurt him.

"One thing you might find interesting," I told Clarence. "PLAYBOY inadvertently aligned himself with the KGB, talking about the KGB as *we*."

"Yes, we already know that. What we need is to know about him as a person—his past and present, his life and work."

"I'm not going to find that out overnight," I warned him. "It will take time . . . and ingenuity."

"I know, we're not pressuring you. Just keep up the good work." Clarence hung up.

Sixteen

We never got to the Met that Saturday. Max brought a bottle of red wine for our lunch, we each had a glass or two and before long we were making love on the living room rug. Slanting rays from the early-spring sun shined in on us through the window and lit up the white blossoms of a pear tree outside. It was heavenly. The lunch I'd prepared became our dinner. It grew dark outside as we sat at the table in the bay window and talked.

"Do you still have the little key I gave you in Moscow?" Max asked.

"Of course, it's in my top drawer. You told me it was the key to your heart. For years I wore it on a gold chain." I took it out and showed it to Max. He looked at it fondly, then fastened the chain around my neck, caressing my neck and shoulders as he did so.

"Please, wear it again, Katya. I like to see it on your beautiful neck."

"Where did you get it?" I asked.

"It belonged to my mother. I found it among her things after she died."

"Oh. I didn't know your mother was dead." Max never mentioned his family; it was as if he had none.

"Yes, she and my father died in an accident, many years before you and I first met." There was no emotion in his voice.

"How terrible for you. I'm so sorry."

"It was a long time ago," Max said, in a way that ended all discussion.

"What about the key?" I asked, changing the subject. "Is it old, an antique?"

"It is Russian, not Soviet. So yes, it is old, one of a kind. I have not seen another like it."

Of course, it would be Russian, I thought. I couldn't imagine a Soviet factory turning out decorative little keys like that for the delight of impoverished consumers. And private artisans didn't seem to exist anymore in the Soviet Union.

"I like it because it's mysterious," I said. "Like you, like Russia. A key without a lock. You know what Churchill said about Russia: *It is a riddle, wrapped in a mystery, inside an enigma. But perhaps there is a key. . . .* I feel that way about *you*."

Max seemed uncomfortable with my analogy. "Let's not talk about Mr. Churchill," he said, then added: "I'm glad you are wearing the key. The key to my 'mysterious' heart."

Churchill had actually gone on to suggest that the key to the mystery of Russia was its national interest. I found myself wondering if the key to the mystery of Max was his own *self*-interest. He seemed so self-contained, reluctant to discuss his feelings and not really interested in mine.

In bed, making love, Max was a different person. Tender and intense, he explored every inch of my body and came to know it better than I ever had. He would play me like a finely tuned musical instrument. I reached highs I didn't know existed and resolutions beyond measure.

That I could give my body so completely to a man who was essentially a stranger to me, a stranger and an *enemy*—I found that incredibly exciting.

Seventeen

"**W**hat do you do as a cultural affairs officer?" I asked Max one day. I had no notion of how Max spent his time when he wasn't with me. It was my job to find out.

"I try to keep up with what American people are thinking. Their politics, their art, their theater. I attend lectures and political gatherings and report back on the state of thought in the US, especially about the Soviet Union. It's a complicated thing, as you can imagine . . . trying to generalize about a population that is so, how would you call it, *diverse*?"

"I could be of some help," I said. "I can make suggestions. We could attend things together."

"Yes, that would be good. Actually, I'd be interested to meet Professor Philip Mathewson. Could you arrange that?"

Philip Mathewson? He was the distinguished director of the Russian Institute at Columbia, a man well into his seventies. He'd spent several years at the State Department during World War II, advising the Secretary of State on Soviet matters and taking part in various post-war peace conferences. He still served as a consultant to the government and had top security clearance at a number of government agencies.

The Institute back in those days had close links to the government, and Mathewson was the connection. Government agencies and the military sent staff to the Institute to perfect their Russian or to learn more about the Soviet system. The Institute, in turn, produced well-trained students ready for government or CIA work, if they were to so choose. Students like me.

I knew Professor Mathewson, of course. The Institute was a small place and we all knew each other. But Mathewson remained rather aloof from the student body, and I found him somewhat intimidating. He gave only one course, in Soviet foreign policy, which I had taken when I was studying for my Masters.

"I'll try," I promised Max, and I did. It was a way of showing him I was on his side.

"Why does he want to meet with *me*?" Professor Mathewson asked. He was a small man with a perpetually preoccupied look. He sounded a little annoyed; I figured he'd had his fill of Soviet diplomats in DC. Then, softening his tone in response to my look of disappointment, "I'll see him, if you wish. Tell him to call me."

Max thanked me for the message, but never said anything further to me about Mathewson. It was Mathewson who got back to me.

"How well do you know this Rzhevsky fellow?" he asked.

"Not very well," I lied. "I met him when we were trying to get some 'real' Russians to a Russian Circle event."

"Well, I'd stay away from him, if I were you. He's clearly KGB. A dangerous fellow, I would say. Very smooth, charming, incredibly good English. A real asset to *them*."

"What did he want with *you*?" I asked.

"He calls himself the 'cultural attaché.' He was trying to strike up a friendship with me. He knows I'm in a position to relay informal messages to the State Department and even higher. Over the years I've had several calls from people like him at the Mission. I always refuse to see them. I'm not interested in playing their game. I made an exception this time as a favor to you. I'm sure he'll get some points from his superiors for gaining access to this office. But that's it. It won't go any further.

"The FBI is keeping an eye on him. After his visit, they asked to sweep my office for bugs. And they found one; they were right to be concerned. It was hidden near the window, not where he had been sitting. So it may have been placed there by someone else. But we suspect it was him. The man's a professional. Don't do him any more favors, Katherine. He's not someone you can trust."

Didn't Professor Mathewson suspect I was working for the CIA? He must have been the one who recommended me to the Agency in the first place. But of course, he never assumed I'd be doing undercover work. He saw me as a young woman with excellent language skills, perfect for Translation.

Eighteen

Someone had been in my apartment while I was gone. I sensed it the minute I got home, even before I saw the pad and pencil on my telephone table, much closer to the phone than usual. Then I noticed the white throw rug in my bedroom, carefully smoothed out, not wrinkled from use as it always was, except on the rare occasions when I straightened it out myself.

"I think my apartment's been bugged," I told Clarence from a pay phone. "I can't find any bugs, but someone's been in there. Maybe I should get a new phone."

"No, don't do that," Clarence said. "It's better if they think you don't know."

"Is it the Russians?"

"It could be PLAYBOY, if that's who you mean. But it's more likely his bosses, checking up on him. They must be getting concerned about his relationship with you. You'll have to be careful what you say in the apartment at all times. And don't *ever* call me from there again. Use only pay phones."

"You know, Clarence, I have a very keen sense of smell. I'm sure it was a woman who broke into my apartment."

"Perfume, eh? That's interesting."

"Something like that."

Actually, it wasn't really perfume I smelled, but something much more subtle—a faint kind of body odor, sexual, definitely female.

A Russian woman, bugging my apartment? Listening to us making love? How can I let myself go during sex when I know we have an unseen audience? And what about Max? Won't he get in trouble if his people discover how close we've become?

I moved the phonograph from the living room to the bedroom and played music the next time we made love. Max seemed surprised and not particularly pleased with the change, but I ignored his queries. After a while, he got used to it.

I became cautious when speaking to Max in the apartment. I didn't want it to seem as if I were pumping him for information. It made my job that much harder.

Max, on the other hand, talked easily and there was no way I could stop him. "One of these days, I'll finish here and go back to Moscow," he said one day, out of nowhere. "Why don't you come with me?"

"Are you kidding? What would I do in Moscow? I'd be a foreigner, I wouldn't be able to work."

"With your Russian and English, it would be easy for you to find work," he replied. "And you wouldn't be a foreigner. We would get married."

"What?" I must have gasped. "Are you serious?" Then I added, teasingly: "I didn't think you were the marrying kind."

That would have been the moment for Max to tell me he'd been married and divorced. But he said nothing. I had told him about Steven early on, and also about other men who'd been in my life, but he had not been forthcoming in return. "There have been many women," he said, "but no one like you."

"Wouldn't a Russian-speaking American be suspect in Moscow these days?" I asked. "Wouldn't you be suspect for marrying someone like me?"

"Not if you defected," he replied.

"Defected?" Despite myself, I started to laugh. "People don't defect *to* Russia, they defect *from* Russia."

"That's what they tell *you!*" Max responded angrily.

I was sorry I'd laughed at the thought of defecting. I tried to make amends. "You know I've always loved Moscow. I love everything Russian—the language, the food, the music, the literature. It's the most fascinating country I know. I'd love to go back again, and yes, even to live there, at least for a while. I may take you up on it, including that marriage proposal," I said lightly, and I gave him a kiss.

Let the Russians think he's turning me. After all, that's what he's trying to do, I realized with a start. Clarence had warned me not to try to turn Max, and I had no intention of doing so. But he didn't say anything about letting Max *think* he was turning *me*. It could only make us closer, and, perhaps, dampen the suspicions of that Russian woman who was listening in on us.

Nineteen

Max and I fell into a pattern. We saw each other every Wednesday night and also spent most of the weekend together. We began going out more, to lectures and the theater, to dinners at quiet little East Side restaurants. I felt more comfortable outside the apartment, now that I suspected it was being bugged.

Max had good taste in food and wine and also in the jewelry and other gifts he bought for me. "You're becoming very American," I teased him. "A real consumer." He seemed pleased when I said this, and it was certainly true. His clothes were now very stylish: He wore well-tailored suits and button-down shirts at work, and madras plaid sports shirts with chino pants at leisure. Gone were his ill-fitting Soviet suits, his windbreaker jacket, and his ugly black shoes.

He was interested in all things American. When I suggested we read some Russian poetry together—Pushkin or Mayakovsky—he said he'd prefer to read American poets. He was interested in American history and geography and asked me detailed questions that I could not always answer. Modern architecture and interior design intrigued him. He made several trips on his own to the controversial new Guggenheim Museum; he loved its circular construction and its winding interior staircase. I bought him a photo book about American architecture; he left it in my apartment but was always thumbing through it when he was with me.

We were lolling about in the apartment one rainy Sunday afternoon when, all of a sudden, he told me he had to leave. "I have some work I have to do back at the office," he told me.

We kissed goodbye and I sat down at the bay window, watching him go down the outside steps. He didn't turn to the left in the direction of the Mission, as I had expected, but rather to the right. I decided to follow him.

I slipped on some boots and pulled a long rain poncho over my clothes. I grabbed an umbrella and my little camera and started out after him. It was easy to hide in the rain: the poncho hood covered my hair and I held the umbrella down so it covered my face. Just to be sure, I affected a slight limp so he wouldn't recognize my walk. That was something they taught me at the Farm. I stayed at a distance, but Max never looked back.

He was heading straight for Central Park. Once in the park, he began walking very slowly. He left a white chalk mark on a lamppost near the entrance, so casually I almost missed the gesture. He had no umbrella and, though the rain was light, I could see he was getting really wet. *What the hell was he up to?*

Max continued walking until he reached an outcropping of rocks. He turned and casually looked around. He didn't see me: I was watching from a distance, standing behind a cluster of trees. I couldn't tell whether he'd left something there or not, but he then began walking briskly toward an exit. I waited until I was sure Max had left the park. Then I retraced his steps, slowing down by the rocks where I saw some white paper, an envelope, that had been slipped in between two stones that sheltered it from the rain.

I didn't disturb anything. Instead I walked to a bench some distance away and sat there watching the rocks. The rain had stopped, so it didn't seem odd for me to be sitting there. Others had entered the park, sitting on nearby benches. I took out the only piece of paper I had in my pocket—my Con Edison bill—and made a show of reading it with great concentration. About fifteen minutes later a man entered the park, following the same route Max had taken. He walked rather slowly right past the rocks, stopping so briefly I could not be sure if he'd taken the envelope or just passed by. I took out my little camera and took his picture, catching his face as he turned to leave. I was startled by what I saw through the lens.

As soon as he was gone, I walked past the rocks. The envelope was gone. I rushed to the nearest pay phone and called Clarence.

"I just caught PLAYBOY making a dead drop," I told Clarence on the phone. "In Central Park, an envelope slipped between some rocks."

"Did you look at what he left?" Clarence asked sharply.

"No. I thought it best not to disturb things. I was more interested in seeing who retrieved it."

"You did the right thing." Clarence sounded relieved. "That was good thinking, my dear."

"Clarence, you'll find this hard to believe but . . . I *know* the guy who picked it up!"

"What?"

"I know the guy who retrieved the envelope. He's an American, not a Russian. A guy I used to see at Agency parties in DC. I was told he was FBI."

"You must be mistaken."

"No, I'm absolutely sure. He's young, about my age, sandy hair, medium build, regulation good looks."

"That could be anyone," Clarence remarked.

"No, let me finish. One of his legs is shorter than the other. He wears a shoe with a raised sole. He walks in a very distinctive way, trying to hide his disability and almost, but not quite, concealing it. And I got a photo of his face."

"Spies often affect a limp to conceal their identities," Clarence commented drily.

"Not this guy. I've watched him in the past. It's very distinctive. The walk and the face. I know it was him."

"Do you know his name?"

"No. We were never introduced. But I could make inquiries. I know people who know him."

"Don't bother. I'll track him down. Send me his picture." Clarence didn't sound pleased. More work for him, I figured.

"Suppose I'm right," I continued. "Why would PLAYBOY be leaving messages for an FBI agent? One of his American assets, yes. But an FBI guy? Do you think that guy's a mole? An FBI traitor?"

"Hold your horses there; don't get so excited!" Clarence answered. "I'll see what I can find out."

"Will you let me know?" I was thrilled by my discovery.

"Not necessarily." Clarence hung up.

***

Max was sleeping in my apartment regularly every Wednesday and Saturday, yet I didn't know where he lived, or where he went when we were not together. "In the neighborhood," he would say vaguely when I asked him. "Not far from here." What could he be hiding? Emboldened by my success in following him to Central Park, I decided to find out.

The opportunity arose when he left one Sunday afternoon, a little earlier than usual. It was a foggy day, quite humid, with occasional drizzles. I put on my poncho, pulled up the hood, opened an umbrella and followed him as he made his way to Lexington Avenue, turning south. He was walking slowly, strolling actually, and stopping at various stores to window shop. I stayed about a block behind him; it was easy to keep him in sight. At 68th Street he crossed to the east side of Lexington and entered a little grocery store, emerging a few minutes later carrying a small bag of groceries. I crossed the street and kept behind him, figuring he must be getting close to home. Two blocks later, he turned east, on 66th Street. I quickened my pace as he turned the corner and disappeared from sight: if he lived on 66th Street, I wanted to see which building he entered.

I turned the corner and was stopped abruptly in my tracks. I found myself face to face with Max! He was standing still, *waiting for me*, a dark look on his face. I pulled back in alarm.

"Are you spying on me, Katusha?" he asked.

Twenty

Max had called me "Katusha," a diminutive form of Katya. It might have sounded affectionate under other circumstances, but at that moment it seemed humiliating, as if he were talking to a child. "You're not a very good spy," he commented, making me feel even smaller.

My only option was to take the offensive, which I did. "You come to my house all the time," I said angrily, "treat it like your second home. And I don't know where you actually live. You never tell me when I ask. Why shouldn't I want to know?"

He stood there quietly for a while, studying my face. Then he took my arm and led me down the street. "Come. I will show you where I live."

We stopped in front of a nondescript brick apartment house, about ten stories high. "Here. This is it. I cannot take you inside because I live with other people, people from the Mission." We stood there rather awkwardly; it seemed so anticlimactic. I began to laugh. "So . . . this is it? An ordinary New York City apartment house? Why all the mystery, Max?"

To my relief, he laughed with me. "I don't know," he said, kissing me lightly on the head. "That's just the way I am."

The front door opened and a pretty blond woman walked out. Pretty was not the word, she was beautiful, with high cheekbones and bright-blue cat's eyes. She was wearing a colorful flowered sundress and high-heeled sandals and carried an umbrella that matched her dress. The umbrella was open, over her head, although it was no longer raining. Barely glancing at me, she came up to Max, kissed him on the cheek and said softly, in Russian: "There's dinner for you in the refrigerator. I'll see you later." And she walked off.

Suddenly, unexpectedly, I was consumed with jealousy. "I suppose that's your roommate," I blurted out sarcastically, "the *people* you live with."

"Yes, she's one of them," Max answered coolly. "I live with a married couple. She is the wife."

Torn by waves of disbelief and anger, I could barely look at Max. "I'm going home," I said brusquely. "I'll see you on Wednesday." And I took off, relieved that he did not try to accompany me.

★★★

What the hell's wrong with you? I asked myself angrily. *Max is the enemy. He's the focus of a job you're doing, nothing more. Okay, so you're having great sex with him; that makes it easier. But you have no reason to be jealous. He should mean nothing to you. You have a boyfriend, a guy you plan to marry.*

I thought of Steven—his openness, his honesty. Steven would never lie to me, or cheat on me with another woman. Yet here I was, sleeping with an enemy spy and fiercely jealous of his every move. It was all wrong. Those feelings had to stop.

Thank God, Clarence would never know about my fiasco today, my failed attempt to follow Max. I consoled myself with the thought that I had successfully followed Max once before, when he made that dead drop in Central Park. Or *had* I been successful? Was Max referring to that episode as well when he asked me if I was spying on him?

I had given Clarence a photo of the guy who'd retrieved Max's envelope, but Clarence hadn't gotten back to me on that. I suspected he never would. It was really irritating. He never filled me in on what was happening unless it directly affected my work.

★★★

Sooner or later, I thought, Max would reveal something important to me. It might take time, but no one was rushing me. Sex was the key—the key to keeping Max's interest—sex without love, without jealousy. I had to keep that separation clear in my mind, the separation between sex and love.

Just thinking about sex with Max, I felt a spark of desire growing in me, anticipating our next date on Wednesday. Max would be as eager and as passionate as ever. He would act as if nothing had happened today. I knew that about him. And I would do the same.

Twenty-One

T he Soviet Union went through a major upheaval after Stalin's death, but Max would not discuss it with me. He dismissed as irrelevant the 1956 "secret speech" by Party leader Nikita Khrushchev, one of Stalin's former henchmen, who revealed the full extent of Stalin's horrifying crimes. Max seemed unmoved by the brief thaw that followed Stalin's death, when dissidents began advocating against censorship and distributing their hand-typed works through underground publishing. In 1964, in a cruel backlash, Khrushchev and his followers were ousted from power. The new leader, Leonid Brezhnev, established a new reign of terror. Max was posted to New York in 1964, a high point in his career. He was, I assumed, a Brezhnev man.

***

"I learned something amazing today," I told Max over dinner one night. I was excited and couldn't contain my news. "Nathalie Babel, Isaak Babel's daughter, is here at Columbia, studying for her doctorate. One of my professors, who knows I'm writing about Babel, offered to introduce us. Nathalie barely knew her father: she was born in France and raised there by her mother. But she must know a lot about him from her mother, and it would be so great to interview her. It would add a personal dimension to my dissertation, something it really needs."

Max did not respond. "Max," I said, "are you listening?"

"What do you want me to say?" Max's tone was surprisingly harsh. "You know what I think. Babel was a traitor. He was executed by Stalin. I wish you weren't writing about him."

"But Max, his sentence was reviewed and revoked after Stalin died. His reputation was restored by Khrushchev."

"And what about Khrushchev's reputation? That man did so many stupid things, including the so-called 'secret' speech he gave, the one you Americans love so much. Khrushchev was forced out by the Party last year. It should have been sooner, if you ask me."

I was taken aback by Max's anger. He saw my response, and his tone softened.

"I try to avoid politics," Max explained, holding out his hand in a conciliatory gesture. "The Party has been good to me. It helped me get a good education and a good career. There are things I don't like in Soviet Union, but I keep that to myself. It would be like criticizing your parents—you just don't do that."

***

I was spending most of my days at the Columbia library, researching and writing about Babel. The long hours were broken by my daily lunch in the Lion's Den on the Columbia campus—the same lunch every day, a cheeseburger and a chocolate milkshake. I ate alone. I had made few acquaintances at Columbia, and most of them had finished their studies around the time I joined the CIA.

Looking up from my lunch one day, I saw a woman carrying her tray across the room, heading for the table next to mine. It took only a minute for me to recognize her. It was Stephanie Evans.

"Stephanie," I called out. "Is that you?" She hadn't changed much since I'd last seen her, at the Smith graduation some years before. She seemed strong, fit, robust. Her wiry red hair was still her most striking feature: it looked like it would be impossible to run a comb through it and she had given up trying. She wore it short, floating around her face in an unstylish but not unbecoming way.

"How are you, Steffie?" I rose from my seat.

"Hello, Kate." She didn't seem surprised to see me, nor did she seem pleased. Neither of us had forgotten the disastrous ending of our Moscow trip in 1954.

But I now knew things about Steffie I hadn't known before: that she, assisted by Jeanie, had smuggled out Soviet *samizdat* for publication in the West. It was Max who had told me what she'd done, told me with undisguised contempt. But I was filled with admiration for her courage and resourcefulness. I'd given it a lot of thought since Max's revelation, remembering how Sy Dulchin, the fur trader staying in our Moscow hotel, had told me he'd "advised" my friends when they were leaving Moscow. They'd probably sent the writings out in the US Embassy pouch, as Dulchin would have advised me to do with my film, had I thought to ask him. I recalled the FBI de-briefer saying: "You girls are quite a crew!"

How had they managed to get those dangerous documents? When? They must have sneaked off at night, I figured. While I, wrapped up in my own little adventure, was sneaking off to meet Max.

How had I missed all that—me, who prided herself on being such a clever spy!

Now I had a chance to make things right. Though I couldn't tell Steffie what I'd learned about her mission in Moscow, I could at least try to explain my own behavior that had upset my friends so much.

"Can I sit with you?" I asked. Steffie nodded, and I moved my tray to her table. I noted the cheeseburger and milkshake on her tray. "We still have some things in common," I said, pointing to my own identical lunch. She gave me a wan smile.

"You look great, Steffie," I continued, and I meant it. She radiated energy and self-confidence. Then I bit the bullet. "I think of you often, about our trip to the Soviet Union. I'm sorry it ended so badly."

"I never did understand what happened," Steffie responded. "Your behavior was—let me just say it—ludicrous and inexplicable. And you never tried to explain."

"I was never given a chance," I said, "at least that's how it felt back then. Let me try to explain it to you now." I took a deep breath and began. Steffie was waiting, warily.

"There was a boy, a Russian boy, I met him when we went to the university and later I spent some time with him alone. I didn't tell you guys, I'm not sure why. I took his picture and promised him I'd keep his photo out of official hands. He was very concerned about that. His photo was on the roll of film I destroyed. I did it to protect him, a stranger, in order to keep my promise. I didn't anticipate what followed—my arrest, the silly story I had to concoct because I couldn't think of any other explanation, and then, all that publicity. I certainly didn't want any of it. I was just trying to keep a promise and not get him in trouble."

Steffie was listening closely. "And that boy, who was he?"

"Just a student. We got together the day after our university visit; he showed me around Moscow. I don't even remember his name now."

"You never told us. Why?" Steffie was sharp, not easily misled.

"I was upset. I thought you and Jeanie had ganged up on me. You seemed critical of me and I assumed you wouldn't approve. They say 'three's a crowd' and that's how it felt to me in Russia. I was resentful, of course. Jeanie was my best friend."

There, I'd said it, and most of it was true. I hadn't identified Max by name, nor could I tell her he was now back in my life. Any more than I could tell her that I knew she had smuggled out documents, that I had learned about it from Max.

"Well, thanks for the explanation," Steffie said. "A little late in the game. I wish you'd told us at the time. . . . What are you up to now? I heard you were in Russian studies, here at Columbia. Is that true? To tell you the truth, I was surprised to hear that. I mean, the Columbia program is hard-nosed, anti-Soviet. And you, well, if I can speak frankly, you seemed rather soft on Communism back there in Russia."

You had to hand it to Steffie; she was not afraid to come out and say what she was thinking. I thought long and hard before answering her. "I was never soft on Communism," I said emphatically. "It was a storybook notion of *Russia* that had me in its spell. But I'm no longer so naive. I've learned a lot about Communist oppression since then. I loathe their system. I hate what they've done to the Russian people."

"I get your point," Steffie said. She seemed to be taking my words personally. "I suppose *I* was kind of hard on the Russians back in '54, blaming the people for what their government has done to them. I'm now working with a bunch of Russian émigrés, trying to help them. I've learned a lot, too."

"What are you doing?"

"I've started my own NGO. It's called the Committee for Human Rights in the Soviet Union and Eastern Europe. A bit of a mouthful, seeing it's just me and a few part-time people. But we're growing, we're just getting started."

"What do you do?"

"We translate *samizdat* reports and publish them so the world can see what's happening there: arrests, torture, and so forth."

"How do you get the *samizdat*?" I was impressed.

"We have channels, secret ones. Sometimes I go to those countries myself. I feel like a spy when I'm there, though all I'm doing is behaving the way anyone would in a free country, calling on people and talking to them about their problems. It's scary because those people—the dissidents—are being watched, and I could be booted out at any time. But it's worth it. I feel like I'm really helping."

Steffie had her own NGO, a *nongovernmental* organization. She was accountable to no one but herself. *How liberating that must be,* I thought, *not to have to deal with government bureaucracy, with rules and regulations, with assignments you only half understand because no one tells you the whole story.*

"Who pays for all this?"

"We have a few wealthy donors, and I'm looking for more. I have proposals in to some foundations. It's a movement, it's growing. . . . Now, tell me, what are *you* doing?" she asked.

"I'm getting my doctorate, working on my dissertation. I'm researching the writer Isaak Babel, a victim of the Purges." And I went on to tell her a bit about Babel's life and work.

Steffie's face had softened. She was listening to me with interest. "You know, Kate, I'm flooded with Russian-language documents. I'm always looking for people to translate them. Would you have time for that? I can't pay much, hardly anything except expenses."

"I can't possibly find time right now."

"Are you sure? Here. Take my card. Call me if you change your mind."

Her printed card gave the name, address, and phone number of her organization. I was glad to have it; I hoped to keep in touch with her. But what would I do with her card? If Max found it in my bag or desk, he'd be suspicious. He saw Steffie as a troublemaker who smuggled out anti-Soviet writings. Well, I'd find a way to hide it from him. It wouldn't be all that hard.

I scribbled my phone number on a piece of paper and handed it to Steffie. We were about to part.

"Are you in touch with Jeanie?" I asked, feeling a small knot tightening in the pit of my stomach.

"Not much. She's married, you know. To a Wall Street guy. Nice guy, a liberal. And they have a little boy."

Jeanie was a mother. And Steffie was an activist. While I, what was I? A woman with a secret life I couldn't discuss with anyone. A woman who was lying, in one way or another, to everyone she knew. Was I really serving a worthy cause? All of a sudden, it seemed sort of tawdry. I felt a surge of envy thinking about Stephanie, the people she was trying to help, the clear, open purpose of her life.

Twenty-Two

Steven was coming for my birthday. "It's been too long," he said. "I've missed you so much." My birthday fell on the Thursday before the Memorial Day weekend. "I'll come on Friday night and stay through Monday evening," Steven said. "Take advantage of the holiday weekend."

"I won't be able to see you this weekend," I told Max. "Steven's coming, on Friday."

"That's okay," Max said, with no sign of disappointment. "I'll go to the Retreat. They've been missing me out there." The Soviets owned an estate in Glen Cove, Long Island, where Russian diplomats and the Mission staff went for relaxation. This wasn't the first time Max had told me he was missed out there.

"Have you told Steven about me?" Max asked casually.

"Not yet," I answered, then added mischievously: "I'm waiting till you tell me about *your* girlfriend so I can ask you the same question."

Max didn't respond. I searched his face for some sign of jealousy or discomfort, but found none. Instead, he became animated with a sudden idea. "Your birthday is tomorrow, Thursday. Why don't we celebrate on the real day, the day before your Steven arrives? I'll make a dinner reservation at Café East. I have a present for you."

I was pleased. Café East was our favorite spot of the moment, a charming French restaurant with candlelit tables, quiet and very private. "Great," I said. "Pick me up here and we'll have some wine first."

I dressed with care on Thursday evening, fussing with my hair and putting on a form-fitting black dress that I'd bought with Max in mind. I didn't wear any jewelry, except for the little key, which I tucked inside my dress. Max had hinted he was giving me some jewelry for my birthday. My new dress with its simple round neckline was the perfect foil for earrings or a necklace. I set an open wine bottle and two filled glasses on the coffee table in preparation for Max's arrival. He came at seven, as promised, and we sat down on the couch. Max raised his glass in a toast to me. Just then, the doorbell rang.

"Yes?" I said through the intercom.

"Surprise! It's me, Steven. Happy Birthday!"

Max and I exchanged startled glances. I whispered to him: "Let me handle this," and he nodded. I buzzed Steven into the vestibule and opened the apartment door.

Steven took the stairs two at a time and entered the apartment in high spirits, his arms enveloping me in a kind of bear-hug. "Boy, have I missed you . . ." he began, then relaxed his grip as he slowly realized we were not alone.

"Steven, this is Maksim Rzhevsky," I said firmly. "Maksim is Russian. He and I meet occasionally to practice Russian and English conversation."

Max rose from the couch. "Very pleased to see you," he said in a direct translation of the appropriate Russian phrase. He spoke hesitantly, with a distinct, slightly exaggerated Russian accent. Steven stood there nonplussed, then shook Max's extended hand.

"I think this is not good time for Russian class," Max continued. "I must leave now."

I walked him to the door. "I'm sorry," I said in a loud voice so Steven would hear. "Steven is my boyfriend. Today is my birthday— *den' rozhdeniya.*"

"*Konechno. Ya ponimayu. Do svidaniya,*" Max replied. ("Of course. I understand. Goodbye.") And he was gone.

I felt proud of Max and the seamless way in which he had carried off our pretense. It was exciting for me, even thrilling. For once, we were lying, not *to* each other but along *with* each other, two professionals improvising to put on a show for Steven. What a team we would make if we were only on the same side! For a minute I felt cheated, cheated of my birthday celebration with Max. But Max was gone. I turned my attention to Steven.

"Who is that guy?" Steven demanded.

"He's from the Soviet UN Mission. I met him up at Columbia when he came to one of our Russian Circle events."

"He doesn't look Russian," Steven commented.

"There are all kinds of Russians, Steven, like there are all kinds of Americans."

"I thought your Russian was perfect. Why do you still need lessons?" Steven was beginning to sound like the prosecutor he might someday become.

"Conversation is the hardest to keep up. I need frequent practice."

"Over a bottle of wine?" Steven asked sarcastically. "And in that sexy dress?"

"Steven dear, the dress is new. I bought it for you, for this weekend. I was trying it on when Maksim arrived; he came a bit early. So I had no time to change. You can see, I'm not really dressed up; I'm not wearing any jewelry. . . . And, as for the wine, I had some left over from a meal I cooked a few days ago. It loosens me up a bit when I have to speak Russian."

I was in my element, one lie following another, some good, some not so good. Steven didn't seem convinced, but he let it drop. Neither of us wanted to begin our time together with a jealous fight.

In the room with Max, Steven had looked pale and ordinary. But now, bemused and upset, he looked sweet and adorable, and I remembered why I had fallen for him in the first place. His thick longish brown hair was a bit tousled, he wasn't grinning his usual appealing smile, but his freckled nose and deep brown eyes spoke to me as they always had, and I found myself slipping into familiar and not unwelcome feelings. He was wearing jeans, a dark blue button-down shirt, and a light blue denim jacket, looking very collegiate for a thirty-year-old law student.

"Please, let's sit down," I said, pointing to the sofa and handing him Max's wine glass. "It's untouched," I hastened to add. Steven accepted it reluctantly, then settled down and began to drink. I joined him on the couch, picking up my own glass. "To your visit," I said. "I'm so happy you're here. Thank you for coming early. What a nice surprise."

"Do you want to go out?" Steven asked without much enthusiasm.

"No, let's save that for tomorrow," I replied. "You must be tired from your trip."

We had a lot to catch up on. Steven was eager to discuss his work, his courses, his colleagues, and his successes. His grades were outstanding, he told me proudly, and he was a leading candidate for the *Law Review*. "But it's all work and no fun," he added. "I'm very lonely out there. I wish you would come out to Stanford and do your research there."

He asked about the apartment, looking around appreciatively. His eyes lingered on the small café table and two wrought iron chairs in the bay window. "Some swell place," he said. "How do you manage it?"

"It belongs to my friend Lizzie, as I told you." I had already told him this lie, in preparation for his visit. "She's away on a Fulbright, and I'm free to stay here while she's gone."

"Wouldn't you be better off up near Columbia? Close to the library and our friends?"

"I have a room near Columbia," I reminded him. "And I stay there most of the time," I lied. "But it's tiny and not very nice. This is much better for your visit."

"And for your Russian lessons, I see." I let his remark pass. I wasn't going there again, not if I could avoid it.

I began telling him about my dissertation, describing Babel as an extremely complicated man. "He seemed to seek out danger," I explained. "He was fascinated by the secret police and frequently visited Nikolai Yezhov, the secret police chief. At the same time, he was having a long-term affair with Yezhov's wife. It was never clear why he was arrested. Some believe it was due to evidence given by Yezhov against Babel after Yezhov's *own* arrest."

Unlike Max, Steven was really interested in my research. It was great to talk to him about it. "Why would Babel do something so reckless, sleeping with the wife of the secret police chief?" Steven wanted to know.

"That's one of the things I'm exploring," I said. "Looking for clues in his letters and writings. He was a wild guy. It's fascinating, a puzzle."

I went into the bedroom to change into some comfortable clothes. Steven came up behind me and put his hands on my breasts. "Not yet," I said. I wasn't ready for sex. But he continued, running his hands along my hips and my thighs. I turned and said playfully: "No, no."

"Yes, yes," he replied. Then we were mock-wrestling on the bed, Steven tickling me into submission. We were laughing, something that never happened with Max. Steven and I made love like two old friends, easily, comfortably, the way it always was with him.

"I've missed you so much," Steven said.

"I've missed you, too," I replied, and realized I really had.

But something was lacking, that dark, intense passion I'd known with only one person—Max. *What's become of me*, I wondered. *What kind of person finds it more exciting to sleep with an enemy than with a friend?*

As if reading my mind, Steven said sleepily: "I don't want you studying with that Russian guy anymore."

That got my back up. "Since when do you give me orders?" I asked.

"How would you feel," he said, "if you came out to Stanford and found me studying with a gorgeous woman? Can't you find some nice old lady to speak Russian with? There must be plenty around."

"I see your point," I said. But I didn't make any promises.

We spent a very busy weekend: a birthday dinner for two at Tavern on the Green, followed by the Broadway musical *Fiddler on the Roof*. We even caught the American Painting show at the Met. We visited my parents who complained to Steven that they rarely saw me. We visited our friends Laura and Frank at their apartment on West 107th Street. "We thought you'd left town again, Kate," Laura said. "You never call. We never see you."

"You seem to be leading a hermit's life," Steven commented. "How do you spend your time? All work, like me?" I just smiled, content to drop the conversation, which we did.

Someday, I thought, *when this job is part of the past, when I'm not pledged to secrecy, I'll tell Steven. Tell him that I worked for the CIA, tell him about OPERATION PLAYBOY.* But how could I ever tell him? He would never forgive me for sleeping with Max or excuse me for all the lies I'd already told him and would continue to tell. Nor would I be able to tell him that I hated being dishonest with him, that I had to lie because of my job. No, that would only be another lie. Because the real reason I was able to tolerate the deception was just beginning to dawn on me. It had little to do with my job. I was under Max's spell, totally, irretrievably.

Twenty-Three

"**H**ow was your weekend?" Max asked brightly when I saw him on Wednesday night.

"Great," I said, trying to provoke him. "We had a wonderful time."

"Did you tell him about me?" he inquired casually.

"No, I didn't. I didn't want to spoil our fun."

"Didn't he ask questions after meeting me?"

"Yes, but I dodged them." Then, realizing he was unfamiliar with the phrase, I added: "I avoided answering them."

I was watching Max closely, looking in vain for some sign of jealousy. Its absence was driving me crazy. Max would often say he loved me, especially in moments of passion when we were making love. He said he wanted to marry me. Yet he never showed signs of possessiveness or jealousy. He had little interest in any aspect of my life that didn't directly involve him. And he revealed almost nothing about himself. There was a part of him I couldn't reach. I began to wonder if it even existed.

I, despite myself, felt jealous of every woman he happened to mention. I was jealous of the former wife he left behind, whose existence he never acknowledged. I was jealous of the beautiful woman I saw at his building, the one he claimed was just a roommate. And then I ran across something really disturbing, something I hadn't expected.

It was Sunday, late morning. Max had gone out to buy a paper and some eggs for our brunch. While he was gone, I ran my hands through his jacket pockets, as was my routine, looking for something interesting. This time I found something: a letter, neatly folded in his inner pocket, handwritten in a feminine Russian script. I didn't take the time to read it: reading Russian script was slow going for me. Instead I photographed it, using my Polaroid camera so I wouldn't have to wait for the film to be developed. I sensed it was personal, and I wanted to see it before Clarence did. I didn't get to read it until evening, after Max had gone.

The letter was short. It read as follows:

Dear Maksim.

I have missed you out at the Retreat. You know I do not like to swim in the cold ocean by myself. And lately you are almost never there.

I know you have been busy with your little American girl. I know you want to use her connections. I know you think you can turn her. I think you are wasting your time. I have seen her and heard her. I cannot prove it yet, but I suspect she is FBI. She probably thinks she can turn you.

I haven't told anyone of my suspicions yet. I'm breaking a few rules to do my own investigation. I'm telling you this, not as your boss, but as your friend. I still love you, Maksim, but I will not hesitate to denounce you if I find you are being foolish – or a traitor.

Vika

I was stunned. I read the letter over and over. Short as it was, every sentence had portent. Vika was his boss, his superior, but she was clearly more than that. A lover? A former lover? Max was trying to turn me. That's what he'd told her and it was clearly true. It didn't necessarily mean he didn't love me as well. But his declarations of love, his desire to marry me, it might all be just a ploy to get me on their side.

Vika suspected I was with the FBI. She couldn't prove it *"yet,"* which meant she was trying. She had *"heard"* me. That could mean only one thing: that she was listening in to my bugged apartment.

And "*seen*" me? Did they plant secret cameras as well? And did Max know this all along, or was this news to him also?

Finally, she was threatening him. Even the words "*I still love you, Maksim . . .*" sounded like a threat. She seemed like a loose cannon, someone who, by her own admission, was "breaking a few rules." She would denounce him if he was foolish (by falling in love with me?) or a traitor (to her or to the cause?).

Late as it was, I rushed to the nearest pay phone and told Clarence about the letter. "Send me the text," he instructed me.

"I will, but let me read it to you now. It's short." I didn't have the patience to wait; I wanted his take on it right away.

"Okay." I guess he heard the urgency in my voice. When I finished reading the letter, Clarence asked me to read it again. He was silent for a bit, then he asked me: "What do *you* make of it?"

"I think it's the writing of a jealous woman," I said. "A jealous woman who's in a position to be dangerous to our operation. I'll bet she's the one who bugged my apartment."

"She sounds a bit unhinged to me," Clarence said. "She clearly has it in for PLAYBOY. And yes, such people can be dangerous. Though sometimes more dangerous to themselves than to others. You're right to be concerned. Just remember, there's no way she can prove you're with the Agency unless you make some mistake. So be careful. I know you always are."

"Thanks, Clarence." I hung up, still feeling upset. A powerful woman, an angry woman, listening in on me and Max. I knew I wasn't being professional, but the thought of it drove me wild.

Twenty-Four

"**L**et's take a trip together," Max suggested. "I'd like to see more of this big country of yours."

"That would be fun, Max. But aren't there limits on where you can travel? Aren't you restricted under US law?"

"You're right, your government keeps us within a twenty-five-mile radius of the UN. But I was thinking: If *you* rent a car and do the driving, no one would know I was with you. As long as you drive carefully and we keep out of trouble."

Didn't Max know that all Soviet diplomats were under FBI surveillance? Especially those who, like Max, were assumed to be KGB? Just to be sure, I would inform the FBI, through Clarence.

"Where would you like to go?" I asked.

"I was thinking of Indianapolis, Indiana," Max replied.

"Indianapolis?" That took me by surprise. "Why Indianapolis?"

"Yes," he said, a little defensively. "You know, it's Middle America, off the track, as you say. And I like the name—city of Indians."

Indianapolis was near Bloomington, the home of Indiana University, which had an excellent program of Russian studies. *Max must have a connection there*, I thought. *He needs me to get him there.*

"I've never been there," I said gamely. "It's a really long trip. It'll be interesting for me as well."

"We're going to Indianapolis this weekend," I told Clarence. "We'll be staying at the Canterbury Hotel. I don't know what PLAYBOY has up his sleeve. I suspect there's someone there he wants to see."

"Thanks, that's interesting. Keep your eyes and ears open. Call me any time if you need advice."

We drove all day Friday and spent the night in a motel in Columbus, Ohio. I was exhausted, having done all the driving. We didn't want to chance being stopped with Max behind the wheel. The next day was easy: in three hours we were at the Canterbury Hotel in Indianapolis. It was a charming, historic place. The high bed in our room with its old-fashioned coverlet and plumped up pillows looked so inviting, I wanted to climb in and take a nap. But I didn't. I had to keep an eye on Max.

"Well, what shall we do?" I asked cheerfully. I'd done a little research on Indianapolis. "There are several museums, a lot of parks, a good zoo."

Max had his own ideas. "Let's just walk around," he said, and before too long we found ourselves on what seemed to be the fanciest shopping street in town. Max was ecstatic. In the first boutique we entered, he bought me a pair of red leather gloves, smooth, supple leather from Italy.

"They're beautiful," I said, but then protested: "They're too elegant for me. I have nothing to wear with them."

"We'll take care of that," Max said.

Three or four stores later, he found what he was looking for—a short black velvet jacket with red silk lining and red piping at the collar and cuffs. It was expensive. I wondered how Max had so much money to spend. Soviet citizens could only bring a small amount of rubles out of the country, and the exchange rate for rubles was not favorable in hard currency countries.

I liked nice clothes but I'd always hated shopping. Max, on the other hand, was just discovering the joys of consumerism. He was like the proverbial kid in the candy store.

"You know," he told me, "when I first saw a supermarket in this country, I was struck by thunder."

"Thunderstruck," I corrected him, but he just went on.

"I could not believe how many things they were selling, the

quantity. It's only now that I appreciate the very fine quality of what you can buy here, articles from all over the world, the very best of everything."

I remembered the long lines outside the Moscow stores, people waiting for drab goods in scarce supply. The billboard I saw that said: DRINK TEA. Max was developing a taste for things he never knew existed. Earlier, when I met up with him in the hotel lobby, I found him totally engrossed in a magazine called MODERN HOMES.

I decided to buy something for Max. After some looking, I ended up buying him a luscious tan cashmere scarf, imported from England. He loved it.

"You know," I said, "it's the beginning of summer. We won't be able to wear any of these things till it's cold again."

"And who knows where we'll be then," Max said, an implicit question in his words.

"Maybe in Moscow?" I asked, teasingly.

"Maybe in Indianapolis," Max laughed. "I like it here."

Our next stop was an automobile showroom. "We're just looking around," I told the eager salesman, who insisted on showing us the latest Chevy Corvette. "Would you like to take a test drive?" he asked Max, and they disappeared together in the car. They returned about fifteen minutes later and, while Max was in the men's room, the salesman took me aside. "Your boyfriend needs some driving lessons," he told me. And he shook his head disparagingly.

Of course, Max was not raised in an automobile culture. It was no surprise that he was not a great driver. For a minute, I indulged myself in a fantasy of Max as he might have been, had he been born in the United States. I could see him as a college student, driving a red Corvette convertible, an adoring, long-haired coed at his side. And that little fantasy, of my own creation, actually made me feel jealous.

We had dinner in an upscale steak house: medium-rare steak, home fries, and a salad. And lots of red wine. Max kept filling my glass before I'd even emptied it.

"You're getting me drunk," I protested. He just smiled.

My knees were weak by the time we reached our hotel room. We were both exhausted from the drive, the shopping, the sightseeing, the wine. For the first time since we began seeing each other, we went to sleep without making love.

"In the morning," Max said. "I promise." He kissed my closed right eyelid; I was sound asleep before he got to the left.

***

I woke with a start. It was 3:20 a.m. and I was alone. Max was gone. His clothes and shoes, piled on an armchair alongside the bed, were gone, too. He'd gone out. I'd lost him.

I was beside myself. All this hard work, only to lose him now. I decided to call Clarence. I didn't care it was so late. He said I should call him any time for advice.

Clarence was clearly asleep. "What's up, my dear?" he asked drowsily. He never used my name on that special phone line. I had no code name, so he referred to me as "dear." It always sounded a bit demeaning. Why *hadn't* they given me a code name? Are code names only for men?

"I've lost him. He slipped out while I was sleeping."

"It's okay," Clarence reassured me. "We've got him covered. You don't have to worry."

"Covered? We? I don't get it."

"Our brother bureau has its people out there. They're on the case." He meant the FBI. "But you told me to keep an eye on him. I should have followed him," I said, confused and bewildered.

"Definitely *not!*" Clarence was now fully awake. "You don't have the training for that. Nor is it the right setup. You'd have to be a Houdini to follow him and then be asleep in bed when he returned."

"So what am I doing here? I've been driving for more than a day, just to get him here. I'm not a chauffeur, you know. Don't you need me for something more important?" I was angry.

"You're forgetting your assignment, dear. By driving him, you're gaining his trust. Your job is to collect info about him, not to follow him. You should be sending us data we can use to determine our prospects with him."

"But Clarence, I'm here. And a clandestine operation is going on right under my nose. Isn't there something I can do?"

"Do you have your little camera? Good. If you get a clear chance, take some photos of whatever papers PLAYBOY brings back with him. *But only if there's a wide window of opportunity.* It's not worth taking a risk and exposing yourself. Be careful."

I heard the elevator stop on my floor, so I put down the phone very softly. I was back in bed, feigning sleep, when Max opened the door. He undressed quietly, crept into bed beside me and was asleep within minutes. He had slipped something into his attaché case before he got undressed.

I tossed and turned, unable and unwilling to sleep. Visions of Max's attaché case swirled in my half-awake dreams. Finally, around 6 a.m., I fell sound asleep.

At 9 a.m. I opened my eyes to see Max standing beside the bed, fully dressed. "I'm going downstairs to find some coffee. Try to sleep a little longer," and he kissed my forehead.

The minute he left, I was out of bed, adrenaline pumping through my veins, exploring the attaché case. It was locked, but the lock was a simple snap lock and I had it open in minutes, using a little tool I had been given at the Farm. I was excited. This was espionage; this was what I'd been wanting to do!

A manila folder lay inside the case. Luckily, it was not sealed. I opened it and removed a document, six pages covered in tiny type with lots of diagrams. I retrieved the mini-camera from my purse and examined it. I'd only used it so far for long-distance shots; now I needed clear close-ups. I adjusted the lens, hoping I had it right, and photographed the first page. I had enough time to finish, I figured, though it would be close. I was on the fifth page when I heard the elevator stop on my floor. My heart skipped a beat and my hand shook. It was too soon; it couldn't be him returning. But damn it, I'd messed up the shot. I photographed page five again, then moved on to page six. Done! I slipped the pages back into the folder, my heart beating faster and faster. Just then, I heard the door open behind me. I snapped down the lid of the case and whirled around to see Max standing in the doorway. He had a cup of coffee in each hand and a look of dismay on his face.

"What are you *doing?*" he asked.

Twenty-Five

Max's eyes were fixed on me as if he was trying to probe my soul. "I have a terrible hangover," I began. "I was hoping you'd have some aspirin in your case. . . ." My voice trailed off.

He put down the coffee and went into the bathroom, emerging a few seconds later with a bottle of aspirin in his hand. "Here. It was in your makeup bag."

"Oh, thanks, I didn't think I had any. My head hurts so much, I'm not thinking clearly."

He hadn't stopped looking at me with that cold, hard look, as if I were an object, not a person, standing in his way. *He knows,* I thought. *The game's up. I'm blown.*

"I'm taking two of these and lying down again," I said. "Maybe I'll feel better after a little more sleep." I had managed to slip the mini-camera into my nightgown pocket without Max seeing it. And this time I fell asleep soundly; I was trying to block out the disaster that had just happened.

An hour or so later I woke to find Max sitting in the armchair beside me, thumbing through an architecture magazine. "Feeling better?" he asked. It was as if nothing had happened. I felt relieved, but wary.

We left Indianapolis soon afterward, driving in virtual silence to Columbus for the night. After a mediocre meal in a Chinese restaurant, we checked into a motel, made perfunctory love and went to sleep. The next day was mainly driving, with very little talking. I kept running through what had happened, turning it over in my head. Was this the end? But I was just getting started. I could not face the fact that I'd fucked up. I could not face the thought of not seeing Max again. Look at it this way, I told myself. We're both spies. Neither of us has been honest with the other. But the cards have been stacked against Max. I've known about him from the start; he hasn't known about me. Now we're even. Maybe the game can go on with new rules.

I was momentarily forgetting Clarence and the CIA, of course. I quickly reminded myself that the CIA mission was the real game, a "game" much larger than just me and Max facing off as spies. I had to tell Clarence the truth, that I had blown my cover, that I had *probably* blown my cover, that I had *possibly* blown my cover. I decided on *possibly*, and I waited until Clarence had had a chance to see the film.

Clarence did not seem overly concerned. "PLAYBOY has that woman—Vika—breathing down his neck. She's a real danger to him. He has a lot more to worry about than you," he said. "But I'm disappointed in you," he continued. "You took a big chance trying to get those photos. I told you to wait for a wide window of opportunity. What you did was reckless."

I was quiet. I didn't know what to say.

"More to the point," Clarence continued, "you haven't produced very much so far. You just keep saying he doesn't talk about himself and doesn't reveal anything."

"What can I do? The man's all zipped up. He doesn't like talking about the past or the present."

There was a short silence. Then Clarence asked: "What did you two do in Indianapolis?"

"We walked around, shopped, he bought me some leather gloves, we went to an auto showroom and he test-drove a Corvette. Then we had dinner in a nice steak house. He pays for everything; he likes to spend money and seems to have a lot of it."

"So there you have it," Clarence said. "That should be your report: *PLAYBOY likes to shop and spend money, he's interested in American cars, he likes nice restaurants.* . . . I think you got off to a wrong start, my dear, looking for skeletons in his closet. That would be interesting to know, of course, but what you can easily give us is data, data on his everyday behavior: what he reads, what interests him, what you talk about. His temperament, his politics, his likes and dislikes. Don't try to process it; just give us raw data and we'll make our own determination."

"Okay, I get it. I can easily do that. I've been trying to dig too deep, I guess. I sense there's a lot of hidden stuff to uncover. But this day-to-day data—that's easy. I'll send you a report tomorrow."

Twenty-Six

"Hello? Is this Katherine? I'd like to speak with Katherine Landau." The woman on the phone had a cultivated British accent, the kind I always wanted to affect when I was back in high school. It was only after we'd spoken a bit more that I detected a trace of Slavic in her voice.

"My name is Marina, Marina Tomashvili. Maksim Rzhevsky is my friend. I've heard a lot about you from Maksim and I would like to meet you."

I was immediately intrigued by her Georgian surname. I knew no one from Georgia, one of the Soviet Union's fifteen ethnic republics. Stalin was Georgian—his real last name was Dzhugashvili—and I had visited his birthplace when I was in Georgia during my 1954 Soviet tour. But I had never met a Georgian person in the States. One of my colleagues at the Russian Institute was studying Georgian language and history; it was considered an obscure specialty.

"What is this about?"

"I'd rather talk in person. Can we meet for a cup of coffee? I won't take too much of your time, I promise."

Why not? I thought. *A friend of Max's? Maybe this will shed some light on Max.* "When would you like to meet?"

"How about tomorrow morning, around eleven? I can meet you at the Lexington Diner at Lexington Avenue and 79th Street. Convenient to your apartment."

So she knows where I live. I agreed to meet her. It was only after we hung up that I wondered how we would recognize each other.

***

I knew her immediately. She was the blond woman I'd seen leaving Max's apartment building the day I tried to follow him. The woman who had made me sick with jealousy. She was dressed down for this occasion, wearing jeans and a T-shirt and looking very young, her hair pulled back in a tight ponytail, her face devoid of makeup. Less showy, but still beautiful, maybe even more so in her natural state. Neither of us acknowledged that we'd seen each other before.

"You're Georgian?" I asked, surprised by her fair coloring. "Actually, no," she responded. "My husband is Georgian, Giorgi Tomashvili. He's the Deputy Ambassador to the UN. I work at the Mission. In an administrative capacity."

There was a long pause; she seemed to be looking for the right words to continue. There was something both childlike and phony about her.

"How did you meet Maksim?" she asked finally, in a girlish, chatty manner.

"We met when I went to his office to invite him to a Russian cultural event at Columbia University."

"You went there just to invite *him*, specifically?"

"Well, he is the cultural attaché, is he not?"

Another long pause followed. She seemed uncomfortable. I smoothed the way by asking her what she did at the Mission. "I take care of things," she answered vaguely. "All kinds of things that need to be done."

"Do you know Vika?" The question just popped out of my mouth. I had misgivings the minute I asked it.

She snapped to attention. "You know Vika?" She seemed alarmed.

"No, no, I don't know her. I've just heard about her." I sensed I was in dangerous territory.

"You heard about her from Maksim," she stated. It was not a question.

"No, Maksim has never mentioned her. Some Americans, up at Columbia, know her. I heard them talking about her."

"Talking about her? What did they say?"

I just shrugged, wondering whether I had said something that would get Vika in trouble. What did I care? It would serve her right.

Marina sighed. "Vika's my boss. She's not easy to please. A very strong woman." She lapsed into a meditative silence.

So she was working for Vika. Of course. Vika had sent her to check me out. "Tell me why you wanted to meet me," I said.

"Because of Maksim. I'm concerned about him spending so much time with Americans. It makes people suspicious."

"But isn't that his job? To get to know American culture, what American people are thinking?"

"American people, yes. But just one American . . . that looks suspicious."

"Why are you so concerned about Max?"

She became flustered, then suddenly switched gears, becoming girlish again and confidential. "I've known Maksim for a long time. I feel like a sister to him. So I worry about him. I don't want him to get in trouble. He's had such a hard life."

"Hard life?" I said. "It seems to me he's had a pretty easy one."

"Oh, but you know about his parents?"

"I know they died in an accident. Nothing more. Max doesn't like to talk about himself."

"Well, who can blame him? Especially about this." And Marina began to tell me the story.

"It happened during the war. Maksim was nine or ten years old. He was in school. There was an air raid. A direct hit on his apartment building. Both of his parents were at home when it happened. The building collapsed in a fiery ball.

"Maksim came home from school to find his parents gone, his apartment gone, all of his possessions destroyed. He had nothing but the clothes on his back. A schoolboy, poor and orphaned in a flash."

"He has a sister, yes?"

"Yes, but she is much older. She was already out of the house, working as a teacher in the provinces. She did not want responsibility for Maksim."

"How terrible for Max," I exclaimed. "How did he manage?"

"He had a relative, an uncle, someone high up in the Party. He made arrangements for Maksim to live and study in a *Komsomol*— Young Communist League—school. Max became a child of the Party. He was a good student, a good athlete, hard-working. He moved from the university to the most elite school of all—the Institute of International Relations. But it must have been really hard for him. He had no money, only an occasional stipend from uncle of his who worked abroad and never came to see him. He was alone on holidays, he had no adult to guide him. But he did so well and had such personal charm, he came to the attention of Party officials who gave him grants to continue his studies. The Party was his family.

"I took the same English-language courses that he did, only many years later. The teacher at the Language Institute still remembered Maksim; she talked about him all the time as one of her star pupils. He mastered the language and it's helped him. Very few get posted to New York City."

"I had no idea," I confessed. "Max doesn't like to talk about himself or his past. At least, not with me."

"Yes, that's the way he is. Much of what I know about him I've learned from others, not from Maksim himself. . . . Now, tell me something about *you*."

"There's not much to tell. I'm a New Yorker, born and bred. I'm a student at Columbia, specializing in Russian language and literature. I like your country very much; I find it fascinating."

I said that last sentence for her benefit. And it worked. Marina smiled and, for the first time, she seemed to relax. Then I took her off guard.

"Are you here today to check up on me? Did Vika send you? To find out all about me, this woman who's been taking up so much of Max's time?"

"Yes, I guess you could say so," she conceded sweetly.

"Well, I can't blame either of you for being curious. But there's more to it than that. You seem to be warning me to stay away from Max, implying that I'm getting him in trouble. And I resent that. What Max and I do is none of your business. It's none of Vika's business either." I was angry, and I couldn't restrain myself.

"Oh, but it is our business," she insisted. "We are working in a hostile environment. Everything we do here is subject to inspection . . . by both sides."

I didn't respond. I'd already said too much.

"You are very naive . . . " she began, but then her voice trailed off. For a minute I thought she might start to cry; she seemed confused and upset.

We were both at a loss for words. I said I had an appointment, excused myself and made for the exit, leaving her with the check.

***

"I met Marina the other day," I told Max when I next saw him. I was eager to hear what he would say. "The blond girl I saw in front of your building a few weeks ago. Marina Tomashvili; her husband is Georgian."

"Oh, her." Max replied. "You must not take her seriously or believe everything she says. She's married to our systems manager, Nikolayev, not to Deputy Ambassador Tomashvili. She's bored; she has no work here, so she puts on airs and makes up stories about herself."

"How does she get away with that? You people run such a tight ship."

"Well, her husband is a good man and does essential work. And she's nice to look at. People like Marina can sometimes be useful, just because they are so, how would you say it, *up for anything.*" Max paused. "But how did you meet her? I'm sure it was no accident."

"She called and asked to see me. She said she was worried about you. That you were seeing too much of me and people were becoming suspicious. She warned me I could be getting you in trouble. She also told me about your parents, how they died. Oh Max, I am so sorry. It must have been dreadful for you." I went to put my arms around him, but he quickly stepped aside.

"Someone put her up to this. I think I know who, and why."

"Maybe it was her own idea," I suggested. "Maybe she's jealous. You know, when I first saw her, I was sure you two were lovers."

"You are my lover, not her."

"Yes, well, you are *my* lover, but I also have Steven, you know. You might have someone else, too."

Max didn't respond. He was thinking, with that troubled dark look on his face. "I wish you hadn't met her. She's up to no good. Please, don't see her again."

"I won't. We didn't hit it off very well."

"Good. Marina and her husband share my apartment. She is not my lover."

I wanted to believe Max. I almost did.

Twenty-Seven

"PLAYBOY is being followed," I told Clarence by phone. I had just finished telling him about my encounter with Marina. "I'm sure it's Vika's work. First she sent Marina to warn me to stay away from him. Now she's put tails on him. Two big, burly men. I've seen them several times, hanging around the convenience store at the Lexington Avenue corner. They're only there when PLAYBOY is with me. As soon as he leaves, they're gone. They're making themselves pretty obvious. I think they want him to know."

"Sounds that way," Clarence said. "Have you said anything to PLAYBOY about it?"

"No. If I'm on to it, he surely must be. I think it's best for me to play dumb."

"Good thinking," Clarence replied. "Thanks for reporting this. It sounds like PLAYBOY is getting a lot of heat over you. He has a real enemy in that woman, Vika. All the more reason for you to be on your guard."

I was now sending Clarence regular written reports, giving him the everyday data he wanted:

Max loves French food and red wine. He spends his money freely. He reads the Wall Street Journal *every day. Max defends the Soviet government's persecution of writers; he considers Babel a traitor, despite his official "rehabilitation." Max loves modern Western architecture and likes reading architecture books. He has asked me to go to Moscow with him when he returns at the end of his posting; this, of course, is part of an effort to turn me.*

I did not report on all the time we spent in bed together making love. Max was always telling me how much he loved me: "I've loved you ever since that night in Moscow," he would say. "I've never stopped loving you." Those words came easily to him, but not to me. Despite all the lies I'd told him, I just couldn't bring myself to say, "I love you, too." I would admire his beautiful eyes, or tell him he was great in bed, but I refrained from telling him I loved him because it just wasn't true. We didn't know each other well enough for it to be real love. Indeed, his glibness on the subject made me question the depth of his feelings. Despite his professed ardor, I often felt like an interchangeable piece on the checkerboard of his life.

Clarence was satisfied with my new tack in reporting, but I was not. I wanted to learn more about Max's past. I was sure he was hiding things.

Marina had described the tragic deaths of his parents. She probably knew more. Why had I let our meeting end so badly? I wanted to see her again, to press her for more information. But I didn't know how to reach her. I couldn't ask Max; he had told me to avoid her.

When Marina called some days later, sounding cheerful and friendly, I was pleasantly surprised.

"There's a Soviet film playing downtown, a very beautiful one," she said. "Would you like to watch it with me?"

So I hadn't turned her off after all, she was back. Of course. She wanted to find out more about me and to warn me yet again to stay away from Max. That was her assignment from Vika; she hadn't fulfilled it well the first time around. We each wanted more from the other. And so, we arranged to meet again.

I had seen the film *The Cranes are Flying* some years before. It was the first post-Stalin film to be celebrated in the West; it had, in fact, received the 1958 Palme d'Or, the top award at the Cannes Film Festival. It was a haunting story of love, loyalty, and betrayal, set against the grim background of World War Two. I looked forward to seeing it again.

Marina had also seen the film before. That didn't stop her from crying, with copious tears and barely suppressed sobs, from the moment the film started. When it ended, she was weeping. I put my arm around her shoulder and ushered her out of the theater. "Let's get a drink," I suggested. "I think we both could use one."

We found a little bar in the neighborhood and settled down at a corner table. I ordered a vodka and tonic; Marina took her vodka neat. It was late afternoon; the place was almost empty. A few young men were at the bar, talking quietly, laughing from time to time. Marina and I discussed the film.

"I'm twenty-four," she told me. "Too young to remember much about the Great Patriotic War. But it touched every Russian permanently, my family included. We had cousins in Leningrad during the nine-hundred-day blockade. One million people died there; two of our young cousins starved to death. Suffering, starvation, death. It seems impossible to recover after all that. But we did. I think it made us stronger."

We ordered a second round of drinks. Marina began talking about the movie again, how beautiful Veronika was, how loyal. "Even though I knew how it would end, I kept praying that Boris would return. Her faith was so strong, I believed it, too."

One of the men left the bar and came over to our table. His friends were watching; it was some sort of dare.

"Why are you lovely ladies sitting in a dark corner on such a bright afternoon?" he began.

Marina answered him in Russian, knowing he would not understand. I chimed in, also in Russian, adding to his growing confusion. Marina turned to me: "I think he's trying to *pick us up*." The words sounded so funny in Russian, we both began to laugh. He retreated to the bar, shaking his head. "They don't speak English," he reported.

We continued speaking in Russian for a while to keep up the pretense. "Your Russian is very good," Marina commented. "You know," she continued in her girlish manner, "we must look very cute to them—you with your long dark hair; me with my long blond hair. The next time we go out together, we should dress alike. That would really drive the boys crazy."

Her cheeks were flushed. She was a little tipsy. I was feeling the booze, too.

"Marina, have you slept with Max?" I hadn't planned to ask her that, I just did.

"Yes," she answered calmly. "But not recently, I assure you. And only once or twice." She paused for a minute before continuing. "Maksim has gone to bed with just about every woman I know. That's how it is. He's good-looking, available. They throw themselves at him and he obliges. Love in Soviet Union is different from United States. In this respect, you have to admit, we are freer than you are." She was making a little joke. I forced a smile.

Is it really that different? I was thinking. *I threw myself at Max, first back in Moscow in 1954, and then again, here in New York.*

Marina must have seen my discomfort. It gave her an opening. "With you and Maksim, it's different. It keeps on going. I've never seen Maksim so committed, week after week. Almost like a marriage. But that is why it's causing him trouble. He should not be seeing so much of you, it makes people suspicious."

So, she knew our pattern. Of course, she knew everything. She was working for Vika.

"Has Max slept with Vika?" I asked.

"Well, of course." She looked perplexed. "Why are you so interested in Vika?" she asked.

"I'm interested in all Russians," I replied. "Their habits, their values. And yes, of course, their sex life. I haven't learned about *that* in my studies. Talking with you about these things is really interesting to me." I was appealing to her love of gossip. It worked.

"Well, Maksim is a kind of Don Juan," she replied. "His big brush with sex fame was with that woman in Hungary, Mrs. Szabo. You've heard about his Hungarian adventures?"

"A little," I said. "Not in detail. When was he there?" I didn't want to admit the truth: Max had never said a word to me about Hungary.

"He was there with our army in '56 and '57, right after their counter-revolution," Marina replied. "Yvette Szabo was a great beauty, older, married to a big shot in the Hungarian government. It was a big scandal. I don't know all the details. They had to send Maksim back to Moscow in a hurry."

"That couldn't have helped his career," I remarked.

"To the contrary. He was promoted right after that. His career took off." Marina was looking at me intently, to see if I got her full meaning.

I was silent, trying to take it all in. Then I asked: "What are you suggesting? That having sex with her was an assignment, part of Max's job?" But the momentum was gone, and she seemed eager to change the subject. She had said too much. Or I had said too little, too late.

Marina took my hand as we left the bar, heading for the subway. We held hands like little kids do. I had seen grown women holding hands in Moscow and had found it rather charming. With Marina, however, it reinforced my impression that she was still very much a child. We got off at the 78th Street station and walked together to 76th Street where I was about to leave her. As I turned to say goodbye, she snapped a photo of me, using a camera she'd been carrying in her bag. "No, no photos please," I protested, but it was too late. She was already putting the camera away, a self-satisfied look on her face. We parted, promising to see each other again, each of us knowing that we probably never would.

***

So Max was not exaggerating when he talked about the "many women" in his life. It seemed he was a master of the one- or two-night stand. Why then was *I* so special? Why did Max continue to see *me* so regularly, despite the disapproval of his superiors? How was I different from all the others? Was he trying to relive that romantic moment we shared in Moscow at an earlier, more innocent time? Max often referred to it, always with nostalgia.

And what about his time in Hungary? He had been there in '56 and '57, in the aftermath of the failed but heroic revolution by Hungarian freedom fighters, a revolution that took thousands of lives and sent hundreds of thousands of refugees abroad. A revolution that might have succeeded if the Soviet Army hadn't invaded Hungary and suppressed it. There was only one reason why Max would have been there at that time—as an intelligence officer with the Soviet Army, helping to restore Hungary to Soviet-dominated rule.

Max was in Hungary during a nasty cleanup operation. He had a scandalous affair with a married woman. I was determined to find out more.

Twenty-Eight

My mother was on the phone asking me to come for dinner. "It's been so long since we've seen you, Katie. We were hoping to see more of you, now that you're back in New York. We're disappointed, we miss you." We made a date for that Friday.

She called again, a few hours later. "If there's someone you'd like to bring with you, Kate, we'd be pleased to meet him." Good old Mom. She really did have a nose for things. The last thing I had in mind was introducing Max to my folks. But suddenly it didn't seem like such a bad idea. *Why not bring Max?* I thought. *It might take his mind off what happened in Indianapolis, make everything seem more normal. Isn't that what "normal" women do, introduce their boyfriends to their parents?*

I called back, this time from a pay phone. "Okay," I said. "I'll bring him. But I have to warn you. He's Russian, a real Russian, a Soviet official. So tell Dad: no politics. And please, above all, don't mention my former work in DC." It was a lot of "don'ts," but I got no protest. My folks were great about things like that. They knew how to keep a secret and they didn't ask too many questions.

Max seemed pleased when I asked if he'd like to meet my parents. He showed up at my apartment all dressed up in a new, pale grey, summer-weight suit, a deep blue button-down shirt and a grey-and-white striped tie. I was wearing a white cotton, full-skirted summer dress and high-heeled sandals. Entering the building on Park Avenue, I caught sight of us in the lobby mirror. A handsome couple, no question about that.

Max was unlike anyone Mom had known before and at first she seemed uncomfortable. But she was soon charmed by his good looks and his attentive manner. Max talked to her about the things we'd done together in New York, restaurants we liked, shows we'd seen. She, in turn, made suggestions of things Max might like to see or do. All the while I could see her trying to assess my relationship with Max—how often we saw each other, our little signs of affection. She was probably thinking of Steven, wondering what was going on with me.

Dad was unusually quiet. He was taking Max's measure, watching him closely, listening to everything he said. After dinner, I helped clear the dishes. When I returned to the living room, he and Max were in deep conversation. Max had asked about the capitalist system. How much capital does it take to start a business, for example? Dad was explaining, using some of his clients as examples, describing the businesses they ran, how they got started, how they grew. Max seemed completely engrossed. I couldn't get a word in for quite some time.

"Let's talk tomorrow," Mom said as we were leaving. Dad seemed energized by his conversation with Max; he loved talking about his work with someone who was truly interested. "Don't be a stranger," Dad called to me from the door. "It's not like you're still in Washington."

My heart sank. *Still in Washington.* Had Max heard that? Of course he had. The words were ringing in my ears as we went down in the elevator. But Max said nothing. He was always the true professional, able to control his reactions, unflappable.

"What a beautiful apartment," Max said instead. "How nice for you to grow up in such a place. I guess your father has always made a lot of money."

"I'm lucky," I agreed. "I had an easy time growing up. Maybe it was too easy; maybe that's why I'm always looking for trouble."

"For trouble? What kind of trouble?"

"Like getting involved with someone like you." I said it lightly, with a smile. Max didn't respond.

"Your parents are very nice people," he said. "I want to thank you for bringing me."

I was surprised and touched by his formality. "We'll go again," I said, though I doubted we would. "They really liked you. I could tell."

***

I felt apprehensive as we walked back to my apartment. Max didn't ask me about living in Washington. He let it pass. That was his way. He had never really asked why I was rummaging through his attaché case in Indianapolis. He never mentioned the time I followed him to see where he lived. I suspected he was letting the facts pile up and that at some point he would take me by surprise, confronting me with the evidence of my treachery. Perhaps this would be the night.

There was a surprise in store for me that night, but not what I'd suspected. I entered my bedroom and froze. On the floor, ground into my white throw rug, was a half-smoked cigarette. The crushed cigarette: it was a well-known KGB calling card, a crude, aggressive way of warning people that the secret police had access to their homes and papers. In my case, there was an additional touch: a smudge of dark red lipstick on the cigarette's filter tip.

I must have cried out because Max came quickly. He stood stock still, transfixed by the sight. "*Bozha moi!*" ("My God!") He picked up the cigarette, examined it carefully, then wrapped it in a tissue and slipped it into his pocket. "I'm so sorry, Katya," he said. There was a brown burn in the middle of my rug, but that was not why he was apologizing. He was tacitly admitting this was the work of his crew.

"Could it be Marina?" I asked.

"No. This is not what she does. Someone much tougher, better trained, more experienced . . ." His voice trailed off. He was thinking of Vika, of course. The lipstick on the cigarette was an intentional giveaway.

"Do you know who it could be?" I asked, as innocently as possible. Max didn't answer.

"Maybe we should call the police," I suggested. "This is America, you know, not the Soviet Union. Someone has broken into my apartment."

"No, no," Max reassured me, having regained his usual cool. "I will take care of this. I know what to do. It will not happen again, Katya. Trust me."

He was heading for the door. "Are you leaving?" I asked. I felt a little shaken. I wanted him to stay.

"Yes, I must," he replied. "I have to take care of this as soon as possible. I'll make sure it doesn't happen again."

I kissed him goodbye and bolted the door behind him. Then I headed for my desk to see if anything had been taken or disturbed. Everything was in order. I checked my filing cabinet; it was locked, as always.

Back in the bedroom I noticed that the drawer in my night table was half open, the drawer where I kept my good watch and my favorite jewelry. Fearing the worst, I went to check it. Everything was there, undisturbed, much to my relief.

Alongside my watch was the plastic case that held my diaphragm. Without really thinking, I snapped it open, then pulled back in shock. The round rubber disk had been neatly sliced in two, right through its center.

I sat there on the bed, stunned, trying to understand an act that was at once so intimate and so violent. My diaphragm had not been torn apart in a jealous rage; it had been cut exactly in two by someone who was sending me an electrifying message: *I have access to your sexual life and I will destroy it with cold precision.*

As I sat there, staring at the damage in my hands, I heard a door slowly opening behind me. It was my closet door; I knew those creaky hinges well. Someone was in my closet. It had to be her! Vika.

Twenty-Nine

Vika had been hiding in my closet. We must have surprised her when we came home and she ducked in there for cover. She had been there all along, listening to what we said when we discovered her intrusion. Vika, hiding with a knife, a knife sharp enough to make that clean cut in my diaphragm. Now I was alone. She could easily attack *me!*

I looked around quickly, searching for a weapon, something to defend myself with. The only thing at hand was the brass candlestick lamp on the night table. As I grabbed it, the cord pulled out of the wall, and the room went dark. I spun around, prepared to face Vika, the heavy lamp in my hand. But I was momentarily blinded by the sudden darkness; I could see nothing but shadows. I caught a whiff of her familiar scent, heard her heavy breathing. Then suddenly I found myself completely enveloped in some huge, heavy fabric that had been thrown over my head with such force I fell back on the bed, trapped in its folds. It was the queen-sized down comforter that I kept in my closet. I struggled to get out from under it, fighting for air.

When I finally broke free, the room was quiet. I waited a few minutes and heard nothing. I groped for the lamp and found it. Slowly tiptoeing to the door, I looked into the living room. It was empty. The front door was slightly ajar. She was gone. I dropped the lamp, its shade already crushed and broken.

I headed for the kitchen. The kitchen light was on and, as I reached the door, I saw my knife drawer wide open. She must have taken one of my knives to cut my diaphragm. I went to see if one was missing.

There was a sudden blow; something large and heavy struck the back of my head. My ears began ringing. I felt myself falling, falling to the floor. Colors danced before my eyes. I lost consciousness.

It was Max who found me an hour or so later. He'd come back, concerned about me for reasons he did not explain. He must have gone looking for Vika and discovered she was not at home.

Max helped me to a chair, put an ice pack on my head, and insisted I stay awake until we could see a doctor. "What happened?" he wanted to know.

"It was that woman. I guess she wanted to get rid of the knife. She went back to the kitchen, and I walked in on her." I told him what she had done to my diaphragm.

Morning came. Max went with me to my family doctor, who diagnosed a mild concussion. He wanted to know what had happened to cause the big lump on the back of my head and did not seem satisfied with my explanation that a big pot had fallen off a shelf and hit me. I could not, of course, tell him the truth—that someone had hit me over the head with full force, using a large, heavy black-iron skillet. As it was, he kept looking at Max with veiled suspicion.

Max was attentive and helped nurse me over the next few days. But he showed no inclination to discuss the mysterious woman who had invaded my premises or what her motivation might have been. "I told you I'd take care of it and I will. Let's not think about it anymore."

I knew him well enough to drop the subject. But I couldn't get her out of my mind. Who was this Vika? Why was she so obsessed with Max? According to Marina, she was strong-willed and powerful. Someone who was not afraid to break rules, as she revealed in her letter to Max, the one I had found in his jacket pocket. She had come alone to my apartment, without any backup—she was on a rogue mission. The lipstick on the cigarette, the destruction of my diaphragm, these were all special touches, her bold signature. I found myself thinking she might be deranged. A crazy woman, out to get Max—through me!

Thirty

I'd promised to visit Steven for the July Fourth holiday. He'd been eager for me to come to Stanford, and the timing seemed right. I needed a break from all the tension. It would be good to get away for a bit.

"I'll be away for the holiday weekend," I told Max.

"Steven?" he asked.

"Yes," I replied, irritated that he seemed so unperturbed.

"I guess I'll go out to the Retreat," he said, thinking out loud.

"Max," I found myself saying, "aren't you a little resentful of Steven? Doesn't it bother you that I have a relationship with another man, an *intimate* relationship?"

Max thought for a minute. "No, it doesn't," he said, smiling. "I know you prefer me."

"How can you be so sure?"

"By all this," he said, pointing to the unmade bed in which we had just made love. "By the way you make love with me."

He was unlike anyone I'd ever known—impervious to deep feelings like jealousy, anger, or loss. Max's life had not been easy, I now knew that. He was orphaned at a young age, abandoned by his older sister, raised and indoctrinated by the Communist Party, trained as a spy to lie and deceive. My heart went out to him for all he'd endured. But it was unnerving to see what it had done to him: he'd lost touch with many basic emotions, so thoroughly he didn't seem to know they existed. If I were to leave him for Steven, I doubted he would grieve. He'd find someone else to love—just as much. It would be easy for him, painless.

***

The first day in Stanford was fun. I was happy to see Steven again, relieved to see us fall into our usual, comfortable togetherness. He showed me his apartment, small and serviceable, then took me on a tour of the campus, ending up in the library where he usually did his work. I met a few of his friends and one of his professors. In the evening we had dinner in a nice little restaurant near the campus, after which we made love and went to sleep.

By day two, I'd done it all. I was bored. There was nothing left to do but hang around, reading the papers and talking. I'd become so used to the electricity between me and Max, not just in bed but in the games we played with each other, me seeking information about his life and activities, he trying to bring me over to his side. Normal life, by comparison, seemed dull.

"I see you're wearing that little key," Steven observed. "Didn't you buy that in Russia? You're so obsessed, Kate, I'm afraid you'll defect one of these days."

"Are you kidding? No one knows more about Soviet oppression than I do."

"It doesn't keep you from hanging out with handsome Communists," Steven answered.

"Fortunately, they are few and far between," I responded, happy that he seemed ready to let it drop.

I was determined to be lively and good company, and I thought I was succeeding. But on the last day of my visit, as we were sitting in the kitchen reading The *San Francisco Chronicle*, Steven said suddenly: "Something's wrong, Katie. I feel like I'm losing you. I think we've been apart too long. I wish you'd seriously consider moving out here, doing your research here."

"Steven, you know that won't work. . . ." I began, then stopped. My eyes became fixed on a headline in the paper I was reading: "Drowning Victim Identified as Russian Delegate," and I quickly began to read the article.

> *A woman whose drowned body was found yesterday on the beach in Sea Cliff, Long Island, was identified today as a high-ranking member of the Soviet Mission to the United Nations. Local police, who listed the death as accidental, followed up on clues from a bracelet the victim was wearing and contacted the Soviet Retreat in Glen Cove. Officials there identified her as Viktoria (Vika) Gruzinskaya, a senior staff member missing since July 2. They claimed her body, which will be sent to her family in Moscow.*

There was a picture of Vika, a rather formal one—a severe, unsmiling face, hair pulled back in a bun. There was something about her, something that troubled me. I remembered Max's description of the person who had broken into my apartment: tough, trained, experienced. She looked all of that.

"Why won't it work?" Steven was asking. "We have an excellent library here. We can live together, study together, cook together. We don't have to wait till we're married. Lots of people don't these days. If you'll feel more comfortable, you can keep your own apartment and we can still be together all the time."

"Yes, I get what you're saying. . . ." I stopped again. My mind was whirling from what I'd just read and there was more to come: a photograph of the charm bracelet Vika was wearing when she drowned. The police guessed she was Russian from the hammer-and-sickle charm on the bracelet. But I saw another charm right next to it, clearly outlined. It was a little key, identical to the one I was wearing around my neck. I buried my face in my hands.

When I finally looked up, Steven had left the room.

I left for home later, on an evening flight. Steven took me to the airport and we parted coolly. Things were not right. He was waiting for some word from me, an apology, an explanation, some reassurance, but I was just not up to it. My thoughts were somewhere else. Max was at the Retreat for the weekend. A woman with a gold key just like mine was found drowned on the beach. The woman who had threatened him. The woman who had ground her cigarette into my rug and sliced through my diaphragm. I kept thinking of Vika's letter to Max: *You know I do not like to swim in the cold ocean by myself.*

***

"Were you at the Retreat last weekend?" I asked Max as soon as I saw him on Wednesday evening. Maybe he didn't go. Maybe he'd have some explanation. "I read about what happened. It must have been awful."

For a moment Max looked blank. "Oh, about the drowning," he said. "Yes, that was terrible."

"Did you know her?"

"Very little. She was what you would call a 'loner.' Very independent. Not very disciplined, I hear."

"Were you there when they found her?"

"No, I'd already returned to the city."

"You must be really upset."

He seemed irritated. "I told you, I barely knew her."

"But still. She was a colleague. A young woman. A tragedy."

Max raised his voice. "Stop asking. I know nothing." He was angrier than I'd ever seen him.

I turned from him to hide my dismay, looking out the window and fingering the key on my neck. That key had been so precious to me: it had symbolized the sweetness and continuity in our relationship. Now all it symbolized was Max's lies. It was not his mother's, not unique, not one of a kind. Was Vika the only one who had a duplicate? Or did Max have a collection of little keys he handed out to all his women? "The key to my heart," he had told me. What bullshit!

I was furious. I wanted to have it out with him. He could not lie his way out of this one. But what would he do? Walk out on me? End our relationship? That would mean the end of OPERATION PLAYBOY. At that moment, I didn't really care.

I turned around, aching to confront him, and found Max seated on the couch thumbing through a magazine. He looked up at me, his face untroubled and serene.

"Where shall we eat tonight?" he asked. My heart sank. I said nothing.

★

Thirty-One

I could hardly wait to call Clarence and discuss Vika's drowning. "Do you think PLAYBOY's dangerous?" I asked. "Vika threatened us, she attacked me, he said he'd take care of it, and now she's dead. He's been warned about me, that I might be FBI, that I'm compromising him. Am I in danger, too?"

"Things are getting hot," Clarence said. "You should come to DC for a briefing. How's Friday, 10 a.m.? Good, I'll see you then."

There were three men waiting for me on Friday in "Clarence's" (Bud Riley's) office: Riley, Jim Baxter from the FBI, and a CIA instructor named Peter Stockton, whom I knew from the Farm.

Riley greeted me warmly. "You're doing great, Katherine. You've gotten close to Rzhevsky in a very short time. It takes our case officers months, even years, to accomplish that. You're providing us with good data. You drove him to a meeting with one of his assets in Indianapolis. That meeting was highly productive for us. We nabbed his asset, and through him discovered several 'illegals,' Russians who've been living in the US for years and spying for Moscow. Those people were about to flee the country. We arrested them just in time. But the arrests we made set off some alarms at the Mission. They've started hunting for a traitor in their ranks. Everyone there is under suspicion now. Vika was running the people we arrested, so she was an obvious suspect. They may have decided to take her out."

"She was out to get Max," I said. "Do you think *he* might have killed her?" I was remembering how Max had said: "I will take care of this. Trust me." Then again, *I* might have cast suspicion on Vika, I realized with a start: I had lied and told Marina that Vika had contact with Americans up at Columbia.

"No, not Max," Riley assured me. "They have people for that: 'chauffeurs' or 'bodyguards' they're called. They do the dirty work. Of course, we don't know what role Max played in casting suspicion on Vika. If he exposed her rogue operation against him, that could have contributed to her downfall."

"Vika was obsessed with Max," I said to Riley. "Yet Max claims he barely knew her. I know that's not true. Why does he lie about it?"

"You haven't connected all the dots, Katherine. Vika—Viktoria Gruzinskaya—was Max's ex-wife."

I was astounded. I couldn't hide it.

"Don't look so surprised," Riley said. "Max lies. You know that."

Baxter handed me a photo of Vika, taken some years before the one that had appeared in the newspaper. It showed a younger Vika, with a wide, expressionless face and long, straight hair. It was the girl I'd seen at Moscow University back in 1954 when I went there looking for Max, the girl with the stringy hair who had shouted out "Maksim" and later watched me impassively as I left the building. She must have been the one who reported on me and Max to the other students. A jealous, vindictive woman, even back then. And Max had married her!

They were together in the "spy school," as Steffie had called it. They were both tapped for the KGB. And they continued to work together, even after their divorce. "*Tough, trained, experienced,*" Max had said about the woman whose cigarette had burned my rug. He would know.

"Let's forget about Vika," Riley was saying. "We're interested in Max, not her. We think Max may be the next to come under suspicion. The person we arrested in Indianapolis was his asset, as well as Vika's. And there's also his relationship with you, which must be raising eyebrows. If things heat up, you may need some protection." He nodded to Stockton, who reached into his briefcase and brought out a small Beretta handgun.

Stockton handed me the gun and a gun permit in my name: "If you want to brush up a bit, we can set up some time for you at a shooting range." He picked up my shoulder bag, examined it closely and then, saying, "This'll do fine," he turned it over and emptied its contents on a table near the window. "We'll make a false bottom for it, a place to conceal the gun."

"Actually, I wouldn't mind some target practice," I said to Stockton. I was comfortable with guns, thanks to those hunting trips with my father and the tin-can target practice we used to have at our country house in the Adirondacks. But the stakes were high now. I wanted to be thoroughly prepared.

"Fine. I'll arrange it right now. You can do that while we're remaking your handbag. We'll be sure to get you on the last plane back to New York."

"Why does Max keep seeing me if it's causing him so much trouble?" I asked, addressing no one in particular.

"Maybe it's your many charms," Baxter replied, with a knowing smile that made me inwardly cringe.

Riley was more thoughtful, and surprisingly in sync with what I'd been thinking. "You have a history with Max, a romantic history," he said. "You met him at a time when he was young, naive, and impressionable. He was carried away by you, a lovely young girl from a country beyond his reach. That was before he got involved with the KGB. You represent his lost innocence."

His lost innocence. I remembered how gentle Max had been that night in the park. Max, reciting poetry to me as we lay on the grass. It was as romantic for him as it was for me. Maybe that's why he's shown so little interest in getting to know me as I am today. He doesn't want to hear about my former boyfriends, he isn't interested in my research, he refuses to take Steven seriously. He wants to turn the clock back, to recreate our first night together. And, I realized, that's just what he is doing, with great tenderness and intimacy, each time we make love.

As I was leaving Riley's office, I thought of something else. "By the way, *I'm* being watched now, not just Max. I see those guys at the corner, even when Max is nowhere around. Not all the time, but frequently. Ever since Marina took my picture. I guess they know what I look like now. Maybe they'll stop tailing me, now that Vika's not around to direct them. Or maybe they're reporting to someone else."

"Are they actually following you?" Riley asked.

"I think they're trying to intimidate me. They followed me once for a few blocks, but gave up when I went into the subway."

"Well, you have nothing to hide. It's not as if you have some secret destination."

Oh, but I did! No one knew it, not even Riley.

I was going to Hungary.

Thirty-Two

I was determined to learn about Max's past and his time in Hungary. He'd been in Budapest at a tumultuous time and had left because of a scandal. If I went there, I could seek out people with information, speak to Hungarians who may have known about him at the time.

Clarence would probably veto such a plan. He'd say it wasn't a job for a woman. Or that I wasn't trained for such work. He'd suggest sending someone else, or using someone from the Embassy to gather information. Or maybe he'd just shoot down the whole idea.

I decided not to take the chance. If I didn't tell Clarence about my plans, then I couldn't be accused of defying an order. Steffie went to those countries on her own and came back with solid information. People trusted her because she was like them, not a government official. I would follow her example.

I knew it was a bit foolhardy for me to go there on my own, pretending to be an ordinary tourist when I was not. As a CIA officer, traveling without diplomatic protection, I could find myself in serious trouble. The police in Communist countries were known to arrest tourists and falsely charge them with being spies. In my case, such a charge would not be false. I could easily end up in a Hungarian prison. I had to be doubly careful.

***

"Have you been to Hungary?" I asked Stephanie over cheeseburgers at the Lion's Den. I'd asked her to meet me there and she'd readily agreed.

"No, not yet," Steffie answered.

"How come?"

"It's a matter of priorities. I have limited funds for travel; I have to choose. I've been to the Soviet Union a few times, as you know. As for Eastern Europe, I've visited Poland and Czechoslovakia, where there are known dissidents and underground groups. Hungary's been quiet since their revolution was crushed. I'm sure there's plenty of dissent in Hungary, but I don't know of any specific people or groups. Why are *you* going there? It's not related to your research on Babel."

"I need a break. I've always wanted to see Budapest."

Steffie wasn't buying it. She gave me a skeptical look and sat there, tapping her fingers on the table, waiting for a better explanation.

"Actually, I'm thinking of writing an article about protest movements against the Soviets. You know, in Czechoslovakia and East Germany in '53, in Poland and Hungary in '56. Hungary's was by far the biggest one, so I thought I'd start there."

"Why didn't you say so in the first place, Kate?" Steffie chastised me. "You're always so evasive, as if you're hiding something, and then you come up with a very rational explanation. You were that way after our Moscow trip in '54; if you had told us what you recently told me—about that Russian boy you were trying to protect—we wouldn't have been so angry with you."

"I'm sorry if I seemed evasive just now. I hate talking about writing projects I haven't started and may not finish."

"Well, as I said, I have no personal contacts in Hungary. I do have one name, got it just a few weeks ago from a Hungarian émigré who came to me for help with his green card. I sent him on to someone else. But before he left, I asked him about dissidents in Budapest. He gave me a name, a woman academic. Said she knew about such things and might be of help. I'm wondering . . . would you be willing to look her up, see what you can find out about her? If it seems appropriate, you could tell her about my organization and that we'll follow up."

"Sure. I'd be happy to do that. Maybe she can help me with the article I'm researching."

"If you're up for this, Kate, it would be great. But I have to give you some ground rules on how to conduct yourself. It's really important that you follow them to the letter, in order to protect any locals you may meet, as well as yourself. I can give you instructions right now."

"Of course. Fire away." I took out a pad and pencil and sat there, ready to take notes.

"First, you should apply for a tourist visa, giving 'student' as your occupation. Remove any compromising material from your luggage and purse—like the name of my organization, for example, or the Russian Institute, or any other anti-Communist groups. Don't carry any books, magazines, or newspapers that could be considered politically controversial. Memorize or disguise the name and phone number I'm about to give you—for that woman in Budapest. When you get to Budapest, do *not* call her from your hotel phone. Go to a public phone booth, one that is at least five or six blocks from your hotel. Tell her you're a friend of Gabor's, whom you met in New York. Say: 'He asked me to call and say hello.' If she doesn't suggest it herself, tell her you'd like to meet her. If she agrees, let her decide the time and place."

She continued, "When you go to meet her, don't take a taxi. Taxi drivers report to the police. Walk or take public transportation. Make sure you're not being followed. If you meet in her apartment, be careful what you say. The place may be bugged. Take your cues from her and, if in doubt, ask her, in writing, if it's safe to talk openly. Ask her about human rights problems in Hungary and if there are others you should see. If you decide to tell her about me and my organization, give her the names in writing, not out loud. Take notes in the tiniest script you can manage; you don't want to be bringing a lot of written material through customs. Don't use real names in your notes, in case they are taken from you; figure out a way to code names so you can recreate them once you're home. You may be searched when you leave the country, so it's important to carry your notes in an inconspicuous place."

Steffie stopped for a moment and took a deep breath. "You're probably wondering how I know all this when I've never been to Hungary. Because all these Communist countries are the same. They're police states, they bug you, they follow you, they search you. If you're lucky, you may avoid some of that. If you're not, it can be quite unpleasant. I've found it pretty easy to get around without attracting attention. I follow the rules I just gave you. It also helps being a woman; they don't take women that seriously. Yet there's always the possibility they may want to create an incident: some stranger slips you a photo or an incriminating piece of paper, then you're immediately arrested and charged with being a spy. The Soviets have done that a lot, especially with Western journalists: they arrest them on false charges and then offer to trade them for one of their own captured spies. I think it's unlikely to happen in Hungary. But I'll get you the name and number of someone at the US Embassy to call if there's a real emergency. Are you sure you're up for this?"

I smiled. Steffie had just described tradecraft she'd created on her own. It wasn't all that different from what they teach at the Farm. She fished around in her appointment book for a piece of paper, then read off a name and number to me, explaining that Hungarians give their last names first: Horvath Tereza—34-21-98.

★★★

My parents were spending the summer in a rented house in southern France. They kept asking me to join them for a week or so. I told Clarence I wanted to take a short trip to see them. I made up a story about my father being sick, and my mother needing some support.

"How long will you be gone?"

"Not long. Under a week. It will hardly disrupt my schedule with PLAYBOY." I told Max the same story, that I would be visiting my parents.

Just in case anyone checked up on me, I booked a direct flight to Paris, using my own money. But instead of going on to southern

France, I took a flight from Paris to Frankfurt where, after an over-night stay, I transferred to Hungarian Airlines, arriving in Budapest early on a Tuesday morning. I had three days to accomplish my mission and only one name to contact.

Thirty-Three

Hungary was the most prosperous nation in Eastern Europe, "the most comfortable prison in the Soviet bloc." Budapest, its capital city, appeared to be thriving with its Old World charm, lively restaurants, and attractive, well-stocked shops. Almost a decade had passed since the Hungarian revolt against Communism. There was now an uneasy trade-off with the Soviet-installed government: people seemed willing to sacrifice their political freedom in exchange for better consumer goods. It was sometimes referred to as "goulash communism."

I found Budapest enchanting. Its two distinct parts, divided by the Danube River, were connected by many picturesque bridges. The Buda side was hilly and medieval, with narrow, crooked streets leading to the massive Buda Castle complex, towering over the Danube. Across the river was flat, congested Pest where most business and commerce took place. Despite some bustling activity, I felt the familiar Communist pall: buildings were pock-marked with bullet holes from '56, and people on the streets seemed uniformly obedient. There was none of the free-wheeling, carefree behavior one might find in a Western city.

I checked into a small hotel in Pest, where I would be close to the action. Not bothering to unpack my suitcase, I bought a map of the city and set out on foot to find a public phone booth at some distance from the hotel. Tereza answered on the first ring. I conveyed regards from Gabor. There was a very long silence; for a minute, I thought she had hung up. But then she asked, in excellent English: "And who are you?" I explained that I was an American student and that I would like to meet her if that was convenient. Again, a long silence before she asked: "When would you like to meet?"

"Today, if possible."

"Will you come to my home? Around noon?" She gave me her address.

I found a little coffeehouse where I settled in, studying the map to find Tereza's street. It was quite far from where I was, too far for me to walk. I continued studying the map and settled on a street about two blocks from Tereza's. At 11:30, I hailed a taxi and gave the driver a slip of paper on which I had written the name of that neighboring street. The driver kept asking me for a specific address, but I pretended not to understand him and insisted on being dropped at a corner. He finally gave up and let me out. Was he trying to be helpful, or did he need an address to give the police? I would never know. Once he was clearly out of sight, I backtracked a few blocks to Tereza's street, found her house number and entered an old but seemingly well-kept building. Her apartment was on the second floor.

Tereza was a philosophy professor in her mid-thirties, a pleasant-looking woman with large, penetrating brown eyes. Her husband, Ferenc, graying and somewhat older, was a professor of economics. Both had been unemployed for nine years, unable to find work since the '56 revolution. They were eager to talk about their situation.

"Of course, we supported the uprising," Tereza told me. "We made placards, drafted petitions, demonstrated in the streets. We did not engage in violence; throwing Molotov cocktails was not for us. But we did take in some students who were injured in the fighting. We supported the uprising to the bitter end. It would have succeeded—most of the army was on our side—but the Soviets intervened and crushed it."

"A period called 'normalization' followed," Ferenc added. "Many of our friends were arrested and sent to prison; others, like us, lost their jobs. I think we escaped more severe punishment because of Tereza's father. He's a Foreign Ministry official in good standing."

"How do you support yourselves?" I asked.

"I do translations for publishers," Tereza explained. "Under a false name. The pay is pretty good. Ferenc writes articles for academic journals, also under an alias. There's not much money in that, but it keeps him engaged in his field, with the hope that things may someday change."

"Is it okay to be speaking so freely?" I asked.

"We're not worried," Ferenc explained. "The worst has already happened. There were massive arrests after '56, but they are now beginning to release some of our imprisoned colleagues. Our government leaders, installed by the Russians after the revolution, feel pretty sure of themselves now."

"And why shouldn't they be?" Tereza asked. "Soviet troops never left. They're still here, backing up the government they installed."

They asked about my studies, about Columbia and other universities in the States. I told them about Stephanie's organization, and asked if there were dissident groups I might meet with.

"Try to understand," Tereza explained. "Hundreds of thousands of people fled Hungary as the uprising was being suppressed. Many were political activists, though some just took the opportunity of open borders to get out while they could. The people who remain, intellectuals like us, voice their dissent in academic journals, using arguments that are too lofty for the average bureaucrat to understand or to fear. We focus on problems in other countries in the bloc, rather than our own, but the message is clear to our readers. Our main problem is that we continue to be punished, driven from the workforce, our apartments bugged, our passports rescinded. We can't travel, even to other Communist countries. Those with children see their kids being rejected by schools and universities."

"We hold seminars in our apartments," Ferenc added, "to keep up with the thinking in our various fields. Some of us also give courses in our homes for young people who can't get into the university, or who don't want a Communist education. We need books from the West. And visits from Western scholars. Our dream is to be invited to be guest professors in the West and to receive permission from our government to go."

I was taking notes in the tiny script Stephanie had suggested. I asked for the names of books they needed and of scholars they would like to meet. I would give all this to Steffie so she could follow up.

I knew they had warmed to me when they offered me lunch and telephoned some friends to come meet me. By late afternoon there were five Hungarian intellectuals in the living room with me, drinking red wine, eating pâté, and asking me endless questions about life in New York City and my views on world politics. Everyone spoke English for my benefit. Most Hungarians, they explained, felt it necessary to know a second language, mainly English or German, because their own language was so difficult for foreigners to learn. They were required to study Russian in school, but were disinclined to use it.

I liked them all and was enjoying their company. But I hadn't forgotten my mission. I took out a picture of Max that I had taken outside the Guggenheim and handed it to Tereza. "Do you know this man?" I asked her.

A cold wind seemed to flow through the room as the picture was passed from hand to hand. Conversation stopped. "You know him?" Tereza asked incredulously.

Sensing trouble, I hastened to cover myself. "No, I don't know him. He's with the Soviet UN delegation in New York. He spends a lot of time at Columbia University and we don't know what his purpose is. Someone told me he'd served in Hungary, so I thought I'd ask, as long as I was here."

"Yes, we know him, by sight at least," Maria piped up. She was a small, dark-haired woman with a sultry manner and a sharp, ironic sense of humor. A social historian, she was the only one in the group who still had a teaching job. "We used to call him the 'Angel of Death,'" she declared.

"That's pretty dramatic," I said.

"It's pretty accurate," she responded. She went on to explain. "The Russians didn't leave once the uprising was crushed. They stayed around to help 'normalize' the situation, using their own intelligence teams to arrest, try, and jail the 'counter-revolutionaries.' Martial law was declared. More than twenty-five thousand people were arrested; most were sentenced to prison here, though some were sent to Soviet labor camps. Hundreds were executed. Our army was purged of suspected sympathizers, as were leaders of the Workers Councils and of other institutions, including the university. We didn't know what was happening. It was total chaos."

She continued, "A number of students and professors disappeared. Perhaps they were in hiding, perhaps they'd been arrested. We were meeting constantly in various groups—to share information, to assess our futures. There was often a stranger among us, a young man with such an innocent, beautiful face we couldn't help noticing him. He was a journalist from England, or so we were told. We called him 'Angel-face.' He hung around our meetings, taking notes, accompanied by a young Hungarian woman who was interpreting for him. None of us talked much with him, as far as I know. He observed, he didn't really mingle, and we had more important things on our minds than making new friends. Then people started disappearing, people in our circle who had attended our meetings. That's when we realized that 'Angel-face' was a Russian spy and he was fingering people for arrest. We began calling him the 'Angel of Death.' When he showed up in our midst, we would pass the word: *The Angel is here, beware.* People would leave. Eventually, he must have found himself in an empty room; he stopped coming around."

Maria took a pause. "But the damage was done. Many of our colleagues were arrested at the whim of this young upstart—those involved in the revolution and others who just showed leadership qualities. He was responsible for purging the university, a cold-blooded guy intent on showing his superiors what a good judge of character he was. And yes, that's the fellow," she said, pointing to the picture. "He's older now, he doesn't look so innocent any more. They say that age gives you the face you deserve."

I thanked Maria for what I called a "terrible story." It was. I was appalled. Then I asked her if she knew anything about his involvement in a sex scandal.

"Oh yes, I forgot all about that. Yes, he became the lover of Yvette Szabo, whose husband, Laszlo Szabo, a colonel in the secret police, was later tried as a traitor and executed."

"Can you tell me more?"

"I don't know the details. You should speak to Miklos Szabo, Szabo's son. He would know. Do you want to meet him? We can call him now. Don't worry, he's one of us. He broke with his father years ago, long before the uprising."

She made an appointment for me to meet Miklos Szabo the following day.

Thirty-Four

I wasn't looking forward to meeting Miklos Szabo. I knew I'd be hearing more about Max, and I was still trying to process the revelations I'd just heard. Max's cold-blooded assessments, based on scant observation, had determined the fate of dozens of students and professors, destroying lives and causing pain and hardship, possibly even death. All this had happened a few years after I first met him. It was probably his trial by fire, his initiation into intelligence work.

***

"My parents divorced when I was five," Miklos told me. "I lived with my mother and hardly ever saw my father. He married again, two more times, and had two sons by his second wife. I would see him once a year at a large Christmas party at his home, where he gave me a big hello and nothing more."

Miklos was slight in build and unassuming. He was an underground photographer who mounted exhibits of his work in his own apartment from time to time, inviting all his friends. He supported himself doing clerical work in an office. We met in a coffeehouse not far from my hotel. He seemed uncomfortable talking about his father.

I showed him Max's picture. "I never knew him," he said. "I only know what I heard through gossip. He had an affair with Yvette, my father's third wife. She was very beautiful and had many affairs, they say. But this guy set her up, used her to get information about my father that led to the charges against him. He was arrested as a traitor during the Party shakeups in '57, tortured until he publicly confessed, and then executed. That's the fate of many Communist police chiefs—they do the arresting, they get too powerful, then they themselves are purged. The Russian guy in that picture—he went back to Moscow right after my father's arrest. He'd gotten what he wanted from Yvette."

"And Yvette?"

"She died a few years later, around 1960. Suicide, or so the rumors go. Maybe she was guilty about her role in my father's arrest. Maybe she missed her young lover. Who knows? I only met her a few times. I can't tell you anything about her."

"I'm sorry. I can see this is all very painful for you. Forgive me for bringing it up."

I changed the subject, asking him about his photography, but I could tell he was restless, eager to leave. I was eager to leave also. I thanked him for his time and wished him luck.

I had planned to look around Budapest that afternoon, but my heart was heavy from all I'd heard and I didn't feel up to sightseeing. I went back to my room and fell into a deep sleep.

***

On my last day in Budapest, I took Tereza and her friends to lunch at a popular restaurant, known for its foie gras. Maria arrived late, announcing with a dramatic flourish: "I'm being followed by four cars." As if to prove her point, two heavy-set men, clearly state security police, entered the restaurant and sat at a nearby table, eating nothing, just staring at us throughout our meal.

"They're disgusting," Maria declared. "Pay no attention to them." But I couldn't stop feeling their gaze.

When we parted, I was dismayed to see that the policemen were following *me*. I hurried back to my hotel, packed my bag and checked out. I had two hours to kill before my flight left later that afternoon. Hailing a cab, I asked the driver to drive me around the city and show me all the interesting sights. I felt a little safer in a car than in a hotel room or walking the streets where I could be easily spotted and apprehended.

The driver rose to the occasion eagerly. There weren't many tourists in Budapest; he may never have been asked to do such a thing before. The possibility of payment in US dollars may have added to his enthusiasm. He drove me around Pest and then into the Buda hills, stopping to point out numerous sights, telling me about various museums, restaurants, and theaters. All the while I was looking, without success, to see if a car was following us. If they used multiple cars for surveillance, as Maria had said, it would make it that much harder for me to spot them.

I'd told no one, no one except Stephanie, that I was going to Budapest. I'd discouraged Steffie from setting up a contact for me at the US Embassy because I didn't want news of my trip getting back to Clarence. Now I realized a grim truth: I could disappear, and no one would know where to look for me.

After an hour or so of driving around, I asked the driver to drop me at the airport. We parted on friendly terms. I doubted he would report me to the police. I had given him twenty US dollars, worth a small fortune on the black market, an illegal transaction he would be loath to reveal.

I melded into the airport crowd feeling relatively safe. In an hour or so I would be in the air, on my way home, my mission accomplished. I had just one more hurdle: Passport Control.

The Passport Control officer examined my passport for a long time. Then he made a phone call and told me to wait. My suitcase was brought back from the airfield and into a curtained room. There two inspectors dumped the contents of my pocketbook on a table and made a show of examining my wallet, my money, my travelers checks, my credit cards, and a letter I had been writing to my parents. They pulled clothing from my suitcase, scattering my things around.

They examined my camera and a book of Hungarian poetry in English translation, a gift from Tereza.

All the while I was intensely aware of my notes, which I had rolled up into two little bundles, tucked in the pockets of the raincoat I was wearing. It was a wise decision to carry them that way. All the "clever" places where I had considered hiding my notes—tucked into the empty bottom of a dental floss container, wrapped in my dirty laundry, or inserted between layers of a sanitary napkin—were the first places they looked. They did not search my coat or my person. Eventually, they let me go.

As I was cramming things back in my suitcase, I realized that neither of the inspectors knew English. They were not equipped to find anything incriminating; the search was strictly punitive, a warning. The only thing they took was the book of poetry.

Thirty-Five

"Tell me about Hungary," I said to Max. Ever since my return, I'd been looking for the right moment, and this seemed as good as any. We had just made love on a quiet Saturday afternoon and were lying in bed together, my head on his chest.

"Hungary?" I could feel his body stiffen. "What about Hungary? What do you know about that?"

"Marina mentioned you were there. Please, Max, don't shut me out. I want to know about you, your life, where you've been. A stint in Budapest must have been interesting."

Max was sitting up now, that dark look on his face. I was sitting up too, looking at him expectantly.

"What do you want to know?" he asked.

"What was it like? Why were you there? How long did you stay?" I tried to make my questions as innocent as possible.

"It was difficult. Not pleasant. That's why I'd rather not discuss it."

"Difficult in what way?" I persisted.

I waited patiently for several minutes before he began. "Hungary had just had a major uprising, a counter-revolution against Communism. There were troublemakers fighting in the streets. The Russian army was asked to come in and calm the situation. I don't know how much you know about all this. Soldiers died, civilians died, people were arrested and sentenced to prison, traitors were executed. It was my first assignment abroad. I was excited to be going there. But I didn't like what I saw, or what I was told to do."

I waited, saying nothing.

"As expected," he continued, "I did my job. But afterwards I gave it much thought. I don't think we Russians should have been there. I think the Hungarians should have been left alone to deal with their problems. The Communists would have won; it would have been a better victory if they had won on their own. Our forces were too strong for the situation; we didn't know or understand the people. A lot of people were punished or killed; some of them may have been innocent. That's why I don't like to think about it, or about my role in it. And that's why I don't want to talk about it, to you or to anyone."

"I'm sorry, Max. I didn't mean to upset you."

"You complain that I don't talk about my life, Katya. My life has not been a happy one. There are many things I want to forget—for myself, for my own peace of mind. If I talk about them, I have to remember. You are my new life; it's a happier life. Let's talk about the future, *our* future, not the past."

"Of course, I understand." I kissed him and we slipped under the sheets again, holding each other close. I had broken through his reserve, not completely but a little. I felt somewhat reassured. Though his overall view of the uprising echoed the official Soviet line, he seemed remorseful about the Soviet role in it and the part he played. I saw no point in pressing him further.

★★★

Finally, I had some real information to send to Clarence. I'd already told him by phone about Max's traumatic childhood, but I began my written report by repeating that information, pointing out that Max, suddenly orphaned, had become a "child of the Party," with Party support, a Party education and, ultimately, a Party career.

His Party loyalty runs very deep. It enabled him to carry out some cold-blooded work in Hungary—singling out professors and students for arrest and imprisonment and seducing a woman to gain information that helped convict her husband. PLAYBOY now seems remorseful about his work in Hungary and is somewhat critical of the Soviet role there. But his ties to the Party remain stronger than his misgivings.

I also reported that Max had a strong interest in learning about American society and seemed eager to enjoy what we had to offer.

If PLAYBOY ever turns against his country to work for us, it will not be on political or ideological grounds. His interest in the good life of the West is the only thing that might turn him.

"I'm impressed," Clarence said in our next phone conversation. "You've gathered a lot of information and presented it convincingly. How did you learn about his work in Hungary?"

"Marina told me he was there and described a sex scandal involving him and Mrs. Szabo. Then I met some Hungarian intellectuals at Columbia, who confirmed what Marina had said and told me about his role in purging the university."

"And your Hungarian sources?" Clarence asked. "You didn't give me their names."

"They wouldn't tell me their real names," I answered. "They were afraid of repercussions. But their stories checked out. I interviewed them separately, and I found them very credible."

"I'm especially interested in your conclusion: that PLAYBOY is indebted to the Party and will not be turned against it. But you also seem to think he might be turned by the promise of money and a better life in the West. Can you give me evidence to support that?"

"I'll try. But my gut instinct is that he's not really turnable."

"Leave that decision to us. You just supply the facts, as you've been doing."

I was pleased to get Clarence's approval of my work, and his implied assurance that it would continue, at least for a while. But I was also troubled. When Max talked about his future, it was in Moscow and it always included *me*. He included me, though I'd never promised to go with him to Moscow. If Max were to be turned and ended up in the United States, would *I*, and the prospect of a future here with *me*, be a factor in his defection? What had I gotten myself into?

Thirty-Six

Vika was Max's ex-wife. Why had he told me he "barely knew her"? Why did he seem so indifferent to her death? Did he have something to do with it? Much as I tried to banish that thought, it often filled me with dread. I was deeply involved with a man I couldn't trust. The strain of it all was getting to me.

Steffie gave me a chance for some respite. She called, eager to hear about my time in Budapest. "Why don't you join me on a working trip to Massachusetts this weekend? You'll find it interesting, and we'll have a chance to talk."

Steffie went on, "It will be a three-day weekend. Bring a sleeping bag. We're going to Vasily Polyakov's house; he's one of the leading Russian dissidents in exile, the one who helps us publish Russian *samizdat* in English. He's invited some recent émigrés to tell their stories. They probably don't know English. I'll need you to interpret."

I told Max I'd be gone from Friday to Sunday, that I was having a reunion in Massachusetts with some friends from Smith. He didn't seem disappointed. Perhaps he needed a break, too. "Have a good time," he said. "I'll see you next Wednesday."

Steffie picked me up early on Friday morning in her Volkswagen Beetle. She introduced the two people in the back seat, Suzanne and Tony. "Now you know my whole staff," she said with an ironic smile.

Suzanne was just out of college, a serious-looking young woman with short, straight, dark hair and horn-rimmed glasses. Painfully shy, she was quick to follow Steffie's instructions, but rarely talked or smiled. Tony was tall and skinny and reminded me of the actor Anthony Perkins. I soon learned, without asking, that he was twenty-five, raised in the Long Island suburbs, had graduated from Queens College and was trying his hand at writing. He looked even younger than he was. I liked him immediately: his cute, snub-nosed face and his easy sense of humor. He kept things lively during the four-hour car trip to Cummington, Massachusetts, where Vasily lived.

Steffie wanted to know about my contacts in Budapest. I described the five intellectuals I'd met, their problems and their needs. "I'm going to send them the books they asked for," I told her. "They're academic books—philosophy, psychology—I think they'll get past the censors. But what they really want is to get out of Hungary for a while as visiting professors here in the States."

"You know, that's possible," Steffie responded. "I could organize some university invitations, that shouldn't be hard. And Hungary, I hear, is looking for better relations with the US; they're interested in expanding bilateral trade. Hungarian authorities might cooperate if the State Department pressures them to issue visas for these people. Kate, you worked for the State Department. You could use your contacts there to get them to help us."

Steffie was trying to get me involved; that's what activists do. I secretly wished I could help her. She didn't know, of course, that I never worked for State, that it was just a cover for my CIA work.

"I'm sorry," I told her. "I have an article to write and my dissertation to finish. I don't have time for that."

"It would just be a day in DC. I'll pay your expenses."

"Sorry, Steff. I can't do that now. Why don't you plan a follow-up trip to Budapest, meet these people yourself, see how they want you to handle things?"

"That's a good idea. I will. I just wish you'd be more helpful." She was irritated.

I was pissed, too. She'd asked me to spend the weekend with her on the pretext of hearing about my Budapest trip, but what she really wanted was for me to interpret for her with some Soviet émigrés. I was happy to do that. But now she wanted more. She was never satisfied.

At just that moment, we pulled into Vasily Polyakov's driveway and our incipient dispute, fortunately, came to an end.

Vasily's house was in a small clearing in the woods, a Russian-style *dacha* that he had built with his own hands. It was made of wood, dark and mismatched; he told us he had scavenged much of it from various building sites in the area. There was a small bedroom and bathroom and a very large living room that served all purposes, with a kitchen area to one side, a long, crudely-built table in the middle and a black, wood-burning stove in the corner that, as Vasily told us proudly, heated the entire place in winter. Some of the walls seemed to lean inward and the room itself was a very imperfect rectangle, yet the house was inviting, reflecting the outsized personality of its builder.

This leading Russian dissident was a jovial, gregarious man who welcomed us with exceptional warmth, accumulated, perhaps, during his mainly solitary existence. He gave us each a bear-hug and sat us down at the table, spooning out huge portions of *okroshka*, a cold summer soup, made with ham, hard-boiled eggs, potatoes, dill, and sour cream. His version was garnished with chopped cucumbers and radishes and accompanied by rich, dark, home-baked bread.

Vasily and Steffie got down to work. The latest batch of *samizdat* had been translated and was ready to be printed and sent out, Steffie told him. They began to discuss their mailing list. "We have to put together a master list that can be mimeographed onto address labels," Steffie declared. "We can't go through this every time." Before Vasily could answer, there was a knock on the door, and he jumped up, opening it to three somber-looking men, the recent émigrés we had come to meet.

They barely touched the soup, despite Vasily's urging. They were waiting, geared up to tell their stories. Steffie led one of the men, Mikhail, into the bedroom, signaling for me and Tony to follow her. I admired the way she handled herself, friendly and businesslike, asking Mikhail clear, direct questions, never hinting at the answers she expected, letting him take the lead. Tony took notes, writing feverishly to keep up with my translation.

When Mikhail told us he was forty-eight years old, I almost gasped. I would have put him at sixty or more. Most of his teeth were missing or broken, his body was thin, stiff and misshapen and his face, the color and texture of leather, was lined with deep creases. He had spoken out against the regime in a bar one evening when he'd had too much to drink. For that, he was arrested and spent seven years at hard labor, chopping stone with a pick ten hours a day and sleeping in a rat-infested barracks, with barely enough gruel to ward off starvation. The KGB officers at the camp were sadists, he said. They were constantly urging the guards on to greater brutality.

Pavel was next. He was in his fifties, a stocky man with a tough demeanor. He had been arrested for distributing anti-Soviet literature, *samizdat* writings like the ones Steffie was publishing in English. Pavel was interrogated and tortured by the KGB in Moscow's Lefortovo Prison where he was held for four years, much of the time in solitary confinement. "They beat me with leather straps, burned me with cigarettes, doused me with cold water. All the time they were asking me questions: who wrote the *samizdat*, give us their names. They threatened to arrest and rape my mother. They handcuffed my hands behind my back and hung me from the ceiling, by my wrists, my toes barely touching the ground. I thought my arms would leave my body. The pain was unbearable. I still feel it in my shoulders, all the time."

I knew about Soviet brutality, but it was different to hear about it directly from victims. It was devastating to look these men in the eye and think about what they had gone through, sickening to experience it, vicariously, through their words. The KGB was an army of terror that kept Soviet people in constant fear—fear of arrest, torture, hard labor, and execution. KGB officers were not above any crime—kidnapping, murder, sabotage. And their reach was international as well, sending out spies to pose as diplomats, or setting up agents as citizens in a foreign country where they wait to be called into action by Moscow Center.

And Max was a KGB officer in high standing. They trusted him enough to post him to the United States. He had passed his first test in

Budapest. What other crimes had he committed to prove his worth? It was my job to find out. But did I really want to know?

Andrei's story was different from those of the other two. He was the twenty-six-year-old son of a high-ranking KGB officer, born into a life of privilege. While most Russian families typically lived in communal apartments, often whole families in one room, Andrei's family had a nice, two-bedroom apartment in a building reserved for the KGB. He attended the best schools and was being prepped by his father for a KGB career. Andrei was seventeen in 1956 when Khrushchev gave his "secret speech" exposing Stalin's crimes. When Andrei asked his father what he had done in Stalin's KGB, his father refused to answer, leaving Andrei to think the worst. Many political prisoners were released under Khrushchev and their stories began circulating. Andrei read and listened and began to hate his country and its practices, even before Khrushchev was deposed and the KGB terror reinstated.

Andrei's family was sent abroad, his father posted to an embassy in a Scandinavian country that Andrei did not wish to name. It was there, in the West, that Andrei decided to defect. He made his way to the United States where he had recently been granted political asylum. He planned to spend his time working for organizations like Steffie's, trying to expose and improve the human rights situation in his country.

"Andrei is not my real name," he told Steffie. "I have to use a false name. I've done enough damage to my family by defecting; I don't want to hurt them more."

He continued, "They say that no one leaves the KGB alive. Yet some KGB guys take the risk of becoming double agents, working for the West. Why would they do that? For different reasons, I think. Some lose faith in the Soviet system and want to help bring about Western freedoms. Like me. Some like living a life of danger. And some just want money and the luxuries that are available in the West. There was one man I heard about, a high-ranking KGB officer, who led a double life working for British intelligence. He was exposed and sentenced to death. They decided to make an example of him. They forced him into a coffin, nailed the top shut and cremated him while he was still alive. His colleagues stood by, listening to his screams. That is how the KGB deals with traitors in their ranks."

My God! That scene would haunt me for the rest of my life. It was especially piercing at that moment, when Max himself might be accused and punished as a traitor. Clarence's words were in the back of my mind: *We think Max may be the next to come under suspicion. The people we arrested in Indianapolis were his assets, as well as Vika's. And there's also his relationship with you.* Suspecting Max because of *me*, me and OPERATION PLAYBOY. I was the one who tipped off the FBI before driving Max to Indianapolis. Max knew nothing.

My stomach heaved. I rushed out of the house and into the woods, where I dropped to my knees, throwing up a sizeable portion of Vasily's soup. Hearing of these atrocities firsthand was devastating in and of itself, without the additional layer of anguish that had to do with Max— Max, as a possible perpetrator of such crimes, and Max as a possible victim of a KGB reprisal for treachery he did not knowingly commit.

I stood up shakily and turned around to find Tony standing there, looking concerned. "Can I help you?" he asked, holding out his arms. I walked right into them and let him comfort me as I slowly regained my composure.

"It's really hard, the first time you hear all this stuff," Tony said. "You'll get used to it after a while."

"I don't want to get used to it," I asserted. "I don't want to accept these things as normal."

Tony was stroking my back with more affection than the situation warranted. But I didn't care. I welcomed some human warmth, some reassurance in a world full of monsters and monstrous deeds.

I told Steffie the next morning that I wanted to go home. It was a day earlier than planned, but my work there was done and I was still feeling sick, unable to eat the *blini* Vasily had prepared for our breakfast.

"No problem," Steffie said, "Tony can drive you to the bus. I hope you'll do this again some time. You were a great help." I assured her I would. Her work was really important. It was something I would have liked to be doing myself.

Tony began a stream of conversation before we even got into the car. He wanted to know all about me, where I was born, where I went to school, what my parents did, whether I had any siblings. His interest seemed real, and he juxtaposed his questions with similar information about himself, much of which he'd already told me on the ride up to Vasily's.

He was especially interested in the Russian Institute. "Who are your professors? What are their backgrounds? Do they all know Russian? Did they spend time in the USSR? When?"

Tony saw himself as a budding writer and was trying his hand at short stories. "Do you write on a regular schedule?" he wanted to know. "How many words a day?"

Babel interested him, too. "I've never heard of him. Why did you choose him as your subject? I'd like to read something he's written. What would you suggest?" I told him about Babel's arrest and execution. He wanted to know why Babel had been killed and seemed upset when I described the arbitrary cruelty of Stalin's purges.

Tony clearly had a quick and lively mind. I was sure he'd remember everything I told him. At another time, I might have enjoyed the conversation. But I was feeling sicker by the minute, and Tony's incessant questions were wearing me down. I couldn't wait till we got to the bus stop.

The bus was late. "You should go back to Vasily's," I said. "I don't mind waiting here by myself."

"It's okay. I'll wait with you. I like talking to you. I'm glad we have some extra time."

"Tony, I'm really not feeling well. All I want to do is close my eyes and rest for a while." I sat down on the bus stop bench and shut my eyes.

"Oh, I'm sorry. I know I talk too much. But I can be quiet. I'll just sit here and wait with you. I want to be sure the bus comes. I don't want to leave you stranded."

I tried to rest, tried to forget the unsettling interviews we'd conducted the day before. Tony didn't say another word, but I could feel his eyes on me the whole time we waited. I had a new admirer, it seemed, the last thing I needed. The bus was fifteen minutes late.

"Here's the bus, it's coming," Tony called out. He picked up my duffel bag and carried it to the bus. "It was great to meet you," he said. "I hope to see you again."

"I hope so, too," I said politely, eager for him to leave me to my thoughts. "Thanks so much for the ride."

Tony remained standing there as the bus pulled out, waving goodbye forlornly, like a jilted lover.

***

I fought off nausea all the way home. I couldn't stop thinking about the testimonies we'd taken at Vasily's. It was the first time I'd come face to face with torture victims, with that dark underworld of evil beyond ordinary experience or imagination. I kept wondering about the torturers themselves, how people could bring themselves to inflict such pain on other human beings. It defied everything I knew and believed about human nature.

Did Max participate in torture? To what lengths had he gone to achieve his trusted position? And what would happen to him now if they declared him a traitor? The KGB didn't bother with trials and imprisonment. Suspected traitors were tortured into confessing, then taken to the basement of Lefortovo Prison where they were summarily executed with a shot to the head.

Thirty-Seven

It was close to 6 p.m. when I arrived home. I took two aspirins, put on a nightgown, climbed into bed and fell asleep, hoping to sleep right through the night. But I didn't. I woke up suddenly around 11 p.m. Something had woken me, sounds coming from the next room.

My heart started pounding. Someone was in my living room, moving around. I reached for my handbag on the floor and noiselessly opened the new compartment, removing the gun. Thank God I had it. I didn't think I'd be putting it to use so soon. I left my bed quietly and tiptoed, barefoot, to the open living room door. The room was dark. I could make out the back of a human figure sitting at my desk, holding a flashlight, rummaging through my filing cabinet, which I always kept locked. My heart was clamoring in my ears. I held the gun in my right hand. With my left hand I groped for the light switch and finally found it. Taking a deep breath, I called out: "Don't move," and switched on the light. The figure froze, then swiveled around in my desk chair. It was Max!

"What are you doing here?" he asked. "I thought you were away."

"What are *you* doing here?" I replied in disbelief. "You broke into my apartment!"

Max remained sitting at my desk, momentarily speechless. I perched on a chair, facing him, holding the gun with both hands, pointing it at him.

"I lost something very important," he began, "a special seal that gives me access to classified materials at the Mission. I thought I might have lost it here, so I came to look for it. Why do you have a gun?"

"My dad gave it to me for protection. I never thought I'd have to use it with you."

"Please, stop pointing it at me. Put it down."

I moved to put the gun on the table between us, but when I saw Max reach for it, I pulled it back.

"I just wanted to see if it was loaded," he explained.

"It is," I assured him, and put the gun in a drawer near my chair.

"Do you not trust me, Katya?"

"Why should I trust you, Max? You've broken into my apartment and you're looking through my papers. It seems like *you* don't trust *me*."

"Should I, Katya? Should I trust you? Just a student, you say, but you have a gun and a very expensive little camera that I've never seen you use." *So*, I thought, *he's been going through my handbag as well*.

"You meet with Marina," he continued, "and press her for information about me."

"And why shouldn't I?" I countered. "You tell me nothing about yourself. You don't talk about your life, about the work you did or the work you're doing. What are you hiding?"

"What are *you* hiding?" he shot back. "You just *happened* to come to the Mission that first day? It was just a *coincidence* that you found me? Do you know how improbable that seems?"

"Talking about 'improbable,' do you really think your missing seal might have fallen into my *locked* filing cabinet?" I asked.

We were glaring at each other with icy eyes and grim faces; the room was charged with anger and suspicion. It wasn't him and it wasn't me: we were like two caged animals, snarling from our separate corners.

"Oh Max," I called out unwittingly. "What's happening to us?"

And Max—cool, unflappable Max—suddenly melted. "I should have left you long ago," he said mournfully. "You're up to something, something not good. But I can't stay away from you. I keep coming back. I can't stop loving you."

He looked young and vulnerable, like the sentimental Russian boy I'd fallen for many years before, the boy who recited Pushkin's poetry to me that night in a Moscow park. The boy I could never forget.

I had since memorized that Pushkin poem. It began: *I loved you once and perhaps I love you still . . .* My eyes suddenly filled with tears as I thought about Max's lost innocence and also about my own. Neither of us would ever again be the naive, romantic kids we once were.

Without thinking, I jumped up from my chair and went to him, cradling his head against my chest. I was crying, soundlessly, and he was too, tears running quietly down our cheeks.

Thirty-Eight

Dear Steven,

*I can't begin to apologize enough for my behavior in Stanford.
I was rude, distracted, self-absorbed. Nor can I begin to explain
why, because I don't understand what's going on with me. I just
know that I'm troubled and unhappy and not myself. You have
been very patient and understanding, but I think it's time to face
up to the fact that it's not working for us these days. It's all my
fault, I know. I think I need freedom, time to be on my own and
unaccountable to you, your needs and expectations.*

*For how long? I don't know. Maybe a few months, maybe a
year, maybe forever. It's not fair to expect you to wait and see me
through this period. You should be free to find new relationships,
get on with your life.*

*You have been, and remain, the only real friend I've ever
had. Whatever happens in the future, I hope we will remain
friends forever.*

Love,
Kate

I hated that letter I wrote to Steven, hated what I said and how
I said it. It sat in my handbag for several days before I got up the
courage to drop it in the mail. I was doing something stupid, ending
a relationship with Steven, one with a real future, for one with Max

that had no future at all. Yet all I felt was relief. I would not be deceiving Steven anymore. I would not be trying to keep us afloat when my heart and mind were elsewhere. And I would see this thing through with Max—I had no choice—through to its inevitably unhappy end.

★★★

Max suggested another weekend trip, this time to Philadelphia. I was relieved when he suggested Philly, only a two-hour drive.

"Give him some space this time," Clarence advised. "We'll have people watching him night and day. All you have to do is get him there and let him off the leash. . . . And don't take any photos. You had a close call in Indianapolis. It's not worth the risk. We have other ways."

We left early on a Saturday morning. It was a lovely, clear summer day in late July. Birds were singing in the tree outside my window when Max arrived, wearing a tan-and-white striped seersucker jacket and khaki pants, looking as American as they come. The car I'd rented the night before was parked on the block. We set off immediately, planning to stop for coffee along the Jersey Turnpike.

Things were strained between us. Our angry, tearful confrontation in my apartment the night I found Max searching my papers was still very much alive, hanging between us. We had gone from anger to tears, from hatred to love, in a very short time, with no understanding of how those conflicting feelings could coexist. And no discussion. As always, we were acting as if the episode had not occurred.

But that didn't stop me from constantly pondering over what had happened that night—the emotion, the tears. There was an unspoken bond between us that seemed to defy all reason, feelings so deep they could not be expressed in words, only through sex or with tears. We both knew our affair was doomed. Neither of us could end it.

Why did Max cry that night? Because he feared, deep down, that his love for me would be his undoing.

And why did I cry? I cried for Max—for the man he might have been—and yes, also for myself—for the person I was becoming.

We had only scratched the surface that night. We hadn't talked about the really damning things we suspected about each other, things that, once said, could never be unsaid. Like Max's suspicion that I was with US intelligence, or mine that he was responsible for Vika's death. I would catch Max looking at me with a kind of probing interest. Sometimes I caught a cold look in his eyes, as if I were some sort of distasteful object. And I could not for a moment forget that Vika, whom he said he "barely knew," was in fact his ex-wife and that she had died wearing a gold key identical to the one Max had given me, saying it was his mother's, "one of a kind."

Did Max have something to do with her death? That thought was too horrible to contemplate, and I kept trying to put it out of my mind. Max certainly seemed indifferent to Vika's fate; if anything, he seemed relieved that she was gone.

Vika thought I worked for the FBI. She had sent Marina to check me out, to warn me. She had ground her cigarette out on my white rug, destroyed my diaphragm. She had slammed a heavy iron pan onto my head; that blow might have killed me. If Max took her suspicions seriously, seriously enough to get her drowned, then he had reason to get rid of me too, the source of all his troubles. No, I couldn't believe any of that. Max was a liar, no question about that, but he wasn't a killer.

***

"I've broken up with Steven," I announced to Max. We were on the Turnpike, just past Newark Airport.

"That's good," Max replied matter-of-factly; we might just as well have been discussing the weather.

"Is that all you can say?" I felt my anger rising. "I've just made the most painful decision of my life, breaking up with the guy I thought I would marry. I probably broke his heart."

"I'm sorry it was painful for you. And that Steven's heart is damaged." Max spoke without any discernible feeling.

I slammed on the brakes, pulling the car off the road, and turned off the ignition. "Do you understand what I'm telling you?" I was almost shouting with frustration. "I had to choose between him and you. I chose you!"

Finally, I had his full attention. "I'm glad you chose me," Max said, smiling. "I always knew you would."

"What made you so sure?" I demanded.

"Because I knew you long before you ever met Steven. Because we have such a special kind of love."

Ignoring his complacency, I found myself explaining: "I had no choice, I had to make a decision. I mean, what kind of girl carries on two love affairs with two different men at the same time?"

"A very sexy girl," Max replied, pulling me toward him and running his fingers lightly over my breasts, down my body and up under my skirt. I found myself wanting his touch, wanting it as fervently as I'd ever wanted anything.

"Come closer," he said, "I'll make you feel better." And there, alongside the Jersey Turnpike, with cars whooshing past us in their morning rush, he did just that. He made me feel better. He made me feel great.

***

I had reserved a room in a hotel on Rittenhouse Square. I wanted Max to see the older, historic sections of Philadelphia, including the park and the handsome row houses. But first, I figured, let him get his business out of the way.

The hotel room was nicely furnished but faced a courtyard. "I'm going to take a nap," I announced as soon as we had settled in. "Do you want to join me?"

"I think I'll walk around outside," Max answered. "You have a good rest, little driver."

I wasn't all that sleepy, so I curled up in an armchair with a newspaper I'd picked up in the hotel lobby. I dozed off, woke again, dozed again. It was almost two hours before Max returned, with very little to report about where he'd been. I asked no questions. *Good,* I thought, *he made his contact, now we can just relax and explore the city.*

We wandered along the streets, admiring the charming town houses. We walked past City Hall, visited the Liberty Bell, and explored Old City. We had planned to visit the Museum of Art, but it seemed a shame to be indoors on such a lovely day. Instead we window-shopped on Walnut Street, staggered by the prices. Max seemed annoyed that everything was so expensive. "I wanted to buy you something," he said.

"It's fine, Max," I assured him. "You've given me so many gifts. I'm afraid you're going to run out of money." Max just smiled.

We made our way back to Rittenhouse Square, its lush green lawns filled with sunbathers on folding chairs or blankets.

"Remember the Aleksander Gardens in Moscow?" I said. Max tightened his arm around me, squeezing my shoulder. I felt a familiar charge between us; he felt it, too. "Let's go back to our room for a while," he said. "We have some unfinished business." And we did.

We ate in an expensive French restaurant near Walnut Street. Max had acquired a taste for French food and wine, and he ordered a complete meal: escargot, onion soup, roast lamb with rosemary and garden vegetables. I skipped the appetizers and ordered coq au vin. We shared Crepes Suzette for dessert and easily polished off a bottle of Bordeaux along the way.

Back in the hotel, I began describing my plan for Sunday. I wanted to take Max to the Franklin Institute, but he had other ideas.

"I've been studying the map, Katya. Why don't we start out really early and drive home along the New Jersey shore? I would like to swim in the ocean with you. We can find a room there and return to the city early Monday morning."

I would like to swim in the ocean with you. His words sparked a feeling of dread. "*You know I do not like to swim in the cold ocean by myself,*" Vika had written. Was she, in fact, alone when she drowned, as the police had assumed? Or was she murdered by the Mission's "bodyguards," as Clarence had suggested? Or had she found someone to keep her company in the cold water, someone like Max, for example?

As always, I agreed to Max's suggestion. Perhaps he had another asset to contact? Would the FBI continue to follow us? Try as I did, I never saw any sign of the FBI tails.

But then Max asked me, "Where is the best place to go?" It seemed he didn't have a special destination in mind. He just wanted to swim in the ocean. I thought of Vika again and felt a sharp pang of fear.

"Let's go to Asbury Park, it's a real American scene," I said. "The beach is great and they have all these rides and arcades, fast food, maybe even fireworks, if we're lucky." We'd brought along bathing suits in case the hotel had a pool. We were prepared.

"I'm going to buy you a floppy beach hat," Max announced. "And some huge sunglasses, like the movie stars wear."

We found a room in a bed-and-breakfast, a nice old Victorian house in Asbury Park, just a few blocks from the beach. We changed into our bathing suits, slipped T-shirts over them and carried towels from our room. Within minutes we were on the boardwalk; it was jammed with happy people, all out for a good time. Max was intrigued by the arcades, the rides, and the vendors hawking everything from souvenirs to beach clothes. We decided to wait and go on the Ferris wheel after dark. It was a very high one, with spectacular views of the surrounding scene.

We spread our towels and sat on the beach. It was a steamy day, perfect for a swim. But I was wary about swimming with Max. I'd decided I'd stay out of the water. "I don't feel like swimming," I said. "Why don't you go in by yourself? Give it a try."

Max didn't seem especially eager himself. "Those waves look pretty high," he commented. The ocean was really rough and angry-looking. "You know, Katya, I learned to swim in the Moscow River. I've never been in such waves." He actually seemed a little scared.

"Don't you swim out at the Retreat?" I asked, carefully watching his reaction.

"The water out there is not rough like this."

He was right. Glen Cove was on the North Shore of Long Island, facing the quiet Long Island Sound. We were on the open Atlantic now, and on a particularly turbulent day. Max's fears put me at ease. I was better prepared to handle the ocean than he was.

"Don't worry," I found myself telling him. "I'll teach you how to ride those waves."

We waded out into the ocean, to a spot beyond where the waves were breaking but where we could still stand. We were facing each other, holding hands, letting the gentle waves lift us from the ground as they passed, then settling down nicely again, our feet touching the bottom. "This is nice," Max said, letting go of my hands. "It's fun."

"Always stay behind where the waves are breaking and you'll be fine," I said, as I backstroked a few feet away from him. "But sometimes a wave will break right where you are," I added. "Then you have to dive under it and let it break over your head. Otherwise it will carry you with it."

Max wasn't listening. He began walking toward me in the gently rolling water. I caught that cold, calculating look in his eyes, the look that always upset me. This time it didn't go away. I froze, unable to move.

Thirty-Nine

Max kept walking toward me. "Come closer," he said, reaching me and placing his hands on my shoulders. I was seized with fear. He was so much stronger than me; he could easily push me under and hold me there. There was no one around to see.

His hands tightened on my shoulders, pulling me toward him roughly. He must have seen the panic on my face as I wrenched out of his grip and began swimming away from him, as fast as I could. Just then I saw a huge wave approaching; it was going to break, right where we were. In the split second it took for me to dive under it, I saw Max standing still, not moving, watching me with a confused expression on his face. That wave was going to hit him.

When I came up for air, Max was not in sight. Before I could even look around, another wave descended on me and I dived once again. When I surfaced, there was no one around. Where was Max? Then I saw him, or someone I assumed was Max. He was lying face down in the shallow water right at the edge of the beach. He'd been carried there, tossed and turned by the first wave, then washed over by the second. By the time I reached him, he had crawled onto the beach and was sitting up, looking miserable and angry. There were little bleeding scratches on his legs, arms, and face. He was covered with sand, and he was shivering.

"Are you all right?"

"If this is what you Americans call fun . . . ." His voice trailed off.

"Let's go back to the room," I said. "I'll fix up your scrapes. . . . Actually, you go back to the room and I'll find a drugstore where I can get some Band-Aids and iodine."

There was a pay phone at the drugstore. I'd been eager to get to one so I could call in.

"Clarence? We're in Asbury Park, New Jersey."

"Yes, 415 Fourth Avenue, second-floor room facing north and east," was Clarence's response. I was impressed.

"I don't think he has any assets here. He just wanted to have a good time. . . . At least I thought that was it," I added. "For a moment just now, I thought he was going to drown me."

"And why would he do that?" Clarence asked lightly. He thought I was joking.

"I'm serious, Clarence. Do you think PLAYBOY's dangerous?"

"The only danger I can see is that he's falling in love with you."

"Clarence, I'm really serious. Something happened just now that had me scared."

"Tell me." Clarence dropped his teasing tone.

"We were in the ocean. There was no one around. There was a sudden calculating look on his face. As if he realized he could hold me under and no one would know. It would be an accident. He was pulling me toward him. Then a wave came along and literally washed him away. That wave may have saved my life." I was speaking calmly, in measured tones, not quite sure I believed what I was reporting.

Clarence was silent for a while. Then he asked: "Are you sure? We can roll up this operation right now if you're in danger."

"No. I'm not really sure. I'm still trying to process it. What I think is that the thought crossed his mind, the thought that he could get rid of me at that moment and end all his troubles. Would he have acted on it if that wave hadn't come along? That is what I don't know. I want to think it was just a passing moment."

"You have to feel safe, if this is to continue."

"It just happened. Give me some time to think about it. And to see how Max handles it. I'll be careful."

"Call me tomorrow," Clarence said. "Let me know what you decide."

★★★

Back in the room, I found Max soaking in the tub. He got out and dried himself. I put iodine on each of his many scrapes, and some Band-Aids on the largest ones. He was quiet and seemed angry. I assumed he'd seen the fear on my face, that he knew why I had been so frightened in the ocean.

"The waves were too strong today," I ventured. "We should have stayed out of the ocean. I was scared, too. You must have seen that." I was inventing a reason for why I had panicked. "Next time you'll dive under the waves, you'll know what to do."

"When you're teaching someone to use a parachute," Max replied, "you send him out of the plane first, make sure he knows what to do, before you jump yourself. . . . But you just left me on my own." Max seemed to be mad at me for abandoning him in front of that first big wave. Did he know I was afraid he would drown me? *Had* he been planning to drown me? As always, he remained an unreadable book.

We never went on the Ferris wheel or the rides. We didn't even return to the boardwalk. We watched a little television in our room, then Max went to sleep for the night and I soon followed. By the next morning he seemed more like himself; neither of us referred to the events of the previous day. We left our lodgings around 7 a.m. and drove in virtual silence. We were back in the city in time for him to start a normal workday.

★★★

I dropped off the car and returned to my apartment. The phone was ringing as I opened the door. It was Steven. "Where have you been? I've been calling for days now, ever since I received your letter. I have to speak to you."

Steven was upset of course, upset and bewildered. "I don't get it, Kate. We're not children any more. We've both had plenty of time to sow our wild oats. We decided a long time ago that we were ready to settle down, into our professions and into marriage. Now, all of a sudden, you're talking like a teenager. You want freedom? No commitment? A chance to be with other men?"

"Steven, I don't understand it myself. I just know I don't want to be in our relationship right now."

"Are you well, Kate? Has something happened to you?"

"I'm fine, Steven. I've just had a change of heart. These things happen."

"Then there must be another guy. Someone you've met. I keep thinking about that Russian guy, the one I saw in your apartment. Are you having an affair with him?"

"Don't be crazy, Steven. That guy's a Communist; you know how I feel about Communists. He's a Soviet official, probably KGB."

Oh my God! I was talking on my bugged phone. As soon as the word "KGB" slipped out, I knew I was in deep trouble. And then it got worse.

There was a short silence at the other end of the phone: Steven was putting things together. "Kate," he said slowly, "are you still doing work for the government?"

"Don't be absurd. I'm ending this call." And I hung up abruptly, letting the phone ring and ring as Steven kept calling back.

Damn, damn, damn! It had all been revealed, right there on my phone! That I knew Max was KGB; that I worked for the government. I was blown. Blown to whomever was taping my calls—Max's superiors in the KGB, or maybe Max himself. After all my careful planning, all the caution I'd used, I blew it all in one stupid telephone conversation! I couldn't *believe* how careless I'd been.

Forty

I lived in fearful anticipation for the next few weeks, not knowing what to expect. Would Max be informed of what had been said on the bugged phone? Or would they (whoever "they" were) assume Max knew all about me and was conspiring with me against them?

As time went on with nothing happening, I began to find reasons for hope. The bugging may have been part of the rogue operation set up by Vika. That is what I had initially assumed. If that was the case, I had nothing to fear since Vika was no more.

***

Max, as always, remained inscrutable. How could I know what was in his mind during that scary moment in the ocean? I never knew what he was thinking, even his most mundane thoughts. As the days went by, I decided I had overreacted. Max could not have been planning to kill me. Yes, he was KGB, capable of horrors I knew nothing about. But he was also my lover. His love for me had brought him to tears. I could not believe he would want to harm me.

And so the Operation continued. But my doubts lingered, especially in bed, making love, when I felt most vulnerable. How could I give myself to Max as completely as I had before? When he caressed my "beautiful neck," I had a sudden image of him wrapping his hands around it and pressing till I could no longer breathe. When passion brought me to the point of oblivion, I found myself pulling back, unwilling to let go of the part of me that was now always watching, always wary.

We kept to our weekly schedule—Wednesday nights and weekends—but our time together had gradually become circumscribed. Max no longer spent long weekend days hanging out in my apartment. Instead, we met on Saturday evening for dinner and a movie or a concert. Max would spend the night and leave Sunday morning after breakfast. Our "weekend" had been reduced to a Saturday-night sleepover.

I was feeling stir-crazy. My parents were still away; I saw no one except Max. My life revolved around him, waiting for the times I would see him, and though that gave me plenty of free time to work on my dissertation, I found it hard to concentrate. I was struggling with writer's block and for good reason.

I had come up against a missing chapter in Babel's life, the very last chapter, as it turned out. Babel had withdrawn from public life in the 1930s, publishing nothing. Had he experienced a change of heart politically? He would have had good reason to do so, for that was when Stalin began consolidating his power. More than a million of Stalin's perceived enemies were arrested and executed in 1937 and 1938 alone. Babel himself was arrested in 1939, tortured until he confessed to espionage, and executed in 1940. His unpublished letters and writings from the 1930s, seized at the time of his arrest, remained missing. Without knowing what was in them, I found it hard to proceed.

★★★

Staring at my typewriter one Tuesday morning, I was startled by my ringing doorbell. No one ever came to see me at the apartment except for Max, and this was not one of his days. I went downstairs and opened the outside door, surprised to see Tony standing there, looking shy and embarrassed.

"Hi. I was wondering how you were feeling."

I was annoyed. Why remind me of my behavior in Massachusetts where, sick to my stomach, I had vomited out in the woods? "I'm fine, Tony, I'm fine. I'm really a very strong person, that episode at Vasily's was most unusual for me." Then I added: "Maybe it was the soup." And we both began to laugh.

"Can I come in?" Tony asked. He entered the apartment, looked around with interest and sat himself down on the couch, his long legs tucked awkwardly to the side to avoid bumping them on the coffee table. I explained that the apartment was not mine, that a friend was letting me use it while she was away. There was an awkward silence.

"What is it, Tony?" I asked. Surely he wasn't there to inquire about the state of my digestive system, weeks after that episode in the woods.

"I want to speak Russian the way you do," Tony blurted out. "I was wondering if you would teach me."

"Oh, Tony, I'm not a teacher. I still need practice myself. You should go to Columbia and enroll in a class. They have excellent instructors there."

"I can't afford that. I have no money," Tony responded. "And anyway, I have a love-hate relationship with languages."

"What does that mean?" I asked.

"If I don't love the teacher, I hate the language." I couldn't help laughing at that. I really liked this funny boy who seemed to have a crush on me.

Tony stood up and went into my little kitchen, giving it a quick once-over. "How about doing barter?" he asked. "I'll make you a meal if you get me started on Russian. I love to cook. And it doesn't look like you're much of a cook," he added, gesturing toward my unused kitchen.

He was right. Aside from the two good restaurant meals I had each week with Max, my daily fare consisted of cheeseburgers or pizza, eaten on the run or brought home for dinner. It was not a healthy way to live; I sometimes worried about it.

"Let's give it a try," Tony was saying. "I'll bring all the ingredients and make dinner for us. While it's cooking, you can teach me some Russian."

It was tempting. A break in routine, some home-cooked food, and a chance to try out my teaching skills, skills that might come in handy some day when my present job was over. I liked Tony's energy, his cheerful good spirits. I needed someone to help lift my own. We made a date for the following Tuesday.

Tony was an enthusiastic cook. He brought me into the kitchen with him and showed me how he made meatloaf, getting me to chop the onions and mix them into the meat. The meal was delicious— meatloaf, creamy mashed potatoes, and gently steamed asparagus. While the meatloaf cooked, we sat down with a Russian grammar book. I showed him the Russian alphabet and gave him some basic vocabulary words to learn. I sent him home with a simple homework assignment, and we agreed that he'd return the following week so I could review his progress.

There was no Russian lesson the following week. Tony arrived with a picnic dinner which we ate on a blanket in Central Park while listening to an outdoor rock concert. It was great to be out on a warm summer evening, dressed casually, the city all around us teeming with life. Tony suggested we try Coney Island the next time, and we did, screaming together on the scariest rides, eating hot dogs and French fries. "This is the life," Tony said, and I had to agree. I felt light and happy, far away from the worries that had been obsessing me.

Tony was the exact opposite of Max. He was very open about his thoughts and experiences and insinuated himself into my life with an unearned familiarity. He asked personal questions without hesitation and was interested in knowing everything about me. At times his brashness was annoying, but he usually sensed when he had gone too far and made things right with his natural candor and earnest apologies.

He was fun to be with, always making jokes and teasing me. We laughed a lot together, something I never did with Max. Max was an intense, serious man. He was as formal when he spoke Russian as he was when he spoke English. Though he smiled easily, a devastatingly beautiful smile that could charm anyone, I never saw him break into spontaneous laughter.

Tony and I spent several very hot days at Jones Beach. I wore a bikini I had bought on impulse, like the ones women in France were wearing but which were not yet popular in the US. People stared at me as I walked along the boardwalk. Tony seemed embarrassed and kept asking me to cover up. I refused, teasing him about his prudishness.

Tony's eagerness to learn Russian had clearly been a pretext. We were doing more and more things together, and Russian lessons were not among them. At times I found myself wondering if Steffie had encouraged him to befriend me as a way of enticing me into their movement. How ironic that would be. The two men in my life, both trying to turn me but in different directions: Max wanting me to embrace the Soviet system, and Tony wanting me to work against it.

One evening we went to a street fair on the Lower East Side. There was a live band and Tony got me dancing with him, a kind of polka that left me breathlessly happy. We shared a slice of pizza that burned both our mouths, then followed it with soft ice cream that dripped down my chin while Tony tried to catch it and wipe it away.

I said good night to him at my front door that night, about to give him the usual peck on the cheek that was our practice. But Tony surprised me by kissing me full on the mouth. His kiss was firm and manly, not at all shy and boyish as I would have expected it to be. I found myself responding for a few seconds before pushing him away. "No, Tony. You're my friend, not my boyfriend. You're my pal, the brother I always wished I had. And anyway," I continued, seeing the hurt expression on his face, "I'm in a serious relationship with someone right now."

"That's okay," Tony responded, his usual grin returning. "I can wait. You said 'right now,' which means it may not be forever."

***

Tony arrived at my place unexpectedly one morning. He brought me some homemade cookies. "I'm on my way to work," he explained. Tony was a volunteer at Steffie's, which meant he could come and go as he pleased. Other than that, he had no job and spent his time writing short stories. He lived with his parents in Hempstead, Long Island, about an hour from Manhattan.

"Why don't you come with me?" he asked. "See Steffie's place. You've never been there, right?"

So maybe my suspicions were correct: maybe it was all leading up to this. But why not go with him? I was curious to see Steffie's operation. And eager to get away from my typewriter for a while.

We took the subway to 42nd Street, then walked east, stopping just one block short of the United Nations. Not a bad spot, I thought; convenient for Steffie's advocacy work.

The office was on the sixth floor of an old but well-maintained red brick office building. I was surprised by how professional it looked, with the name—Committee for Human Rights in the Soviet Union and Eastern Europe—stenciled on the milk glass panel of the front door. Inside was a good-sized entry room that housed a mimeograph machine, a secondhand sofa, and a few chairs. Off to the right was Steffie's office. We walked right in.

Steffie didn't seem surprised to see me with Tony. She greeted me warmly and thanked me for coming by. "I'll leave you two to talk," Tony said, and slipped away to "do some work." Her office was quite large, the walls covered with bookshelves and filing cabinets. Every horizontal surface, including the books on the bookshelves, was covered with papers, piled high in no discernable order. Her large desk was also stacked with papers and books. She had to clear a space to look out at me from her desk chair.

"I'm so glad you're here, Katie. Can you stay awhile? I have a new document that just came in, it needs translating." I said I'd be happy to help out and that I could give her a few hours.

"Great. Come with me. I'll find a desk for you to work at." Steffie picked up some papers from her desk and led me outside. Suzanne was sitting at a desk in an alcove outside her office, out of Steffie's sight but close enough to hear her orders which, I suspected, came frequently. We walked through the entry room to another room with three desks;

"for our guest workers," Steffie explained. Tony was sitting at one of them, his feet up on the desk, reading a pamphlet. Steffie was about to set me up at another desk when the front door banged open and a man entered, yelling: *"Gde nakhoditsya Stefani?"* It was Andrei, the man we had interviewed some weeks before in Massachusetts; he was demanding to see Stephanie. He looked like he had just run a marathon, sweaty and disheveled. "Something terrible has happened!" he announced in Russian, which I quickly translated. We both rushed to him and made him sit down. Steffie called out to Suzanne: "Bring some water, quick."

Andrei collapsed on the couch, gulping down the water; after a time he quieted down. The four of us gathered around him—me, Steffie, Suzanne, and Tony. I questioned him in Russian and translated his answers. Andrei was clearly in no state to use his faltering English.

"What happened?" I asked.

"My father. The KGB demoted him. Because of me. I'm sure of it. Someone must have revealed my real name, the name behind the signature 'Andrei' in the publications you've been circulating. Someone must have broken into your files and found out who 'Andrei' really was!"

"I very much doubt that . . ." Steffie began, but Andrei interrupted: "Do you keep your files locked? Has my real name been kept in a locked file?"

"There's no way anyone could get your information from us," Steffie assured him. She did not say the files were locked. I thought of all the papers scattered around her office. Nothing there seemed secure to me.

"And anyway," Steffie continued, "if someone broke into our office, we'd know it."

"Please bring me my file," Andrei demanded coldly.

"Go get it, Suzanne," Steffie said. And, to my surprise and relief, Suzanne returned a few minutes later with a file marked "Andrei" in her hands.

In it was a transcript of the interview we'd done with Andrei at Vasily's house and copies of several articles they had published, based on Andrei's revelations. In the back of the file was a slip of paper with nothing on it except a name, written in Russian, Andrei's real name. Andrei took that piece of paper and tore it into little pieces.

"I don't think it's wise for me to come here again," he said. "And please do not quote 'Andrei' anymore in your articles. I support what you are doing, but I have to protect my family. I am sure you understand." He got up and walked out, turning at the door to say a rather frosty good-bye.

Stephanie and I went back to her office. "You know, Steff," I said, "even if you can't afford a real security system, you have to protect your sources. Maybe you should get a safe with a combination lock, keep your confidential stuff in it."

"No one's been in here looking for his name," Stephanie assured me. "This place may look messy, but I know every paper in it and just where it is. If anything had been moved or taken, I'd know it. Anyway, I don't give a damn about his old man, a KGB colonel, getting demoted. I wouldn't care if he got kicked out altogether."

"You forget what Andrei told us," I reminded her. "*No one leaves the KGB alive.*"

Stephanie changed the subject. "I'm awfully glad you were here to interpret for us, Kate. Thank you. I guess it's too late for you to do that translation, but I hope you'll come again."

"I will," I promised, but I knew I would not. It would be a disaster if I were to be seen there—by Max, or by others from the Mission who might be following me. Or, for that matter, by Clarence and his FBI pals. Involvement in the human rights cause was not part of my cover.

Forty-One

Tired of our regular French restaurant routine, I suggested a change to Max. "Let's stay home tonight. Have some simple American food." I had some leftover macaroni and cheese, prepared by Tony a few nights before. It seemed perfect.

We had just sat down to eat when the doorbell rang. "It's me, Tony!" I heard over the intercom.

"This is not a good time, Tony. I'm sorry. I'm having dinner with a friend."

"That's okay, I'm not staying. I'm just dropping something off."

"I'll be right back," I told Max as I hurried downstairs to see what Tony had for me. I was greeted at the outside door by a huge, beautiful flower arrangement, so large it obscured Tony's face. The flowers were sitting in a glass dish full of water that Tony was holding at his waist. Water was sloshing onto my front steps and onto Tony's shirt.

"I was at a fancy luncheon today. This was the centerpiece. They said I could have it and I thought I'd bring it to you."

It was the last thing I wanted at that moment and I was about to say so, but Tony was so pleased with himself that I found myself relenting. "Thank you, Tony. You really shouldn't have gone to all this trouble. Please, bring it upstairs," I said, leading the way. There was no way I could carry it myself.

Tony followed me into the apartment. "I'll just put it here on the coffee table," he said. I gave Max a smile, thinking he'd be amused by Tony's lavish flowers. But Max looked furious, his face red with anger. I'd never seen him quite that way before. He leaped from his chair and confronted Tony, grabbing his shirt collars with both hands and bringing their faces close together. "What are you doing here? Who sent you?"

Max was speaking Russian, but Tony got the drift. "I'm just . . . dropping off . . . some flowers," he stammered. He pulled away from Max and the next thing I knew, the two of them were wrestling. Max had him in a chokehold within minutes. Tony's face was red and he was gasping for air. Max kept asking: "Who sent you? Why are you here?"

"Max!" I called out. "You're choking him."

As Max slowly relaxed his hold, Tony mumbled meekly: "Directorate S, Maksim. You know, Maksim, Line N. Let me go, please. I didn't know, I didn't know you were here. I didn't know you knew her. I'll leave. I didn't know."

I fell back on the couch, stupefied. Tony was speaking in Russian— fluent, perfect Russian. Russian much better than mine!

Max let him go with a terse warning: "Get out of here, Anton, and don't let me see you here again. You have no business here, do you understand?"

"Yes, yes. I understand." And Tony was gone.

Max went into the bathroom. I could hear him washing up. I sat there in a state of shock, trying to understand what had just transpired.

When Max returned, his face washed, his clothes set straight, he was full of apologies. "I am so sorry, Katya, I really lost my temper. That guy just gets into, *gets under* my skin. Please forgive me."

"How do you know him?" I asked.

"Oh, I see him around. At parties where he doesn't belong. Sometimes out at the Retreat, where he shouldn't be either. He's a fool, always looking for attention when he should be keeping quiet. . . . How did *you* get to know him?" Max was looking at me with that dark, probing expression that had become familiar to me.

"I met him at Columbia," I said, my stock answer when I wanted to dodge the truth. "He's friendly with people I know up there."

I don't know how I got through the rest of the evening, my mind was in such a state. It wasn't until Max had left that I could finally sort things out.

Tony, who came to me seeking Russian lessons, could speak perfect Russian. He and Max knew each other. His full name was Anton, not Anthony as I'd assumed. He crashed Russian diplomatic parties and showed up at the Soviet Retreat. Tony was *Russian*. But he couldn't be! He was so quintessentially American, with his Queens accent, his hip mannerisms, his love of American pop culture, his cooking repertoire of chocolate-chip cookies and mac and cheese. We sang songs together, songs we both knew from high school, some of them pretty obscure to anyone but a New York City kid. Tony was as American as apple pie.

***

"What do you know about Directorate S, Line N?" I asked Clarence during our phone call the next day. "I think it's a division within the KGB."

"I don't know," Clarence answered, "but I can find out." I was relieved when he didn't ask me why I was asking.

Actually, I already knew the answer to my question. I had figured it out. Directorate S, Line N was the KGB division that handled the "illegals." And Tony was an "illegal." His Russian parents must have come to America when they were very young, bringing Tony along as a child. They assumed fake identities and lived as ordinary American citizens, waiting for orders from Moscow if and when they were needed. Tony was given a typical American upbringing, but he was programmed to work for the USSR.

I found it hard to accept, remembering Tony at Coney Island, eating hot dogs and French fries, or stretched out on a blanket with me in Central Park, listening to a rock band. He was so full of fun, so carefree and happy. It was hard to believe he was concealing dark secrets, leading a double life and a very dangerous one at that. And part of that life was spying on *me*. He wasn't trying to recruit me for Steffie's organization, as I had once suspected: he was trying to undermine her group and everyone connected with it.

And then I thought of Andrei. Someone had revealed Andrei's real name to the Soviets, and his father had been demoted. Andrei had been right. There was a mole in Steffie's tiny office, and the mole was Tony.

I had to tell Steffie. She needed to know at once.

Forty-Two

Steffie, always a cool one, showed no surprise when she saw me at her office door. "C'mon in," she said. "Tell me what brings you here."

"I need to talk to you, but not here. Is there somewhere private we can go?"

Steffie grabbed her bag and told Suzanne she'd be back soon. We took the elevator to the lobby where there was a coffee shop and settled down in a booth in the back, away from other patrons. "What's on your mind, Katie? You look upset."

"I *am* upset. Very upset. I've just discovered that Tony is a spy, a Russian spy."

Steffie started laughing. "Oh Kate, that's crazy. Tony . . . a spy? Come on!"

"No, really. I caught him speaking Russian, perfect Russian. He's been hiding that from us, not letting us know. And that's how Andrei's real identity must have been leaked. He's been spying on *you*. How did he come to be here in the first place?"

"He just walked in one day and volunteered. Said he supported our cause and wanted to help. Kate, he's no more a spy than *you* are. You've been reading too much about the Great Purges; it's gone to your head."

"Tony's what they call an 'illegal,'" I explained. "Soviet spies who pose as Americans but are here to sabotage us." I couldn't tell Steffie the rest of what I knew: that Max knew Tony, that his name was Anton, that he worked for Line N. Steffie didn't know about Max, and she never would.

"I don't believe this," was Steffie's response. "I don't know why he would have concealed his knowledge of Russian. I admit that's very odd. But there must be some explanation. We should ask him, right now." She began thumbing through her address book, and then headed for a pay phone near us. *Fine,* I thought. *Let's see what happens.*

She was back a few minutes later. "His number's been disconnected."

"I'm not surprised," I told her. "He knows that I know, and that I would tell you. I don't think you'll be seeing him anymore. Steff, you've got to get some security for the office. The Soviets are on to you. There may be others coming around. Get a safe for sensitive documents. And have the place swept for bugs. I'll bet your phone is bugged, and maybe other parts of the office as well."

Steffie was quiet, coming to grips with it all. "I guess I should thank you," she said without much enthusiasm. Then she added: "I know there's a lot you're not telling me, Kate. Maybe someday you will."

"Listen, Stephanie. No matter what you think, or hear, or see— you and I are on the same side. Please remember that."

"I will. Yes, I will." We were about to part. I moved to give her a kiss on the cheek, forgetting that Steffie was not one for such gestures. She pulled back instinctively, offering me her hand instead, a firm, meaningful handshake. I think she knew I wouldn't be coming back again soon.

Forty-Three

It was August, the height of summer. And a very hot New York City summer it was. The sidewalks seemed to sizzle in the blazing sun; people walked about in a daze; workers in hard hats, chopping up Lexington Avenue with their jackhammers, seemed like sinners consigned to Hell. My parents were still in southern France, urging me to join them, but I kept saying no, citing the need to keep working on my dissertation. I found myself missing Tony; he would have found ways to enjoy this hot weather.

My apartment wasn't air-conditioned, so I made do with a few fans. I could have asked for a government stipend to buy an air conditioner, but I decided not to. I had a feeling that OPERATION PLAYBOY would soon be coming to an end.

I filled my time with Max by suggesting various cultural events to attend—movies, concerts, ballets, lectures. Max went along willingly, but without much gusto. What he really liked was window-shopping at some of his favorite stores. He loved wandering around Conran's, a new store in New York featuring stylish modern furniture and accessories.

"Are you planning to take that couch back to Moscow?" I asked in Conran's one day, as I watched him check the measurements and test it for comfort.

"Unfortunately, no," he said, "I can only take what I can easily bring with me. Fortunately, that includes you."

"It sounds like you'll be returning soon," I remarked. I ignored the part about my going with him. He didn't press me.

"Not at all. I really like it here."

We seemed to be running out of conversation. Max didn't want to hear about my work: Babel remained a traitor in his eyes. And needless to say, he never talked about the work he was doing.

Our sex life had also been losing steam, for me at least—ever since that episode in the ocean at the Jersey shore. I was afraid of losing control during sex with Max, and Max, though he made no comment, must have sensed that things had changed. I also found myself missing the cozy intimacy I had come to expect after sex, the way it had always been, afterwards, with Steven, when we would lie close together in the dark, sharing our most personal thoughts, dreams, and fears. With Max, there was no talk, just a few words of appreciation, followed by sleep.

"This seems to be going nowhere," I told Clarence as we began one of our weekly phone calls. "I'm not getting anything new from PLAYBOY. He reveals nothing. I feel like I'm just marking time. . . . And," I continued, "I think I've lost his trust. He knows I have a gun."

"What?" Clarence was startled. "How did that happen?"

"Oh, it was a bad business. I thought I heard a burglar in my apartment, so I took out the gun, but then I saw it was him. He was going through my papers, so it's clear he didn't trust me, even before he saw the gun."

"When did this happen?"

"A few weeks ago."

"And why didn't you tell me about it before? This is important."

"I was ashamed to tell you. I shouldn't have been so quick to grab the gun. It was over in minutes. And PLAYBOY, in his usual fashion, acts like it never happened."

Of course, I should have told Clarence. But I was afraid he'd want to know more. And the rest was too emotional and confusing to share with anyone. One moment we were glaring at each other, the next we were crying in each other's arms. I still wasn't sure what to make of it myself.

"You should have told me." Clarence sounded severe, disappointed in me.

"I know. I'm sorry. I was embarrassed. I put it out of my mind."

"Well, be more precise in the future. And try to hang in there a little longer. We're not quite finished with PLAYBOY yet."

***

Could it be? Those long legs, that awkward posture, it could only be Tony, sitting on my front stoop, waiting for me as I returned from the library one day. "What are you *doing* here?" I exclaimed.

"I have to explain . . ." he began, but I cut him off.

"There's nothing to explain. I understand it all. You should not be here. I can get you in a lot of trouble." Actually, that was an empty threat. I didn't know Tony's real name or where he lived. I could not send the FBI his way if I wanted to, and I had no intention of doing so in any case. "You should leave, Tony, immediately. And don't ever come back."

He just sat there looking at me, a puppy-dog expression on his face. "Tony, I'm serious. You have to go."

"I'll go. But first, there's something I want you to know," Tony said, clearing his throat and looking downward. "I loved you; I still do." He was paraphrasing that Pushkin poem; I wondered if he knew it.

Our eyes met. I could see in his a mixture of emotions: confusion, fear, and yes, also love. "Go, Tony. Go, go, go." And he did, walking away slowly, without the usual spring in his step. I watched him walk off. He was an imposter, but then, who was I to condemn? Wasn't I an imposter, too? But I was serving a righteous cause, for a country that stood for free expression and human rights. His allegiance was to a regime of repression and terror. I wondered if he had ever been to the Soviet Union. Did he have any idea of what life there was like?

I went inside and sat there motionless for a long, long time, watching the afternoon light fade away. I felt unbearably sad.

Forty-Four

"We're going to Boston this weekend, staying at the Copley Square."

Clarence seemed amused. "The Copley, eh? Nothing's too good for the PLAYBOY. . . . Well, you know the drill, my dear. Give him his freedom, no photos. We'll be on the case. And Katherine . . . be careful."

He'd used my name. Why? It could only have been for emphasis. He was stressing the need to be careful.

***

I'd booked a room at the historic Copley Square Hotel where my parents used to take me when we visited relatives. I didn't tell Clarence I was paying for the hotel myself. I wanted to make up for all the gifts, hotels, and restaurants Max had paid for in the past. I should have paid my own way all along, but Max so enjoyed being the big spender, it seemed pointless to protest. It was different now, when our affair seemed to be coming to a close. It didn't seem right to be behaving like a married couple.

When my assignment ended, our relationship would end, too. I was ready to let it end. I would go back to DC. I would lie and tell Max I was moving to California, getting back together again with Steven. He would never know I was with the CIA, that he'd been an assignment, a job. But how would Max take it? He seemed so complacent about our future together in Moscow.

And what would I do once it was over? I found it hard to contemplate a life without intrigue and excitement. Would they send me back to Translation? That would be odious.

★★★

Max liked luxurious things, and our room at the Copley was just that—large, bright, and furnished all in white: plush white carpeting, white upholstery, and a king-sized bed with white sheets and blankets and lots of white pillows in various sizes and shapes.

It was close to 9 p.m. when we arrived. We took off our shoes before walking on the thick carpeting. "How in the world do they keep it so clean?" I wondered out loud.

Max went to the window, opened the draperies and stood there, looking out at downtown Boston. Then he called room service and, without asking me, ordered champagne, oysters, and a Caesar salad for two. "I'm going to shower now," he said and went into the marble bathroom. He emerged a little later, looking scrubbed and handsome and wearing a white terry-cloth robe with *Copley Square* embroidered on the pocket. "There's one of these in there for you, too," he said.

"How was the shower?" I asked. "It was okay," he answered without any zeal. "The towels could have been larger and thicker."

Fresh from my shower and wrapped in the other robe, I found Max sitting on the chaise, thumbing through a Boston guidebook and grumbling because room service was so slow. Our food arrived soon afterward, wheeled in on a carefully set table, its crisp white cloth decorated with several small vases of fresh flowers, the oysters chilling over crushed ice in a silver bowl. But Max was complaining: the oysters didn't taste fresh, the croutons in the salad were soggy. He had become a connoisseur, and a highly critical one at that. I wistfully remembered his early innocent awe at the abundance and quality of American goods. Now he spoke with an air of entitlement that I found irritating. We were at the Copley, for God's sake. And I was footing the bill.

The champagne, the oysters, and the enveloping softness of the huge white bed should have made for some very special lovemaking that night. But it didn't, not for me at least. I found myself faking an orgasm, just to get it over with. Max went right to sleep, without his usual words of praise. He must have sensed my waning passion. Was his waning as well?

When I woke the next morning, Max was gone. "Out walking," said the note on the night table. It was a familiar routine by now. I assumed he'd be gone for hours. I showered again and dressed, then ordered a light breakfast to be sent to the room. Curled up in an armchair, a cup of coffee at my side, I began reading the *Boston Globe*, which had been included with my breakfast tray. The United States was protesting the Soviet Union's unlawful detention of a US citizen, accused of being a former German spy.

I had just dozed off when I heard Max enter the room. I opened my eyes and saw him, sunk in an armchair near me, looking ashen.

"What's wrong?" I was alarmed. "You look like you've seen a ghost."

"I'm being followed," he announced. "*We're* being followed."

"Followed? That's ridiculous. Who would be following us?"

"There were two of them. They were clearly following me."

"Do you think it's because we've gone outside the city limits?" I was thinking fast, trying to invent some explanation for the FBI tails.

"No, it's not Americans. They're Russians."

"Russians? Are you sure?"

"Believe me, I can tell a Russian thug when I see one. They're after me."

"Why, Max? Why would they be?"

"I'm not sure," he spoke slowly. "There's a lot going on in the Mission these days. They think there's a traitor, an informer in our circle. Because some Americans were recently arrested, Americans who are friends of Russia. Someone exposed them to American intelligence. First they thought it was Vika, the woman who drowned. Now I think they suspect *me*."

I knew the FBI had arrested some American spies after Max met up with them in Indianapolis. Why had they been so heavy-handed? Of course Max would come under suspicion.

"That's crazy," I said.

"It may be because of you, Katya. They know I've been spending time with you, that we are lovers. They've questioned me about you. And they've bugged your apartment, I'm sure of it. They think you're FBI."

He gave me a penetrating look. "Are you? Are you FBI?"

I heard Clarence's voice: *Deny, deny.* "Of course not, that's absurd!"

Max kept searching my face. "You're working for something, for someone," he said. "I just don't know who."

I held his gaze until he finally dropped his eyes. I'm good at that; it was a game we played in school.

"Let them follow us," I said as cheerfully as I could. "We're doing nothing wrong."

"You don't understand," Max said. "This is not ordinary surveillance. These are the dangerous guys, the ones who cause accidents, use poison, make people disappear."

It was like a hand clutching my heart. Vika, killed at the beach. And now Max? Because of me? Because the FBI followed us and arrested his American assets? My job was to befriend Max and evaluate him. I never thought I'd be putting his life in danger!

"What are we going to do?" I asked.

"Be quiet, I'm thinking." He shut his eyes. After some minutes, Max turned to me. He was calm. I could see he had a plan.

"There's a gift shop right next to the hotel. Go down there and buy me a baseball cap, and a sweatshirt, whatever you can find, something a kid would wear. And a gym bag. Then, stop at the desk and order a car to be waiting at the back entrance to the hotel at nine o'clock tonight. It will be dark by then; I'll slip out that way. They don't know I've seen them, so they won't expect me to be leaving. We'll stay close to the hotel today. Eat in the dining room, act normal."

The day went by very slowly. We rested. We read. We didn't talk much, though my mind was racing. I followed Max's directions, buying the sports clothes he wanted, ordering the car. At eight forty-five Max put on the sweatshirt and the baseball cap. Then, quickly and right before my eyes, I saw him subtly change his posture and his walk. Just like they taught me at the Farm. But he did it so easily; he was a pro. If I had seen him from the back, I would not have guessed it was him. He looked like a kid.

"After I've gone," he told me, "keep the lights on, walk by the window a few times and talk out loud as if someone else is in the room. Turn on the TV. Around midnight, turn off the lights and go to sleep. Tomorrow, you should be careful. They won't hurt you. They deal with Russians, not Americans. But don't take any chances. Take the plane, don't drive back to New York. You can turn in the car at the airport. One of them may follow you from the hotel. The other will stay back to look for me. Don't worry. Just get on that plane to the city. And stay away from your apartment. Go to your parents' house. I'll be in touch when things settle down."

"But where will *you* go?" I asked.

"Don't worry about me," Max answered. "I have friends, people who trust me. I will be safe. I will work this all out. . . . I'm leaving my clothes for you to take back."

He gave me a quick peck on the cheek and left, carrying only his attaché case, concealed in the gym bag. I remembered his lecture about the parachute instructor: always let your student jump first, then follow. This time *he* was leaving *me* in the lurch.

★★★

Much as I liked mental games of danger and intrigue, I was not prepared for brute, physical force. I was scared. *Where were the FBI tails?* I wondered. Probably following Max. I carried out Max's instructions, walking past the lighted window, adding my own touches, such as gestures with my hands, to give the impression that someone else was there in the room.

I called Clarence, careful to sound calm and strong as I told him what had happened. "Those guys are after PLAYBOY, not you," he assured me. "Still, you should be careful getting home tomorrow. And yes, it's best to avoid your apartment; they may look for him there. Call me when you're back in the city."

At midnight, I turned off the lights and pushed a dresser against the locked door, thinking they might decide to surprise us when they thought we were asleep. I kept my clothes on and sat all night in the armchair, dozing off, then jerking my head up, wide awake. I kept my gun close to me, on the arm of the chair. It seemed like morning would never come.

Forty-Five

I checked out at 8 a.m., skipping breakfast. *I'll have coffee at the airport,* I decided. Our rented white car was parked down the block from the hotel. I headed for it, carrying my little suitcase.

The sidewalk was suddenly blocked by a large man, facing me, standing in my way. When I tried to move around him, he shifted his position so I could not pass. "Excuse me," I said.

"Where?" he asked in heavily accented English.

"I don't understand," I said.

"Where Rzhevsky. Where?"

"I don't understand," I said again. "Please, let me pass by."

"Rzhevsky," he repeated, holding his ground.

He was tall and heavy, about six-foot-two, with broad shoulders and muscular arms. His hair, cut short, was coarse and black, and his skin was swarthy. I assumed he was from one of the Soviet republics. I decided to hide the fact that I spoke Russian. Let him struggle to make himself understood; it gave me an advantage.

"He in hotel?" he asked. I looked at him blankly.

He grabbed my upper arm in a viselike grip, turned me around and headed back toward the hotel, pulling me along. When I started to struggle, he put his mouth close to my ear: "Careful. I have big knife."

A few yards from the hotel entrance, he stopped briefly to confer with a crony, another large man though not quite as imposing, with pale, thinning hair and a face badly scarred from disease or acne.

"We go to room," he told me, pulling me toward the hotel door.

"I've checked out," I said.

"We go to room."

He accompanied me to the reception desk and stood close behind me as I asked for the key. "I may have left something in the room; I want to go back and check," I explained.

"You don't need a key," the receptionist told me. "The room is being made up right now; you can take a look." I fixed my eyes on hers with a pleading look, hoping that she would see I needed help. But she took it wrong and assumed I was asking to bring my thuggish companion to the room with me. "Just you," she said with disdain and went back to her papers.

"Just me," I told him. But when we got to the elevator, he walked in with me and no one seemed to notice or care.

The door to the room was open. A maid was making up the bed. Without ever letting go of my arm, he searched the closet and the bathroom; he even got me on my knees as he knelt to look under the bed.

On the way down in the elevator I asked him what his name was. It was a question he didn't expect, nor did he intend to answer it. After a minute though, he gave me an ugly grin and replied: "Ivan Grozny."

Ivan Grozny—Ivan the Terrible—was the feared and powerful Tsar of All Russias who reigned in the sixteenth century. It was a stupid, grandiose joke. I decided to play along and sound really dumb.

"Mr. Grozny," I began. "Rzhevsky is not here. I don't know where he is. I have to go now. I am expected home." He did not respond. He just kept walking, pulling me along with him.

Outside the hotel, he conferred again with Scarface. I gathered from their conversation that there were others on their team, that they suspected Max might still be somewhere in the hotel and that they had both exits covered, waiting for him to emerge. Grozny had let go of my arm, and I began walking away, carrying my suitcase, heading for the car. I walked fast, without running or turning around, hoping they weren't following me. *If I can only get in the car, lock the doors and drive away.* I fished in my shoulder bag for the car keys, planning to take off as quickly as I could. But as I opened the car door, Grozny was upon me, snatching the keys from my hand. They threw my suitcase in the trunk, opened the back door and pushed me in. Scarface climbed in after me. He was holding a long stiletto, the largest switchblade knife I'd ever seen, snapping it open and shut like a kid's toy. Grozny took the wheel and drove off, heading north. My shoulder bag was strapped at an angle across my chest. In it was my little gun.

We were on a fairly deserted two-lane highway, driving away from the city. After ten or fifteen miles, Grozny pulled the car into a rest area bordering the road. It was a small, paved area without any facilities; just a place where drivers could stop to adjust something or to rest. They climbed out and, pulling me along between them, made off into the woods, leaving the car behind. There was no clearly defined path. We stumbled through tangled underbrush and brambles. I was wearing sneakers, but my legs were bare. My skirt kept catching on brambles and tearing as they pulled me along. A big thorn tore into my thigh and I yelled "Stop," but they didn't listen. Another thorn ripped my shin: blood was streaming down my leg, but still they pulled me on. Finally we stopped in a small clearing. They pressed me up against a tree, raised my arms above my head and tied them to the tree with Grozny's belt. They left me there and went to sit on a nearby log, smoking and mumbling to each other with words I couldn't catch. Scarface was still playing with his knife. He didn't seem to speak any English, but he appeared to be the boss.

They were going to hurt me. Why else would they bring me here and tie me up? I felt surprisingly calm. All my life, it seemed, I'd been preparing for something like this, something that would test my bravery and strength. I would not give in to them.

My arms were in pain. There was a little give in the belt that held them, and I found that if I kept inching my arms down, the belt moved also; each small move released some of the pressure. Given enough time, I would be able to free my arms completely, but I had to move slowly and carefully so they didn't see what I was doing. My shoulder bag was still strapped diagonally across my chest. If I could free my hands and get to my gun . . . but how would I use it against two huge men armed with knives and maybe guns as well? It could end in mayhem, with me as a victim. I had to bide my time, and wait for just the right moment.

Grozny walked back to where I was standing, pinned against the tree. From the malevolent grin on his face, I knew I was in for it.

"Rzhevsky. Where?" he asked.

"I don't know."

He slapped me across the face, not all that hard. I could take it and I would. I was determined not to cry out.

"Where?" he asked again, and I said I didn't know. Another slap, this one much harder, then more repeated questions, followed by more slaps. Each time the slaps became more brutal; I could feel my face swelling and burning and my eyes filled up inadvertently with tears. He was destroying my face, counting on my vanity to bring me to my knees.

Then, suddenly, he grabbed my crotch. I kicked him very hard on the shins, which made him grin even more maniacally. *That's what he wants,* I thought. *A fight, one that he can easily win.* He put his hands on my breasts and leaned into them with the full weight of his body. The pain was excruciating and I couldn't help but cry out. "Where Rzhevsky?" he asked again, maintaining the pressure.

"I don't know." I was crying now, from pain and fear. "He left last night. By plane. He's probably back in New York City now."

Grozny turned and walked toward Scarface, his back to me. My hands had worked themselves free. I could open the compartment, reach for my gun, but should I? Scarface had not taken his eyes off me. He could throw a knife faster than I could shoot.

"She doesn't know anything," Grozny said to Scarface in Russian.

Scarface stood up, ground out his cigarette with his foot and replied in Russian: "Okay. It's enough. Let's fuck her and get the hell out of here."

★★★

I heard those words and I bolted, running as fast as I could through the woods, back in the direction of the car and the highway. I had to get away. Brambles scratched and tore at my legs but I didn't even feel them. I stumbled and fell but was quickly up again, barely touching the ground. I just kept running, adrenaline pumping through my veins. I was faster than they were and I had a head start. The car gleamed white through the bushes; if only I had the keys, I could jump in and drive away. But of course I didn't. My heart was pounding wildly as I ran toward the highway. Please God, let there be a car coming, make it stop for me. And yes, yes, there was a car, driving slowly toward me. It was easy to flag it down.

I pulled open the passenger door and climbed in, breathlessly appealing to the man at the wheel: "Please, drive fast, get me out of here, anywhere, anywhere that's safe."

He looked at my torn clothes, my bleeding legs, and my bruised face, and he nodded. But he continued driving at a slow pace.

"Go faster, faster, please," I begged him, but he continued driving slowly, his eyes fixed on the rearview mirror.

"What the fuck . . ." I turned around to see what he was looking at and there was my white car, with the two thugs inside it, driving fast, bearing down on us.

"*Khorosho,*" said the driver of my car, quickly picking up speed. He was Russian. He was one of them. I'd walked right into a trap.

Forty-Six

He drove to the next rest stop. Both cars left the highway and pulled into the tree-shaded area. This time they didn't bother to drag me into the woods. They pushed my seat into a horizontal position and raped me, right there in the car.

Grozny was first. I fought him with every bit of strength I had. I scratched him, I kicked him, I bit him; nothing altered that horrible grin on his face. He was more than twice my weight, and when he threw his full body on me, I was pinned like an insect under a boot. He was perspiring profusely, his smelly sweat dripping all over me, and his breath exuded a nauseating mix of garlic and nicotine. I threw up all over myself. He ripped off my skirt and underpants, tossing them out of the car. When he plunged himself inside me, the pain was unbearable. I felt like I was going to die.

The rest is blurry. By the time Scarface climbed onto me I was wasted, unable to move, drenched in blood, vomit, and tears. Nauseous with pain, I was sobbing, pleading for them to stop. It's no wonder that the third man, the driver of the second car, declined to take his turn with me.

They lifted me from the car and rolled me onto the grass. Someone dropped my pocketbook alongside me. *This is my chance,* I thought, my mind suddenly alert. *Get the gun, shoot them each in the back while they're returning to the car, aim low, hit them where it will really hurt.* My fingers reached to open the secret compartment where the gun was hidden. There was time; I could do it.

Then I passed out.

★★★

I woke to find a woman with kindly eyes gingerly cleaning my bruised face with a warm, damp cloth. She was a nurse. I was in a hospital room. I tried to talk, but my lips were cracked and dry and my throat parched. She brought me water with a straw and urged me to take small sips until my mouth was wet again and I could speak.

"Where am I?"

"You're in the Free Hospital for Women. In Boston," she replied. "You've had a bad time of it. But it's okay now."

I moved slightly and felt sharp pains throughout my body. I moaned.

"You're getting pain-killers," she said, motioning toward an IV stand and a tube connected to my hand. "They should kick in soon."

I closed my eyes and drifted off. When I woke again, it was morning. The pain had subsided somewhat and I had questions.

"How did I get here?" I asked a different nurse who was now in attendance.

"Someone found you and called an ambulance. Don't talk too much. You should rest. The doctor will be here soon." I closed my eyes and slept some more.

I awoke to a woman shaking me gently by the shoulder. "I'm Doctor Grisham," she introduced herself. "Are you up to talking now?" I nodded.

"First, please tell me if there is someone we should contact. I know you're from New York City. Is there a family member? A friend?"

I shook my head. "My parents are in Europe. There's no one else."

"You're going to be all right. You've been badly bruised and torn, inside and out. We're treating your wounds. But there's no serious internal damage. You'll need time to heal, but you'll be fine. And," she added, "you were wearing a diaphragm." She raised her eyebrows in an unasked question. "So you don't have to worry about an unwanted pregnancy."

My diaphragm. From that last night with Max. With all the excitement, I had forgotten to take it out. Max! Where was he? Was he all right? It all came rushing back to me: the hotel room, his quick departure, our foolish expectation that I could walk out the next day and return home unharmed.

"You'll have to stay here for a while to recover," the doctor was saying. "And the police want to question you as soon as possible. They want to file a report, find the person who did this to you."

Police! That could be complicated. I needed time to think that through. "I'm not ready to talk to them yet," I said, closing my eyes. She pressed my hand and left me to sleep.

When I awoke that evening I asked for a telephone. "And some privacy, please." They brought me a phone and plugged it in. "Dial 9 first to get dial tone." They pulled the curtain shut around my bed, a mere semblance of privacy.

"Clarence?" My voice was thin and shaky.

"Oh, Katherine, I've been worried about you. Where are you?"

"I'm in the Free Hospital for Women in Boston. Those bodyguards really worked me over."

"Are you all right?"

"I'm not, but I will be. It'll take some days, they tell me. The police are here. They want to file a report, go after those guys."

"No," Clarence said sharply. "Keep the police out of this. I'll send someone to you at once, someone who'll take care of everything. Till then, refuse to talk to the police."

"But I want to get those thugs. They're rapists. They should be punished."

There, I said the word, answered the question that Clarence was too timid to ask. *Yes, Clarence,* I said to myself, *I was raped. That's what happens to women, even tough women like me, women who are trained and armed.* I fought against a rising feeling of shame, shame for a weakness I could do nothing about. Men could easily do things to women that we could not, in turn, do to them.

"We're the ones to deal with those guys," Clarence was saying. "The police can't do anything. We'll have them out of the country pronto."

"That's not enough," I muttered.

"It's all anyone can do. They have immunity; you know that, Katherine. If we get the police involved, it will blow everything wide open—you, Max, the Operation, the FBI. We don't want that now, do we?"

"Do you know what's happened to Max?" I asked. "*He* was the one they were after, not me. Is he okay?"

A long pause. "Don't think about him right now. Just think about yourself, about getting better. Talk to no one about what happened. I'll have someone there by morning, someone who can handle everything. Call me again, if you need me. Any time."

There was something he wasn't telling me about Max, something bad. He was sparing me. Was Max hurt? Dead? In handcuffs on a plane back to Moscow? Damn it, Clarence. Always dealing in half-truths. Always so secretive. It was frustrating. Especially now. Was Max alive or dead? I had to know.

I checked my answering machine in New York to see if Max had called. Nothing. Surely, if he was okay, he would have called. He would want to know how I had made out.

***

Clarence was true to his word. FBI agent Sara Eastlake was at my side the next day, just as I had begun my first solid-food lunch. Slender, fortyish, with just the right blend of professionalism and warmth, she told me she had been there since early morning and had already dealt with the police. "They won't be coming around anymore. As for the hospital staff, you should answer only those questions that deal with your symptoms. Don't talk to anyone about what happened, by whom, how, or why. I'll be here with you until they're ready to release you. Is there anything I can do for you right now?"

"Yes, there is. The car I was driving. It was a rented car. They probably abandoned it along the highway. They had another car with them. There's a suitcase in the trunk with my clothes in it. Do you think you could track it down? I have nothing here to wear." I had told the nurse to throw out what remained of what I was wearing when they raped me. I never wanted to see those clothes again.

"Here's the information from the car rental place," I said, fishing in my bag. "And yes, there's something else. My gun is missing. They must have x-rayed my bag and removed it when I entered the hospital. Do you think you can find out about that?"

"Sure. Will the gun need some forensics done?"

"No. I never got to use it. The situation wasn't right . . ." I trailed off. Why was I making excuses to her? She wasn't there, she wasn't the one being attacked. The more I thought about it, the more convinced I was that I had done the right thing. Using my gun to hold off two huge men with knives would have resulted in disaster. And police. And publicity. If I had managed to survive, my career would have ended.

"Sara," I asked, as she was leaving. "Do you know what's happened to Max?"

"Max? I'm sorry, I don't know who that is. Should I?"

"No. It's okay. Forget I asked."

***

The hospital staff was polite and attentive. People came by frequently to ask if I had any pain. But no one asked what was going through my mind. No one acknowledged the trauma I'd experienced. They didn't ask how I was feeling emotionally; they probably didn't know what to say.

My brain protected me from experiencing the worst. It blanked out much of what had happened, except for the very beginning, when I tried to fight off Grozny, and the end, when they dropped me in the grass. I welcomed that amnesia and had no desire to remember other details.

Instead, I obsessed about something I could never really know. Who had found me and called the ambulance? Was it a man? A woman? A family that had pulled over to have a little picnic on the grass? Or maybe a bunch of teenage boys on bikes. What did they see?

A half-naked woman, bloody and beaten. Did they look at me with horror, with disgust? Did they check to see if I was breathing? Did they touch me? Did they cover me up? Did they feel awe at how fragile the human body is, how vulnerable a woman's body is to abuse?

***

Sara Eastlake was quick and efficient. She found my suitcase and brought it to me the next day. The gun, she reported, was being held by security at the hospital and would be given to me when I left.

The following day, she told me we were leaving. "That's impossible. I can't leave yet. The cuts on my legs are oozing pus. I'm using a catheter to pee."

"I know, but we have to go," she replied. "The press has gotten wind of this. Some blabbermouth policeman, I'm sure. There were two reporters here today. They know there was a rape and that the FBI is involved. One of them got past security with a camera and almost got to photograph you in your room. And they're pumping the hospital staff for info. We're leaving tonight when there's no one around to see. I've arranged for an ambulance to transport us, with you in a bed. There will be a nurse on board to take care of you. She'll give you a sedative so you can sleep through the night. We'll be in DC by mid-morning."

"I don't want to go to Washington," I said angrily. "I live in New York. I want my own apartment, my work, my things."

"That apartment is no more," Sara told me, then added quickly as she saw my dismay: "All your things have been carefully packed and will be sent wherever you wish. The apartment has been vacated. The Operation is over."

I thought again of Max. How would he ever find me, if he *is* still around? I didn't miss him, nor was I that eager to see him. What I felt was guilt. He was being hunted as a traitor because of what we did to him, "we" being OPERATION PLAYBOY, mainly *me*. I was the one who betrayed him when I drove him to Indianapolis and to Philly where he unknowingly revealed his assets to the FBI.

I, a novice operative, had bested Max, an experienced spy. It gave me no pleasure. I remembered what the FBI guy had said at the outset: "Every man has a weakness and his weakness is pretty women."

Forty-Seven

They put me on a movable bed and wheeled me into an ambulance. The drive was smooth. I slept all the way to Washington. There I was put up in a small, out-of-the-way hotel, more like a bed-and-breakfast, with a cheerful dining room looking out on a lovely flower garden. I had a two-room suite; the nurse slept in one room and I in the other. Within a few days I was walking around easily, taking my meals in the dining room and well on the way to recovery. The nurse left, and I stayed on.

Riley called me every day. "Clarence is over," he told me. "Call me Riley now. Everyone does." Our talks were short. He asked about my health and my accommodations. He put no pressure on me, but ended each conversation, saying: "Whenever you're ready, call my office and make an appointment to see me."

I was in no hurry. I stayed there for almost a week, by myself with no visitors except for Sara, who dropped in for a few minutes each day to see that all was well. One day she brought me some pancake makeup to cover up the remains of the bruises on my face. It was a subtle hint, I assumed; she was telling me it was time to face the world again.

But I wasn't ready. I ate my meals in the dining room, walked in the garden, and occasionally took a book to read from the hotel library—poetry or short stories. The weather was comfortingly warm. Most of the time I just sat in the garden, thinking.

The Operation was over. It was far from a success. I'd given them data on Max, inconclusive data that would now be meaningless, since Max, thanks to us, was being hunted as a traitor and, at the very least, would be sent back to Moscow for punishment. A handful of American spies had been captured in the course of the Operation; thus a few less military secrets would be smuggled out to Russia. I took no pride in this. I hadn't done anything meaningful to me. To the contrary, I felt complicit in Vika's killing and maybe in Max's as well. It all seemed ugly and sordid to me, culminating with my rape.

I thought long and hard about my passion for Max and why it had slowly dissipated. I thought about Tony, how unsuspecting I'd been, cavorting with a youthful Russian spy. I thought about ebullient Vasily in his lopsided house in Massachusetts, devoting his life to helping his less fortunate friends in Russia. I thought about Stephanie and the important work she was doing, the courage it took for her to travel secretly in Russia and smuggle out *samizdat*.

I took stock of all the lies I'd told to everyone I knew: my parents, Steven, Max, Tony, Stephanie, and even Riley, my boss and supposed confidant.

I'd used sex to get information from Max. Was that any different from what he'd done with Yvette Szabo? Was it okay because I was infatuated with Max? Maybe Max had been infatuated with Mrs. Szabo.

What job would they give me next? What kind of job would I want? Would I eventually become a cipher, like Max, so full of deception I would no longer know who I was?

I wanted to stay in that garden forever, pondering what I had done and what I would do next. But Riley ended it all with a summons. "It's time," he told me curtly. "Be in my office tomorrow morning at ten."

***

"Katherine, you've been a real trooper," Riley welcomed me. "I want to thank you and also tell you how sorry I am that it ended so badly for you. That should not have happened. The FBI tails had been told to follow Max, so they did. They didn't think there was any danger in leaving you alone. A very bad miscalculation."

He showed me some photos and asked me which men had attacked me. It was easy to identify Grozny and Scarface, though the sight of them made me want to puke. "There was a third man, driving the car. I don't think I'll be able to identify him, I barely saw him with all that was happening at the time. He was a minor player, anyway." Riley assured me they would follow up.

"Do you know what's happened to Max?" I asked. "Where he *is?*"

"Max is fine. He's in a safe house here in DC. He managed to dodge them and came right here to Washington."

"Here? Max? Why would he come *here?* I don't get it."

"There's a lot you don't know, Katherine. I have a lot to explain. You see . . ." He paused. "This may come as a bit of a shock to you . . . Max has been working with us from the start. That's why we've been so successful."

"Max?" I thought I'd misunderstood him. "Working with *us?* How?"

"Max was a walk-in. He got in touch with the FBI when he first came to the US, said he wanted asylum, wanted to defect. We convinced him to become *our* agent, to stay in his job long enough to lead us to some of the American spies who were passing info to the Soviets. Which he did. In return, we promised to protect and reward him."

I was stunned. "Why didn't you tell me this before? I don't get it."

"We thought it would work better if you didn't know about Max. Max didn't know about you, either, that you were with the Agency. We figured there'd be less chance of slipups that way. And Max might not have been so open with you if he knew you were with the Agency."

"Then what was I doing all this time? If Max was already on our side, what was *my* role? I thought I was evaluating him for you, getting information so you could determine whether he might be convinced to work for us. But he was already working for us! So what the hell was I *doing?*" I could feel the blood rushing to my face. I felt humiliated. I had concluded that Max was not turnable. How could I have been so dumb?

Riley saw my upset. "You were doing something important, Katherine, telling us things about Max that were useful. We had to be sure he was the person he purported to be and not a plant. Walk-ins are always suspicious, more so than those we recruit ourselves. We *needed* your reports on him."

"But I concluded he was *not* likely to be turned."

"We weren't looking for conclusions from you. The raw data you provided confirmed what he had already told us and that he was on the level."

Riley went on: "You also provided cover for him, got him to the places where his assets were. That wasn't initially part of our plan: it was actually Max's brainstorm to have you drive him out of the city. As you know, we've been working hand in hand with the FBI on this. Remember when you spotted that FBI agent picking up Max's drop in Central Park? You were right, of course, but I couldn't tell you then. Max kept in touch with the FBI through drops like that. They followed him when he visited assets in Indianapolis and Philadelphia and ended up arresting four Americans who've been spying for the Russians. There are several more they have under surveillance. We got all the evidence we needed, including copies of documents they passed on."

He continued, "We initially thought you might photograph the documents and send them to us, but that proved to be too dangerous. We didn't want you to blow your cover with Max, not that early in the game. So the FBI did the camera work instead."

My anger was mounting by the minute. "I thought I had a clear cut assignment, to evaluate Max as a possible agent for us. Now you're telling me *what*? I was just doing a little cross-checking for you? And some chauffeuring on the side? You didn't even want my conclusions. You didn't trust me to do anything important!"

"Remember, Katherine, you were untested. A newcomer to the Agency, with no knowledge of tradecraft. We took a big chance on you because of your previous relationship with Max. That saved us a lot of time. And don't take yourself to task because of your conclusions.

You behaved like a true professional and demonstrated courage and resiliency."

"That's bullshit!" I declared. "You never took me seriously. You said yourself that dangerous jobs were not for women. You didn't trust me with the truth. You didn't even try to protect me. Those FBI tails looked out for Max, not me. Does Max know about me now, about my role in all this? Where is he? I want to see him."

"He knows everything now. We've been debriefing him since he arrived here. He's providing us with valuable material about KGB operations, here and abroad. And yes, you can see him. I'll get someone to bring you to the safe house. Come back here again tomorrow morning. We have to talk about your future."

Riley was eager to get me out of his office.

Forty-Eight

T he man who drove me to the safe house insisted I wear a blind-fold. "It's standard procedure," he assured me. "That's how we keep it safe." When I removed the blindfold, I was in the basement garage of a large apartment house. We took an elevator to the 14th floor, and my guide let us in with a key. "He's expecting you," he said. "I'll wait here in the foyer." He sat down on a small couch, while I entered the apartment through the living room door.

Max was alone in a small, sparsely furnished room. Slumped in a chair, he was gazing out the window and did not hear me enter. I stood near the door, overwhelmed by conflicting emotions.

My first response was one of relief. Max was alive; he was well. I had spent the past few weeks fearing the worst—that he was dead or arrested, and all because of me. But with my relief came a strong sense of let-down. Stripped of his air of mystery, no longer a Soviet diplomat or a KGB spy, Max seemed somehow diminished.

"Max," I said softly. He turned around and brightened immediately, standing up and holding out his hands in a familiar gesture. He was wearing a shirt that was too big for him. His arms, below the short sleeves, looked thin and pale. I stood there facing him, without taking his proffered hands.

"Katya, I am so happy to see you." He smiled, then added affectionately: *"Moya malen'kaya shpiona."*

"My little spy." What a put-down! And what bad taste, to be making a joke about the lie that had driven and sullied our relationship.

"I can't believe you're joking about that," I said, incredulously. "There's nothing amusing about it. I was spying on you, Max, and you didn't know it. Doesn't that make you *mad*?"

"The truth is, I always suspected something. At times I even thought you might be KGB." Max sat down again. I settled on a couch, facing him. "I also wondered if you might be FBI," Max continued. "But it didn't make sense: Why would your government have you spy on me when I was already working for them? Now they've explained it. I understand."

"Well, *I'm* upset," I announced. "Upset that they didn't tell me the truth about *you*. I feel like I've been used. And . . . I can't forgive *you* for leaving me the way you did in Boston. Those thugs really worked me over. In the very worst ways. They thought I knew where you were. I was in the hospital for days. I'm still recuperating."

Max was taken aback. No one had told him what had happened to me. "Yes, it figures," he said slowly. "They were frustrated because I got away from them. They took it out on you. I am so sorry, Katya. Those guys are forbidden to get involved with Americans. What you report was not expectable."

I decided to spare Max the details. What was the point? He didn't press me. I assumed he didn't want to know.

There was an awkward silence as we took each other's measure, each seeing the other in a new light. I was seeing Max as a defector, a Russian working under cover for the FBI. And he was seeing me as a CIA operative, a spy.

I found it hard to absorb this turn in our relationship. Not so for Max, however. He seemed ready to take up where we'd left off. He was smiling, beckoning me with his hands, inviting me into an embrace. But I wasn't falling for it. There were things I needed to know, and this was the time to ask.

"Max, did you have something to do with Vika's death?" I asked.

"No, of course not!" he exploded. I had taken him by surprise. "It was those thugs, the same ones who attacked you."

"But you'd been married to Vika. Why did you hide that from me? Why do you seem so blasé about her death?"

"You have to understand," Max began slowly. "It was a bad marriage from the start. She was a mean, angry woman. And she never forgave me for leaving her. She did everything she could to make my life miserable. So yes, I don't miss her. I'm sorry things ended for her in that way, but I'm glad she's out of my life."

"And me?" I continued. "I made things hard for you, too. Did you want me to end up like she did?"

"Never!" Max was really upset now. "Yes, there were times when I wanted to shake you, to threaten you, to force you to tell me what you were up to, who was behind you. But I never did. I would never hurt you. I love you, Katya."

I thought about my panic in the ocean with Max—the look on his face that had scared me so much. He had me in his power then, he could have tried to make me talk. But that wave came and washed him away.

"Like that time in the ocean at Asbury Park?" I asked. "Were you planning to scare me and force me to talk?"

But Max wasn't listening. His mind was elsewhere. "Katya," he said, "they're giving me a new name, a new identity. I will move many miles away, settle in the West, in Arizona or New Mexico. They're giving me money, lots of money, enough to buy a house and start a business. I will become an American. Come with me, Katya. We'll start a new life together. Live in a nice house with a backyard barbecue grill, just like the pictures."

"No, Max, I could never do that. It wouldn't work. Don't you see, we have nothing to build on. Our entire relationship was based on lies. I know nothing about your real life, past or present. And you know little about mine. We've been in some dream world that wasn't real."

Max looked surprised. "We can start to know each other now. I know you love me. You said you would move to Moscow and marry me. There is a much better life here. We can get married in United States."

"Those were all lies, Max. I never planned to move to Moscow or to marry you."

"Well, I was lying, too," Max confessed. "I never planned to go back to Moscow. I was planning to stay here—with you. That talk about Moscow was for Vika's ears. She was listening in on us. I wanted her to think I was turning you."

"And how horrible that was! How could you make love to me and say all the things you said when you knew your ex-wife was listening?"

"It was much worse for *her*. Hearing us making love, talking about marriage, it drove her crazy. People at the Mission saw she was acting strange. They suspected she was conducting a secret operation. They thought she was the mole. That's what finished her."

Max moved to the couch and put his arm around me. I rested my head against his shoulder for a minute; it felt comforting, familiar. When he tried to kiss me, however, I pulled back. "I'm a wounded warrior," I said, my body stiffening.

Max understood. "I'd like to kill those guys," he said.

"So would I," I answered. "I wish I had."

There was another long silence before Max spoke again. "Let's forget everything that happened and start fresh. Come with me, we'll make a new life."

"No, Max. That's not what I want. Don't you see? We don't have a real relationship at all."

"What about the love we had? In bed, all those nights?"

"That was lovemaking, but it wasn't love. You've been a complete mystery to me. A stranger. You've never opened your heart to me. You've been leading a double life for so long, I'm not sure you can open your heart to anyone."

I was seeing Max in a new light: his love of shopping, his interest in home improvement magazines, his talk with my father about starting a business. Max wanted a better life for himself, the kind of life he could find here—with kitchen appliances, a television set, and all the other middle-class comforts of modern America.

Max wasn't leaving Russia because it was a police state. He was leaving for a backyard barbecue grill! That was the *key*, the key to understanding Max. It wasn't all that complicated. It was really very simple.

Max had every right to want nice things, things I'd always had and took for granted. But it wasn't what *I* wanted. I wanted to do something more with my life. I wanted to do something meaningful, something that would help others less fortunate than me.

I stood up and moved toward the door. Max rose and moved toward me. I knew what he had in mind. He wanted to hug me, to hold me, to bring me back under his spell. But I kept backing away. It wasn't going to work this time.

"You'll be fine, Max. It's better if you start a new life without me. You'll find another woman, that will be easy for you. Here," I said, opening the chain around my neck and slipping off the little key. "Take this to give to her, whoever she will be. Maybe she'll have more luck than I did in opening your heart."

I pressed the key into his hand and quickly left the room. The man I left behind was a stranger. The Max I had loved was nothing but a fantasy, a romantic dream. From the very start.

★★★

Back in Riley's office the next morning, my mind was clear, clearer than it had been in months.

"I've been thinking of what to do with you now, Katherine," Riley began. "What kind of work would be right for you . . ."

"Don't bother," I interrupted. "I'm quitting. This work is not for me."

"Now, Katherine, don't be hasty. You've been through a lot in the past few weeks. You're not thinking clearly. You have a big future here. It would be a shame to squander it."

"You don't get it," I said. "I've been living a life of lies. I've been lying to everyone because of my commitment to you, to the Agency. Now I learn that *you've* been lying to *me* all along. It makes the whole thing seem like a farce."

"We all lie," Riley said. "That's part of life, this life, anyway. I'm sure you've kept plenty from me. Like your little side trip to Hungary, for example. I could have fired you for that."

He was right, of course. I never told him about Hungary, about Tony, about the work I did for Stephanie, about the many times I'd screwed up. I never told him about my passion for Max, about the intense nature of our relationship.

"We have a mission," Riley went on. "You mustn't forget the mission. That's why we do the things we do. It's for a good purpose. It's what we're all about."

"That's the biggest lie of all." I was angry, but I kept my cool. "I joined the Agency to help promote our country's values. I wanted to help people in Russia, people suffering under Communist rule. But this work, this spying, it would go on even if the Soviet Union became the most humane country in the world. It has nothing to do with their evil system. It's all about great power politics. It's in the nature of governments. But it's not in *my* nature. It's not what I want to do with my life."

Riley was studying my face. He wasn't moved by what I said, I knew that. He was just assessing me. He didn't try to dissuade me.

"I'm not going to change my mind. I'm resigning, as of today. . . . Please, have my things delivered to my parents' home," I added, and wrote down their address.

We shook hands. Riley wished me good luck. I couldn't wait to be out of Langley, out of DC.

***

Out on the street, I thought of Steven for the first time in many days. We hadn't spoken since I'd hung up on him after that compromising phone call. No, I thought, I can't deal with him now. Maybe there would be time for that in the future. Time to see if the scattered shards of our relationship could be repaired.

Right now I was going home, home to my parents' apartment, home to the room in which I'd grown up, the room they'd kept unchanged for me over the years, a place for me to go if I needed refuge.

The afternoon sun was shining through the white lace curtains when I arrived. In the top left drawer of the desk, the desk at which I'd done my high school homework, there was an unopened envelope, addressed to me in my own handwriting, care of my parents. In it was a little white card. I took it out. It read:

Stephanie Evans, Director
Committee for Human Rights in the Soviet Union
and Eastern Europe

Such a long name, cumbersome, a bit like Steffie herself. Well, I could help her with that. We could change it, find a better name.

I stretched out on the bed as the sun gradually moved through the room. I was luxuriating in a feeling I hadn't known in years, a feeling of peace.

Tomorrow, I decided. Tomorrow I would call Steffie and tell her I was ready, ready to begin work.

Acknowledgments

I am indebted to the two institutions that enabled my writing and my human rights career: the Russian Institute (now Harriman Institute) at Columbia University, where I learned about Russian culture and Soviet oppression, and Human Rights Watch, the organization I helped found and for which I carried out more than fifty human rights missions, most of them clandestine ones behind the Iron Curtain.

The Russian Key, though decidedly a work of fiction, draws very loosely from some of my student and professional experiences.

I appreciate everyone at Arcade Publishing who brought this book to fruition. My special thanks go to Arcade's gifted publisher Jeannette Seaver, who told me "I love it!" as soon as she read my book, and to Lilly Golden and Elena Silverberg, who cheerfully and expertly guided it through to publication.

Lisa Kaufman, who edited my memoir *The Courage of Strangers: Coming of Age with the Human Rights Movement* (PublicAffairs, 2002), brought her talent and enthusiasm to this book as well, making important structural suggestions that vastly improved the story.

Friends and family pitched in from the start, as the book grew from a story to a novel. I appreciate all their comments and suggestions, many of which were incorporated in the final work. Thanks to you all—Joe Weisberg, Pat Jaffe, Zeke Faux, Peter Osnos, Susan Osnos, Joel Bell, Steve Persky, Sarah Faux, and Jerry Katcher.

Thanks most of all to my daughters—Emily, Abby, and Pam—for reading different versions of the manuscript more times than I can remember, always with helpful suggestions and always urging me on.

And, of course, to Charlie, whose presence—and absence—I feel with every word I write.

About the author

Jeri Laber is a founder of Human Rights Watch, where she served as executive director of the Europe and Central Asia Division during the Cold War until 1995. She completed dozens of missions, in which she went undercover in the Soviet Union and Eastern Europe, dodging the secret police and bringing hope to dissidents. After the fall of Communism, she received the Order of Merit from Czech Republic President Václav Havel. She has published her memoir *The Courage of Strangers: Coming of Age with the Human Rights Movement* and *A Nation is Dying: Afghanistan Under the Soviets, 1979-87*, as well as more than one hundred articles on human rights issues in *The New York Times, The New York Review of Books, The Washington Post, The Chicago Tribune, The Los Angeles Times,* and others.